HAZARD'S WAY

For John Robinson

HAZARD'S WAY

A novel

by Roger Hubank

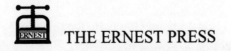 THE ERNEST PRESS

Published by The Ernest Press
© Roger Hubank 2001

ISBN 0 948153 63 6

Type-set in 11 on 15 point Goudy by Stanningley Serif
Printed by St Edmundsbury Press

Prologue

Wastdale Head. 8th June 1924.

Several hundred of us turned up for the ceremony. Real Bank Holiday weather we had for it, too. Squally rain, gusting to gale. Gable, of course, was draped in cloud. As we slogged higher up the ridge the rain turned to a dense white mist. No visibility. All one could hear were boots, slithering and sliding in the scree as we converged upon the summit. I went up with Mason. Still the quicksilver charmer as of old. He'd had an 'exciting' war, whatever that might mean.

The names are inscribed on a bronze tablet set in the rock. Jeffcoat's there. And poor Slater, my contemporary at Caius. Montague, thank God, survived. Mason recalled how we all laughed at him dyeing his hair in his eagerness to join up. Poor Oppenheimer was not so lucky. Nor Herford, killed at Ypres. Sellars wrote to me after the news of his death appeared in *The Times*.

'Yes, we shall miss him. But then, what do we matter ? For him it is an honour and a victory beyond anything he could ever have won for himself on Pillar or the Pinnacle.'

As if Herford dead was somehow to be preferred to Herford living.

A watery sun came out for the service. A hymn, the usual prayers. Then the 121st Psalm, as one might have expected. A misreading, of course. The mood is interrogative, not indicative. There is no help in the hills. *Help*, if I read the text aright, *cometh only from the Lord.*

A bugle sounded the Last Post. Then Young addressed us. Geoffrey Young, perched on a great rock.

Cold, wet, scattered about in sodden groups, we gazed up at him. Some of the women were in tears. Heaven knows what they were expecting. Though the golden tongue was more than equal to the occasion. *During the appalling years of war the Wastdale hills shone like a grail across the valley of the shadow.* No doubt that elegiac light of early autumn. That low slanting sunlight that makes luminous every detail – the white-washed inn, stone-walled fields washed green – the pure golden glow of a morning when the world was young.

Throughout those dark years, he went on, his voice blown about by the wind, these hills still spoke to Wastdale men of all that their hearts held dearest, all that they'd ever dreamed of manliness and truth.

Gazing out over our heads in that rapt, unseeing way of his, the speaker seemed to come and go in the mist.

"He might be addressing the other mountains," Mason murmured drily in my ear.

Yet even in the midst of present sorrow, would you believe, there is cause for joy at the realisation of what, for many of our comrades no longer with us, would have been their dearest wish – the Wastdale fells now established for all time as some sort of Never-Never land, where men might become boys again and have adventures. At least, that was the gist of it.

Then we sang *Lead, kindly light.* After which 'the encircling gloom' fell on us with a vengeance.

I managed to get back to the inn without going astray. Though it was more by luck than judgement. A good many didn't. Quite a few blundered about till nightfall, coming down at last in the wrong valley, a long way from where they'd started.

Lord, how they'd have laughed, those dead men.

I

It was, if I remember rightly, a morsel of cake soaked in tea that called into being Proust's vast *Remembrance of Things Past*. For me the rather more robust smell of ham and eggs invariably brings to mind a long refectory table. A door opens into a small dark hall. A floor of black-and-white linoleum squares. Rows of nailed boots oozing oil. And with the hall, a staircase festooned with ropes pulled tight over the newel posts. A fug of drying clothes.

Suddenly I'm filled with a wild longing to be flying north again – gazing from the blue carriage window of the little toy train chuffing in and out along the coast by Morecambe Bay.

What we loved once, and shall never see again, we love for ever.

*

To dream of the still-lingering sweetness of those days is to bring to mind a timeless perfected place, or else a childhood of blessed memory. I remember a bank where two becks joined to run into the lake, one in full sun, the other rippling under dipping branches: bathing pools running hot or cold, with grassy bays and a shingle beach with coloured pebbles lying ready to hand.

No thought, then, of reputation or ambition. Only that sudden blaze of astonishment at being alive – the wonder of a creation still waiting to be explored. For the dale then was filled with a primordial light. Becks, running with the first water, sparkled like veins of crystal. Heather and wild thyme, bruised under foot, gave off the warm scent of something freshly made. We sallied forth in our flannel shirts and peat-smelling Norfolk jackets, pockets stuffed with prunes, raisins, bread and butter, potted meat and chocolate, caps turned back to front – caps, tweed hats, tam o'shanters draped with scraps of moss, or floppy felts from the Tyrol pinned up at the front or side – whatever best expressed a mood. We sought out the steepest fells to savour the operation of newly discovered bodies: the thrust of legs as, hearts thudding, we attacked the slope, matching stride to steepness or, jinking downhill, feet darting nimbly, instinctively, over boulder fields untouched since the creation. In every lungful of air, in every droplet of moisture, we breathed and tasted what we were.

So day was added unto day. We plunged in icy tarns. We sprawled on the soft warm turf. We floated over sun-soaked slabs still radiant with the glow of that first morning. A single movement skilfully performed, the feel of it as one made it, was to step into some new dimension of existence.

And what splendours attended the aftermath of each ascent – hunger, that transformed every mouthful – the joy with which we gazed at a seemingly inexhaustible prospect of forms, shapes and patterns – the excitement of a delirious treasure hunt as we sped from crag to crag, probing the depths of mossy ghylls and lichenous gullies, stripping away the covering of grass and moss, to discover what a benevolent Providence had planted there expressly for our happiness. For a climb then was a gift of Nature – not a route forced up the fiercest, the most forbidding faces. And we couldn't fall. We couldn't fall. No one would ever fall.

*

My mind goes back to the turn of the century and an evening in Mosedale when, much to my embarrassment – for it was evident my clumsy struggles on the Y boulder had been observed – a voice addressed me out of the blue.

Had I, it enquired, come to Wastdale for the mountaineering ? Due to my inverted position on the boulder (I was attempting to ascend it after the manner of Dr. Collier – that is to say, upside down) it was only by a considerable craning of the neck that I was able to bring into view my questioner's upper half. I had a somewhat disorientated impression of a stovepipe hat, a purplish face and venerable white whiskers – no less a luminary, as I discovered later, than Prebendary Iremonger.

Had I, he repeated, *come to Wastdale for the mountaineering* ?

On being assured that was indeed my purpose, he replied that he was glad to hear it. Every healthy Englishman, he impressed upon me, would be improved, morally and physically, by mountaineering. Disinclined to persist in my struggles under inspection, I dropped to the ground. We walked back together to the inn.

It was, he averred, a grand school for prudence, self-reliance: indeed, for all the qualities that made up manliness.

A school was what it was. Though no school like it existed anywhere in England. Where 'pupils', overflowing from the bedrooms, slept on chairs and sofas, or on the billiard table, or in the bath. Where dozens of pairs of stockings hung nightly over the stair rail, with piles of sodden clothing flung down in a great heap on the landing. A school where high jinks and japes were never frowned on, with genial masters (every one a famous old boy) whose deeds, recorded in the Climbing Book or on the photographs that covered the walls of the dining room, led us to feel that youth could have no finer privilege than to follow where they led.

It still strikes me as remarkable that an obscure inn, in a remote region far from any cultivated centre, should have witnessed such a gathering. Scholars, mathematicians, lawyers, Fellows of the Royal Society, men for whom it was a moral duty to make something of their lives. Many of them belonged to an earlier generation. Yet their names, the tale of their achievements, were as familiar to us as the great names of old. Some of them were still to be met with in the smoke room at Wastdale Head.

It was small for a public room. A few chairs, a single sofa, though upwards of a score of fellows would cram into that tiny space, sprawled on the floor, propped against one another's legs. Here the great ones gathered: Slingsby, Hastings – veterans of innumerable Alpine triumphs – Collie, who had climbed with Mummery on Nanga Parbat; gods, each one of them, whose approval, hinted at the corner of a mouth, or twinkling in an eye, would truly crown the tale of our own small doings.

I can see Collie now, sitting in his chair by the fire, one leg thrown over the other, a lean silvery-grey figure in knickerbockers, that long pointed face, pipe in mouth, looking for all the world like the pictures of Sherlock Holmes in the Strand Magazine. The coffee passes round, the room fills with smoke, the talk (punctuated by crashes from the billiard room next door) rising and falling with the flickerings of the fire: talk about guides and glaciers, couloirs and crevasses, of stone-chutes notorious for broken skulls, and the deathly chill enveloping lower limbs plunged through a snowhole – and the laughter rumbles round. The tale is told for the hundredth time of Mummery's crack, and Hastings' boot, jammed descending the precipice of the Grépon. And the laughter rumbles round again.

*

One dank, depressing day in Cambridge, when my senses

yearned for crisp cold air and the crunch of frozen snow in Hollow Stones, I came across a book on a stall in the market place – *The Lake District*. I picked it up, curious to see what the writer had to say about Wastdale. I almost recoiled with astonishment to read of the 'oppressive loneliness' of the place. Its 'deathly silence'. The suggestion of 'a cut-off, cornered sort of life'. Of sunshine piercing the shadows of great gloomy mountains, 'like music from the outside filling the death chamber'.

Only then did I see that the writer was a Mrs. Lynton.

Well, what could a woman know of our rough-and-tumble sports, the good-humoured banter, the laughter of young men at home in their world, and at ease with one another. Heedless, high-spirited young fellows, we were there for the fun. For the adventure. Though our efforts weren't always well regarded. Some of the older men had come by their hard-won skills through a long apprenticeship on Alpine snow and ice. Their experience was of a different kind from the climbs that were just then beginning to be attempted in Wastdale. They shook their heads over our audacity.

One Easter I was sitting in the smoke room listening to an elder laying down the law.

"It is the climber's bounden duty," he was saying between pulls at his pipe, "to execute every expedition in the safest and most orthodox style possible."

"Then how," a voice made innocent enquiry, "would you ascend the arête from Low Man to Scafell Pinnacle ?"

Widdop loved to tease the older Alpine men.

"Astride it, of course."

The old fellow must have shuffled, à cheval, across innumerable Alpine crests.

"Indeed ?"

The inflexion of that languid voice, its affectation of faint surprise, was calculated to a nicety.

"Surely the proper way is to walk along the edge ?"

"That is precisely the kind of irresponsible exploit one has a duty to suppress."

"On the contrary, it is the only gentlemanly way to do it."

Of course Widdop, with that jaunty facetiousness of his, was being deliberately provocative. Stepping along that knife edge was never a thing he would have done himself.

"And if you slipped ?"

"I shouldn't," came the prompt reply. "But if I slipped, I very much hope Lockhart would jump over the other side."

"That sort of thing is not funny. It is not a joke."

But indignation was swallowed up in a gale of laughter. For a joke was what it was. The 'near things' one had survived, recounted by the fire, after a good dinner with one's friends, were things to laugh about.

II

At that time I scarcely knew Widdop, except by reputation as the partner of the celebrated Lockhart. For some reason Lockhart's arrival that weekend had been delayed. Next morning, finding himself at a loose end and hearing me say something over breakfast about leading the North if only I had a second, Widdop rather alarmingly volunteered his services.

"I'll come along and hold the rope for you, if you like."

No doubt Pillar Rock by the North Climb is little enough to shout about. Small beer indeed compared with the fierce routes the young men make these days. Yet at the turn of the century it still enjoyed some notoriety. Ten years in the making, it was one of the great achievements of the founding fathers. Its great length and soaring situation, to say nothing of its well documented terrors, made it a supreme challenge for a young aspirant like myself. Widdop was exactly the companion I needed: not only an experienced second man, but one who'd been on the climb before.

He was a man of what was then considered an admirably Anglo-Saxon appearance: blue eyes, a silky smooth moustache of the same degree of fairness as his well-brushed hair, and a healthy glow that suggested an addiction to cold tubs. His fussiness with regard to his equipment was something of a standing joke at Wastdale Head. He was most particular about his boots. Widdop rejected the conventional wisdom of that time, according to which the best mountaineering boots were Swiss. His were specially made for him in South Molton Street, and nailed according to a pattern of his own devising. Each one was packed away after use in its own canvas bag. After a day's wetting in the hills he used to fill them with oats which, he claimed, kept them supple and prevented them from losing their shape.

We set out early, for a long climb lay ahead of us. It was a cold, grey day. The raw wind carried flurries of snow. The cracking pace at which Widdop set off up Mosedale did little to stem his flow of conversation. The conditions afforded him an opportunity to draw my attention to some of the more practical aspects of mountaineering dress: the buttons sewn on all his jacket pockets, the tabs to close the sleeves against blown snow, the anklets of elasticated cloth circling the tops of his boots as a barrier to stones. It all spoke of an impressive competence, certainly. The long muffler of Shetland wool, wound round the neck, then over the ears and head, securing a wide-brimmed floppy felt hat, completed the picture of a methodical mountain man. Blowing hard as I followed him up the last steep pull to Looking Stead, I congratulated myself on my good fortune. Widdop was exactly the companion I needed.

Dropping down again from Looking Stead, we set off along a rough winding path traversing the steep north-east side of the fell. Half-an-hour's walk brought us to a rocky belvedere where we halted, pulled up short as one always is by that first sight of Pillar Rock, like a towering headland jutting out into the sea. Confronting us, across a deep wide cove, lay our objective. The north-east face.

Shivering as the sweat cooled, I felt the first flutter of nerves, conscious of the sullenness of the sky, and that flat cold light which, on grim walls of rock, impresses gloomier fears and questionings. Ruinous scree and boulders, tumbled about the cove, completed a cheerless scene.

"Most courses look at their worse when seen *en face*," said Widdop cheerfully.

For him it was just another outing. He pointed out the line

taken by the North Climb. It appeared to run up the side of a steep shallow gully, moving from one vertical flute of rock which looked bad, to another which seemed no better. Widdop, though, seemed more interested in the gully – Savage Gully, as it was called, then still unclimbed, and the subject of much speculation among Wastdale men. I was preoccupied with other, more imminent, terrors. I began to question Widdop about some of the more notorious features of the climb. The 'Strid', for instance.

"Oh, nothing very terrible. Just a long stride from the top of a block. 'With a drop into nothing beneath you, as straight as a beggar can spit.' "

To climb with Widdop was to be plied liberally with quotation.

We scrambled easily up the introductory walls and ledges in the lower part of Savage Gully. I was heartened by the sight of copious scratches on the rock. The passage of so many nailed boots somehow humanized the place. Confidence growing, I led the way. Widdop came up after me, chatting lightly of the abomination of darned stockings ('A blister one's first day out may be the ruin of a holiday') and the importance of lining the back of one's waistcoats ('Flannel, George – thick flannel').

The famous Stomach Traverse had loomed in my imagination as something grotesque and terrible. 'Crawlbelly ledge', Widdop called it. His jaunty phrase conveyed, as well as the method of progression, a disturbing suggestion as to the craven condition to which I might find myself reduced while negotiating its terrors. Yet, when the moment came, I might not have recognised the place had Widdop not pointed it out, so very safe and easy did I find it. Ten years earlier, with the deep groove at the back of the sloping ledge packed with earth, no doubt the pioneers had a nervy struggle. That day, with the earth removed and one leg well buried in the rift, I felt perfectly secure, though the position with half one's body hanging out over a smooth blank wall, was wonderfully exciting.

My glee at having so easily vanquished one of the principal terrors received a further boost at the next passage – a short cave pitch where the chief difficulty consisted in pulling over a large capstone forming the roof of the cave. This I managed at the first attempt. Though of only medium height, I was blessed with strong arms and fingers. Wherever my hands could take a good grip I flattered myself the rest of me would follow.

We had reached a point where a series of grass ledges formed an open area in the very middle of the crag. Still roped together we clattered up small scree towards the next pitch. I was in high spirits. The day was going well. One by one my dragons loomed, and submitted. I wriggled up the deep fissure to the top of the Split Blocks and stepped, with fine carelessness, across the Strid. So we came to the Nose.

No one who ever stood there is likely to forget it. That narrow platform, overhung by crags. Behind you, as you edge along it, is the Strid. Below, a sheer drop into the dripping depths of Savage Gully. To the left, bulging out over the gully and blocking further progress, is the famous Nose. Even on a rope it looks alarming. You step out to a spike of rock, reaching up at full stretch for a wrinkle on the sloping top of the Nose – then a long swing of the leg, up and round, for the good ledge you can't see and have to take on trust.

To lower Widdop into the gully it was necessary to descend to a grassy platform at the base of the Nose, where a sharp pinnacle of rock offered a belaying pin for the rope. Thus protected, Widdop climbed down twenty feet to a turf ledge. He then crossed the gully to ledges on its further side, retrieved the rope, and began a circuitous detour that would eventually bring him to the top of the Nose above my head.

Alone now and unroped, I examined my surroundings. This was a famous place. Lurking beneath the terse accounts in the Climbing Book, I'd detected the thrill of fear experienced by earlier climbers. It was indeed 'impressively dangerous and sensational'. I became aware of the silence. No sound, save for a stealthy trickle of meltwater somewhere in the gully. A faint murmur, rising and falling, was the river Liza two thousand feet below. Ten feet or so above my head a thin edge of rock – the famous hand traverse – ran like a broken gutter across the bulging wall to the top of the Nose. Mentally I rehearsed the opening moves: the step out on to that thin flake of rock, the left arm groping. The thought of committing myself to a hold I couldn't see was more than I cared to contemplate. It struck me that the hand traverse, however demanding, was at least visible. Though that too had an awesome history. I knew men had fallen off it. Only a handful had succeeded. It demanded strong arms and a stout heart.

As I stood uneasily debating, a sound of boots on stones somewhere above the Nose announced Widdop's arrival. Then an airy voice came floating down.

"What ho! George."

I caught sight of a wide-brimmed hat. Then, with a scattering of pebbles, the end of the rope arrived.

"Look here," I said, affecting a casualness I was far from feeling, "I think I'll have a shot at the traverse."

A moment's pause.

"Good for you!" The cheery voice radiated all the assurance I was lacking.

It was, I suppose, that unfailing confidence which made Widdop, as second man, such a tower of strength to an able leader. I was too inexperienced to recognize the insidious inducement it represented to a novice like myself.

"I say! I shan't take the rope in unless you want me to. Give you a chance to do it under your own steam. It'd be quite a feather in your cap."

No doubt it was well meant. Widdop's schoolmasterly way of encouraging a young aspirant. No doubt, too, he presumed I knew what I was doing.

I looked up at the traverse – the acute edge of the flake. More satisfying, I seemed to remember someone saying, than a horizontal bar.

"Just sing out if you want the rope."

Somehow or other I managed the few feet up to the flake. Then I set off, swinging along the traverse, toes pressed against the rock. In this fashion I managed half-a-dozen feet. Perhaps more. I might have gone further, who can say, had it not been for a break in the guttering, the upper, continuing edge perhaps a foot or so away. It needed a good pull – a reach – then another swing.

Suddenly I knew with absolute certainty I would not be able to finish the traverse. I glared up at Widdop.

"Come on," he cried. "You're doing splendidly!"

Desperately I glanced back, trying to gauge my chances of retreat. Yet when it came to it I couldn't budge. My hands seemed welded to the edge of the flake. I knew if I attempted to move in either direction I would fall. I was aware of noises, a scraping that must have been my boots scrabbling against the rock, Widdop's voice, as if from another world.

"Take in the rope," I screamed. "Take in!"

Then I was plunging backwards, the ledge rushing up to fling me out by the heels, it seemed, the very instant an unseen hand snatched me up again.

That night at dinner, amid much hilarity, the tale was told
of Hazard's narrow squeak.

" 'From morn to noon he fell, from noon to dewy eve.' "

Widdop's jests were gauged exactly to match the mood of a
company for whom laughter was the natural accompaniment of
a good dinner, as necessary as seasoning. A newcomer at the
table, a slender man in glasses, smiled quietly as if in deference
to the general mood. Though I fancied the eyes behind the
lenses were not smiling. Lockhart knew the place.

"What happened ?" repeated Widdop. "Why, he let go.
Now why, do you suppose, would a fellow want to do a thing
like that ?"

Let me say, I laughed with the rest. I have always loved
laughter. It is still, for me, one of the dearest things in life – the
warm, deep-throated laughter of men rejoicing together over
the day's adventure. Yet no man believes real fear – his own
heart-stopping terror – is ever experienced by others. Later that
night, as I took my candle, I confessed the terror of that traverse
– a terror so extreme that the fall, when it came, had seemed
almost a relief. It was out of my hands. It was over.

Widdop looked thoughtful. Then, as we went up the stair
together, he took my arm. Again I was made aware of that
remarkable self-possession which, in a tight corner, somehow
assured security.

"There's no shame, George, in feeling afraid. Fear is there
to be faced. What one makes of it is what matters. Afterwards
such things are best forgotten."

III

If I were to sit now under Scawfell Crag and look back to those halcyon days before the turn of the century, and see in my mind's eye the little party of friends toiling up Brown Tongue, it would be to pick out one in particular, moving faster than the rest – a lean, long-striding figure – slender, not much more than ten stone – who, without stopping, might greet you as he passed: *'Well, old fellow ! How about Collier's for a start ?'* Even after twenty years, Lockhart seems no less an enigma: that austere, enquiring face, the face of the solitary thinker, and the rangy whipcord figure of a man of great physical endurance, a man who must press on to the world's end if need be.

He'd arrived earlier that evening. Scorning the use of the hotel trap he'd walked, with rope and rucksack, the thirteen miles from Drigg.

Lockhart was a physicist. Though it was as Widdop's celebrated climbing partner that he was known to me. A less likely partnership could scarcely be imagined. Lockhart's field of interest lay in the primary constituents of matter. Or, as Widdop was wont to put it, 'the insides of things', a preoccupation for which he affected the utmost scorn.

"No doubt Lockhart was one of those odious small boys who are forever taking things to bits to see what makes them tick."

"Quite wrong, as usual."

Lockhart never seemed anything but amused by his friend's sallies.

"We can hear the ticking. We can even watch the hands going round. But we have no way of opening the clock. Not our kind of clock, anyway. So we must form theories to explain our observations."

Widdop, though, had little time for 'theories'.

"Oh, *science*," he would say. "Science might exercise a boy's intelligence, but it contributes nothing to the formation of his character. I'd rather a boy of mine believed the earth was flat than take up science."

They came from different worlds. Though the urbane Widdop would have taken care to seem at ease even in the rarified regions of the Cavendish laboratory, Lockhart would have been a fish out of water amid the rough-and-tumble of Widdop's public school.

In fact, they rarely met, except at Wastdale Head. For they were famously known never to invade one another's territory.

"The secret of a happy marriage," Widdop would say airily, "is to avoid one another's company. Lockhart and I meet only now and then at a remote hotel."

Yet Christmas and Easter they were the staunchest of companions: the daring leader, the safe, dependable second man. It was the *sang-froid* Lockhart valued. That cool control. In those days, when any form of inwardness was regarded as unhealthy, manner served as a protection. It stabilised the man.

Meanwhile, our climb on the Pillar was still a topic of conversation. More than once I'd had my arm taken after dinner, and been assured that the traverse had defeated 'some very good men'. I received the plaudits, still somewhat dazed at the shifting fortunes of a day which had seen me first frightened out of my wits (and made to feel foolish into the bargain), now declared a daring fellow. By this stage the evening was well advanced. Second sitting had long since finished, and to judge from the jovial din coming from the billiard room the sporting activities were in full swing. I fully intended joining them later, for I knew that whatever ribbing I might have to endure would be tinged with envy and admiration. Besides, I'd promised Slater over dinner to make up a pair for a challenge match on the billiard table.

I was expecting any minute to be summoned thither when a slim figure slipped quietly in at the smoke-room door.

Widdop introduced us. "Lockhart, I want you to meet George Hazard."

I ventured to say how sorry I was he'd not been with us earlier in the day.

"Don't apologise," said Widdop tartly. "He wouldn't have come. Lockhart takes little pleasure in repeating climbs he knows."

"Oh, they're too comfortable. One should always attempt the unfamiliar, don't you think ?"

Lockhart's eyes fastened on me in a scrutiny as intense as it was disconcerting. I had the sense of being weighed up. At the same time I felt I was being mocked. Or perhaps rebuked. I didn't know which.

At that moment the door was suddenly flung open.

"Ah, Hazard, there you are. We're on."

Slater had come to claim his partner. Relieved, I went to join him.

*

Fives, as played at school, was never so thrilling or exhausting as when battled out on the billiard table at Wastdale Head. The room was never heated, not even in the bitterest weather, and our bodies steamed like cattle as we barged back and forth. The ivory ball flew about like a bullet. If lamps and windows suffered more casualties than players and spectators it was due to sheer good fortune: that, and the speedy reflexes of

youth. The ball flew, and we leapt after it, heedless of danger.
Back it came, hammered by our opponent, Slater leaping aside
from the flying missile which buried itself in the chimney breast
behind his head, to be recovered only after lengthy gropings up
the chimney. On it went, back and forth. At last, to wild shouts
of exultation, and a great cheer from the spectators packing the
doorway, the ball, flying true from a well-aimed blow by Slater,
lodged in one of the pockets for the winning point. The
challenge match decided, we now vied with one another in feats
of strength or agility, wriggling through chair-backs, or vaulting
over the corner of the billiard table. My own party piece
consisted in passing underneath the table from one side to the
other, without touching the floor. I lacked the strength and
stamina necessary for the real *pièce de resistance* – a complete
circuit of the room. Only one man had so far managed that.
Indeed, in all these feats and strivings there was, if half the stories
told of him were true, but one supreme champion and exemplar.
A half-legendary man.

*

Strange to say, I never knew Jones. The Easter of '98, when
he made his epic climb from Lord's Rake to Scawfell Pinnacle,
found me laid up with a bout of 'flu. That Christmas the usual
family gathering summoned me to my grandfather's estate in
Scotland. The following Easter Jones was in Snowdonia, while
I was at Wastdale Head. Before the end of the summer he was
dead.

Though I never saw him in the flesh, that buttoned cap,
the thick round spectacles, the coil of rope slung over a shoulder
were as familiar to me as the many stories told about him. The
Only Genuine Jones. Though that breezy gloss on his own

initials drew from Widdop a tart rejoinder.

"There's no such thing as a genuine Jones. All Joneses are thoroughly spurious."

By any account OGJ was not without his shortcomings. Even the legend admitted to failings. He fell off fairly frequently. He had little sense of direction. He often got lost, while claiming to know precisely where the party was. He was also very short-sighted. Indeed, Widdop held that Jones's myopia actually constituted an unfair advantage, since it prevented him from recognising the perilous nature of the positions into which he got himself, situations from which only a man as formidably equipped as he could have emerged unscathed.

To the older generation at Wastdale Head there was something coarse-grained, even flashy about Jones. Deprived by natural science of the religion of their childhood they found a reflection of its transcendent mysteries among great mountains. OGJ's ape-like antics, swinging from the girders of the university laboratory, scampering across the rivets in railways engines, mocked exalted sentiment. In London, denied the mountains, he'd been known to climb church towers. Cleopatra's Needle and the facade of the Albert Hall were said to number among his conquests. Everything he did suggested to some a man whose chief interest lay less in mountains than in his own performance. Nonetheless, whatever they thought of Jones, none of them would have expressed their detestation as unreservedly as Crowley.

*

By the time I first began to visit the mountains Crowley was no longer to be seen in Wastdale. His name was never mentioned. Later however, long after the events referred to in this narrative, our paths were to cross.

It was in Paris some years after the turn of the century. For several days running I'd noticed a man of striking appearance sitting outside the Café du Dôme in Montparnasse. A man a little older than myself. Shaven-headed, with curiously pointed ears and dark staring eyes.

"Un sorcier notoire," I was informed in a whisper. "Un anglais."

The effect was certainly impressive. Svengali seated at a pavement café. Though the sinister pretension was rather undermined by a certain theatricality of dress and manner – the black cloak, the wizard's staff. Evidently Crowley was appearing, so to speak, 'in character'. Clearly the situation called for a striking entrance. Swiftly I sketched on the back of a menu card a rough but unmistakeable outline of the Napes Needle, scribbled *Greetings from Wastdale!*, and sent it over to his table.

Crowley studied it a moment then, turning his heavy features in my direction, lowering his head and opening his eyes wide, he fixed me with a prolonged, penetrating stare.

It was a tactic, as I swiftly realised, designed to unsettle. I continued to smoke, keeping my gaze an inch or two above his head. Eventually he beckoned me over.

I was perhaps lucky to encounter him when his astral plane (if that is the right term) was in the ascendent. Certainly he radiated an aura of malignant satisfaction, having triumphed (by his own account) in some battle of spells with a rival sorcerer whose occult missiles, deflected by Crowley's superior defences, had rebounded on their perpetrator. *Naturally the man was doomed.* This sentence he pronounced in an unusually husky, rather sibilant tone, no doubt cultivated to convey a sense of menace.

However, I soon realised that the advantage lay with me.

Evidently Crowley was eager for news. (It was long after the Kangchenjunga scandal had put an end to his career. No one, not even his friend Eckenstein, would have climbed with him after that.) Eventually the talk turned to the tale of his own exploits, his climbs on Beachey Head and the Needle, his seasons in the Alps.

Jones ? Oh yes, he'd climbed with Jones. A fraud – a mountebank – a self-seeking publicist who went about with his own personal photographers.

Much of what Crowley had to say might have been put down to spite, the jealousy a man might feel for a rival, a man of the same sort as himself. One, moreover, who had surpassed him in achievement. Yet some of it had a familiar ring. I'd heard others, men of unimpeachable integrity (as Crowley most certainly was not), raise questions with regard to Jones' methods.

"You know, of course, how he won his reputation ? He had himself hoisted up and down a climb repeatedly by his photographer friends. Then, when he'd learnt the sequence of holds sufficiently well, he made what he had the brass neck to claim as a 'first ascent'. Now all the merit of a first ascent rests on its having been precisely that. It does not allow for being held on a rope while making a prior inspection."

Be that as it may, I pointed out, surely Jones must have been a superb climber ? After all, one only had to look at the climbs he made.

It was a concession Crowley was by no means prepared to allow.

"No one can be a good climber," he went on, "who is not at the same time a safe climber. Jones' methods were highly dangerous. If he couldn't reach a hold – he was very short, you know, little more than a dwarf – he would simply jump for it."

However, what struck me as truly rich was to hear Crowley (sworn enemy of everything the age held sacred), as well as evincing a horror of anything remotely infringing the notion of fair play in a matter of sport, invoking that cardinal rule of gentlemanly conduct, our detestation of 'brag'.

"Oh yes," he said. "That too. Jones was abominably conceited."

Not everyone took that view. Lockhart, for instance, while admitting to a certain self-regard in Jones, saw the matter rather differently. Not surprisingly, perhaps. They were, after all, both physicists.

"Yes, he talked a good deal about himself. And of course some men disliked him for it. But Jones took a scientist's interest in what was after all only another physical system. He only spoke of what, in his view, had been tested by experiment, something he'd been able to verify for himself."

Yet even the most reticent of men could be drawn on the subject of Jones. One evening in the smoke room a few of us, half-serious, half-ragging, were extolling the superior achievements of the younger generation. Naturally OGJ's name figured prominently. At length Professor Collie, a man given to listening rather than talking, unexpectedly entered the conversation. Leaning back in his chair, all the while staring into the fire, pipe in hand, he began to tell the tale of a day at the Napes years earlier, and of a man stuck on the top of the Needle, stranded, quite unable to move; a man who might have been there to that very day had not he, Collie, climbed up and helped him down.

He turned his head and looked at us significantly.

"That man," he said, "was Jones."

Collie replaced his pipe in his mouth with the air of a man who'd said all that was needful.

To restrained, cultivated men like Collie, Jones remained a reckless and flamboyant exhibitionist. But legends accrue wherever men gather, and fireside tales are told. And we were young. We had a taste for such things. Whatever his short-comings, Jones defined all our aspirations. He was our universal man, our hero and our inspiration.

Shortly before his death he'd surpassed everything he'd done before in a brilliant display of skill and courage. With darkness coming on, he'd climbed from Lords Rake to the top of Scawfell Pinnacle, stepping up in stockinged feet over slabs so smooth and steep they were generally considered impossible.

"Of course, if Jones could have seen it," said Widdop in his flippant way, "he would never have done it."

The simplest, yet most telling, tribute came from an unexpected quarter.

"He went," a sober voice said quietly, "where no other men would go."

Coming from Lockhart there could be no higher praise.

IV

That summer of '99 war was in the offing. I went up as usual to the Blackmount. It was the time of year (Hogmanay being another) when my grandfather expected a visit from his sons. I say 'his sons'. I dare say he was indifferent whether or not wives or daughters joined the party.

We were a largish company. As well as my own family, there were my Uncles Guy and Giles, my Great-Uncle Rufus, plus the usual bevy of aunts and cousins. Behind us we left a city buzzing with the coming conflict. In London men talked of nothing else. As the exchange of demands, conditions, charge and countercharge dragged on, ominous reports had begun to filter back from Natal. In the Transvaal the Boers were collecting horses and distributing rifles. Dutch farmers from the Free State, accustomed to grazing their cattle across the border, had driven them back behind the barrier of the Drakensburgs. The veldt, it was said, had been fired earlier than usual to hasten a fresh grass-crop after the first rains. Yet, come what may, August was August. Not even the proximity of war could be allowed to divert Father and his brothers from the shooting of stags.

An army of porters was required to load our mountain of luggage, piled on the platform at King's Cross: rods, rifles, boots, sticks, dogs – all the impedimenta of a Highland visit. Two sleeping carriages were reserved for our party. The maids and cooks came too, dressed in their Sunday best.

Grandfather usually came in state to meet the train at Bridge of Orchy. A short stocky figure with grey close-cropped beard, his eyes hollowed out by years of exposure to Highland weather, he seemed indistinguishable from the wild-looking band of retainers who clustered round the wagonettes.

Then followed six bone-shaking miles over rutted tracks before the welcome sight of spires and turrets coming into view above the pines beside the loch. Then it was stiff drams for the men, and a clatter and bustle of water lugged upstairs for steaming baths.

My mother dreaded these forays north. I believe she would gladly have taken to her bed for the duration of the visit, had not duty decreed otherwise. Even so, she remained in her room for most of each morning.

But for the guns it was promptly down to breakfast, and then out to the hill. The gong would sound, a low urgent clamour. Then, with a clatter of boots on bare boards, in they came, Uncle Guy clapping his hands and rubbing them together as if through sheer excess of vigour, of zest for the day.

Indeed, my father and his brothers were very like that earlier generation I met at Wastdale. They too were buoyant, energetic men. To my boyish mind they seemed the very embodiment of industry and inventiveness, men who might have accomplished anything to which they set their minds. My Uncle Guy built ships. Uncle Giles was a partner in a merchant bank. Father was a Queen's Counsel, and a Bencher of Lincoln's Inn.

Fond though he was of describing himself as 'a refugee from marine engineering', Father remained intensely proud of the family industry and inventiveness. In the dining room at home hung a family icon: Tuke's painting of the 'Northumbrian Star'. It was one of the first steam ships built in the Hazard yards. *True, I chose a different life for myself. In every generation men have their dreams. And they are not always the dreams of their fathers.* Then the great grey eyes set deep in their sockets would take on a distant look. I liked to fancy Father had a look of Collie about him. He was a fine-looking man, certainly, with his dark silky hair curling in the nape of his neck, his shrubby eyebrows, straight nose, thin, lawyer's lips.

That night at dinner, instead of 'points' and 'heads', all the talk was of a likely show-down.

"It was bound to happen," rumbled old Rufus. "The country's paying now for Gladstone's shameful capitulation after that fiasco at Majuba Hill. This time, at any rate, we shan't make the mistake of underestimating an enemy."

"At last," said fat Giles Every, my cousin, "they're going to get the lesson we should have taught them twenty years ago."

He seemed to relish the prospect of the Boers getting a hiding. His home was in the Cape, and his people had not forgotten that old humiliation before their Dutch neighbours after Majuba.

"Kruger will climb down," said Father. "You'll see. Always providing, of course, the government stays firm."

"They'll fight," grunted my grandfather morosely. "They fought in '81, and they'll fight again. In their place I'd fight too."

He was a moody, unpredictable man. In an age when behaviour was governed by a complicated code of manners, grandfather made people feel uneasy. He outraged my mother. *It's quite deliberate. Everything he does is calculated to cause discomfort.* Certainly his was a disconcerting presence. Some men give off light. With grandfather it was darkness. Just why it should seem so is difficult to say. It had perhaps as much to do with the sombre setting of his life. So many years of barbarous isolation, my mother used to say, had destroyed his capacity for cultivated contact. She hated the lowering skies. The dark looming hills.

And yet that gloomy soul was lit by the extraordinary grace and floating beauty of red deer.

My grandfather was one of those men whose lives are

changed by a book. Though the change took many years to put into effect. As eldest son he could not refuse his place in a great family concern. Half the trade of the world was carried about the seven seas by British tonnage, a fair proportion of which was built in the Hazard yards. But grandfather never forget Scrope's *Days of Deerstalking*. In middle life, chancing across an impoverished young laird with a taste for the high life, he bought an estate, turned the shipyards over to a younger brother, and devoted the rest of his days to the study of red deer.

Since I hated shooting I usually spent my time roaming the hills. That summer, though, I'd brought my books with me. While Father and his brothers were out chasing the deer I sat at the library table struggling with the elements of Morphology. Two years of grinding application had seen me through my 2nd MB. It had been a dour struggle, for I had done no chemistry and little of the biology required for the first year Medical course. The family showed little enthusiasm for my choice of career. My mother had grown up with a notion of medical students as low fellows with whom she would not wish her son to associate. Indeed, I was still ashamed to think of the indecent jokes and obscene mnemonics I'd encountered in the anatomy rooms. I thought it vile that elderly men should talk so to boys scarcely out of school.

But, since I flatly refused to contemplate life as a lawyer, Father had regretfully settled for medicine. It had become his habit to refer to it as if it were a disappointment with which he was struggling to come to terms. *Ah well, it's no bad thing, I suppose, to have a sawbones in the family.* Uncle Guy was rather less accommodating. One evening I came across him in the library glancing through one of my books.

"Seems a damned squalid business," he muttered. "Only one remove from poking about in people's mouths."

After breakfast on Sundays, since local susceptibilities forbade the slaughtering of deer on the Sabbath, the male members of the party retired to the library to pore over maps and gazetteers. Now, all attention was focused on Natal. The vulnerability of its northern border, a sprit of mountainous country sandwiched between the Boer republics, was much remarked upon as my uncles formulated a defensive strategy. The most popular theory had a Boer force driving in from either side, severing communications and cutting off retreat.

It was the position of Ladysmith in particular that gave cause for concern.

Father had evidently given some thought to the deployment of his forces. He dug out a large atlas from the shelves to demonstrate his plan. "The only feasible line of defence," he said, "is here. The Tugela. A dozen miles to the south."

He traced it on the map.

"And here," (tapping with a finger) "you have Ladysmith. These" (circling brown heights) "are hills. You see my point."

My Uncle Guy frowned as he peered over Father's shoulder.

"You intend to abandon Glencoe to the Boers?"

"That'll put them about a dozen miles from where we're sitting now," I muttered. It was a flippant, foolish remark. One I instantly regretted.

Uncle Guy stared blankly. Uncle Giles was lighting his pipe.

"Glencoe, *Natal*," he murmured, between puffs. "A railway junction."

"I don't suppose George knows that."

Father's voice was ominously jocular.

"I don't suppose George could even name the capitals of the Boer republics."

Cold grey eyes bored into mine.

"Well, George ?"

Mr Roderick Hazard QC was cross-examining a witness.

"I'll settle for just one."

As I sat silent, smarting.

"It's not clever heads we need," old Rufus growled from the depths of an armchair. "Good Lord! Any old cabbage will do for a head. What England needs is hearts. Eh, George ?"

It was a somewhat back-handed intervention. Yet I was grateful. Dear good old man. He was always a true friend.

Back in London I was still smarting from Father's savaging. Though it was nothing new. Father's forensic skills were more than a match for those who were neither learned friends nor hostile witnesses, but merely members of his family. Yet his onslaught had shamed as much as it had wounded. For it was true. I was only too conscious of my lack of general knowledge. I had no interest in politics. I rarely read a newspaper, except to study the cricket scores. I knew more – it wasn't much – about topographical anatomy than about the Uitlanders or the Boer republics. Yet I was no different from most other undergraduates of my generation. The world of affairs meant little to us, the charge of it being vested then in men so old that any responsibility we might expect to inherit seemed infinitely distant. Sometimes, on my way to a dissection class, I used to pass a venerable old gentleman out and about in his bathchair, Master of Clare since the Crimean War. At Magdalene my cousin Giles had for Master of his college a man whose office had been filled once in ninety years. Nevertheless, I resolved from that day forward at least to glance through *The Times* each day.

V

It was Father's habit to refer to Cambridge as 'the city of idle youth'. It used to irritate me intensely. Of course, he had a point. Certainly there was no great pressure to work. A good many men went up with little intention of doing anything very serious. A neighbour of mine established himself in his rooms with such self-effacing idleness as to escape the notice of the authorities for several weeks until an unfortunate encounter with the Dean drew attention to his presence. All this was very hard on a medical student like myself. For we had to work. The sheer quantity of material to be mastered was truly daunting. My constant anxiety was that I should never be able to cope with it all, and the fear of failure kept one up to the mark. Examinations punctuated the course like fences. To fall at one was simply to have it tacked on to the next round. I was now approaching my last year, and the relief of having passed my 2nd MB was of small consolation when set against the continuing drudgery of Chemistry. It was a subject which reduced me to despair. Particularly galling was the fact that, acting on my tutor's advice, I'd chosen it as my third subject for the Tripos. My own inclination had been towards Zoology. *No, my boy, atoms and molecules, atoms and molecules. That's what you should study.*

At the end of August I returned to Cambridge. I was determined to pull in a thorough revision course in Chemistry prior to the start of Full Term in October. Slater had agreed to join me in this enterprise. He was a carroty youth with long bleached lashes, that gave him somewhat of a sly look. Circumstances had rather thrown us together. We'd worked in harness from the moment it first became clear that I was the possessor of a fine skeleton about which I knew next to nothing, whereas he seemed already to have got off the significance of every groove and nodule. He was also rather a dab hand at dissecting. Since we were in the same chemical boat we'd agreed to follow the same programme of revision, share the practical work, and go to the same coach. Furthermore, we could test each other's progress. As he lived in the set above mine, it was a convenient arrangement. Our routines would be identical: breakfast in our rooms, a quick glimpse of the cricket scores (like me Slater was an avid follower), then down to business.

The morning had begun as usual. Mrs Stubbings arrived with hot water. A porter brought round our copies of *The Times*. The day's work lay ready on the table: *Alkaloids; their chemistry and detection*. Well satisfied with Yorkshire's progress at the Oval, I'd finished breakfast and was just folding the paper, when a headline on an inside page caught my attention.

DISASTER ON THE DENT BLANCHE. Even as my eyes raced through the paragraph, I heard Slater thudding down the stairs. I met him at my door. Thunderstruck, we stared at one another. Jones dead ! It wasn't possible.

Over the next few days, as more details were made public, there emerged a familiar pattern of events: a falling guide sweeping away the party, the breaking of the rope, a lone survivor ... it revived memories of the Matterhorn disaster thirty years before.

Many were the tributes paid to Jones, from fellow climbers, as well as colleagues at the City of London School. OG's landlady spoke of him as the kindest, most considerate of lodgers. The sense of shock and incredulity was almost universal. Slater, in particular, was stunned at the news. He'd actually once climbed with Jones, a man, he said, so recklessly, unstintingly alive as to make allegations of his death seem scarcely credible.

Only the *Manchester Guardian* struck a dissonant note:

Many climbers hold, we rightly think, that to take the risk of such places is bad mountaineering, bad mountaineering being a kind of gambling with nature for your life. Good mountaineering means the unfailing maintenance of a clear balance of precaution over risk, the very worst that can happen only bringing into action a safeguard pre-arranged to meet it.

The following day the same paper published a letter from Widdop. He took a different line altogether. Not surprisingly, given the alarming nature of the views expressed, it caused something of a stir. Yet to me, at twenty, its note of gay defiance, its call to live life to the full, was wonderfully stirring. I was so impressed that I cut out the piece and kept it. I have it still. Reflecting on it now, after twenty years, I'm struck by its remarkable candour.

Life is fragile. Men are vulnerable. Moreover, there are forces, eventualities beyond our reckoning or control. So let us set up an ideal. Let us recognize our mountaineering for what it is – a way of life. What matter, should it be death and not victory which awaits us in the end ? It is the quality, not the mere brute fact, of our living that must be the end of all our striving. Then let us commend reck-lessness: that is, not reckoning the loss. An Englishman can prove his pedigree by showing that he is not afraid of anything, that he can rise to any challenge, even the challenge of Death. In so doing, he exemplifies the spirit of a race that will not die.

At the same time, well aware of the distaste he felt for Jones, to say nothing of the animus he cherished towards the *Manchester Guardian*, I was rather surprised that Widdop should want to write at all.

Slater put it down to his combative nature.

"It's obviously Montague who wrote the *Guardian* leader. Widdop's just having a smack at Charley Montague."

I've no doubt that behind it loomed the coming war. At the same time it pointed to something I certainly hadn't grasped, though I came to understand it later: that in recognizing what had to be defended was the loss of life itself, Widdop went to the very heart of our ideal of manly courage.

Full Term began in a ferment. All that week sabres had been rattling in the press: the Army reserve called out; pages filled with lists of postings. From Bombay and Calcutta, from Alexandria, Malta, Crete, British troops were steaming ever closer towards Natal. Like most young men I was caught up in the general excitement. I'd discovered that the issues were quite clear. The Dutch way, apparently, was to put every obstacle they could in the path of progress, while exploiting everything that was being done for them, and grabbing every penny they could squeeze out of it for themselves. One's duty in the matter seemed beyond question. It was what one would expect of any straightforward, honest Englishmen. Men like my great-uncle Rufus. Britons were being ill-treated. A great wrong was being done. It should be put right.

Then, one morning over breakfast, I saw that the Transvaal Boers had issued an ultimatum. *The Times* declared itself uncertain whether to laugh or cry. Nevertheless, it seemed clear that we would be at war by tea-time. That probability, taken in with the toast and marmalade, struck me as quite extraordinary. I was still ruminating on it when my bedder, Mrs Stubbings, announced a visitor.

"Buck up, George," a voice cried. "You're coming to the races."

It was my cousin Giles, bombastic as ever. His uncle had a horse running in the Cesarewitch. Very well. He ordered a hamper, hired a carriage, and then informed his friends that they were coming to the races. Of course he would brook no refusal. "No more excuses, George," he said. "You're coming to the races!" There was more than a touch of Toad about Giles Every.

Outside the porters' lodge, quivering and snorting as though impatient to be gone, stood a Daimler motor car. I regarded it dubiously, for I knew my father looked on motoring as a very low affair quite unworthy of a gentleman.

"It's a double phaeton," said Giles impressively. "And of course the Daimler is a very reliable machine. We should arrive at Newmarket in under the hour."

In an instant I found myself propelled into the back of the vehicle, wedged beside a whiskered youth. Giles took his seat next to the chauffeur. Minutes later, we were bowling through the flat fen country out beyond Fen Ditton.

"A very good level road all the way," Giles turned to yell.

It was just as well. Seated over the rear wheel, I was receiving a jolting lively enough to churn butter. The dust flew up, the air rushed in our faces, the great car plunged forward, sweeping us along in a state of high excitement. Our thoughts soon turned to the coming war. Though it seemed scarcely possible to take, for serious adversary, a farmer on a horse.

"From what I hear," shouted my whiskery neighbour, "they're quite outraged by the use of dynamite bombs to bring down rain. It's firing on God. Isn't that it?"

"Oh yes," yelled Every. "That's quite true. It's absolutely against their religious beliefs to dip their sheep, or to take measures against cattle plague. Locusts are as sacrosanct to them as a cow is to a Hindu. You see, they figure in the Bible."

This image of ignorance and superstition was embodied for

us in the person of Kruger, whom we knew for a surly peasant, who disdained to speak the language of Shakespeare and Milton, and whose only reading was the Old Testament. How we vied with one another in itemising his absurdities. The silk hat. The puffy oyster eyes. The frock coat covered with stains.

"They say his personal habits," the whiskery youth spluttered, "are no more salubrious than his appearance."

Every, whose brother-in-law was an aide to the High Commissioner, could confirm every detail. "That's right," he shouted. "The man spits at random. He blows his nose through his fingers. He actually arrived for lunch with Milner with a filthy pipe sticking out of his breast pocket."

Enclosed in a gale of ridiculing laughter, we swept on towards Newmarket Heath.

The weather was perfect. Autumn that year had blessed us with the most Indian of summers. And how we revelled in it. We strolled with the crowd in the warm sunshine. We feasted on game-pie and champagne. We cheered the Prince of Wales, and hissed the Liberals. In the paddock before the race, helpless with laughter, we smote one another's shoulders at the sight of Lily Langtry's colt lashing out at a rival. Plucked so unexpectedly from the arid zone of practical chemistry and set down on this great expanse of heath, under an empty bowl of blue sky, I felt as if I were floating off into some wondrous anarchic space. It was all too extraordinary for words.

It had been a warm day, and as the afternoon drew on the atmosphere began to thicken. The start of the race was delayed for some twenty minutes. We gazed expectantly through our glasses, but runners and riders were indistinct, blent together in an autumn haze. I could make out little beyond a smudge of smoke rising from burning stubble somewhere over the horizon. Then a great shout announced the 'off'. Still there was nothing to be seen. The field entered the Rowley Mile all together in a cluster. Six furlongs out the line began to break. Neck and neck the leaders raced, stride for stride, to a great storm of cheering as the winner crossed the line. Every's uncle's horse, I noticed with some satisfaction, trailed in well down the field.

Afterwards, I commiserated with him.

" Did you lose much ?"

"Good heavens, no. I backed the winner."

The general acclamation as the triumphant owner led his colt into the enclosure had not yet subsided. Still it went on, cheer after cheer.

I noticed men around me examining their watches. Then Giles, bending close, was yelling in my ear that the Boer ultimatum had expired.

"Kruger's asked for war," he shouted. "War he must have."

VI

Even as a child I had a passion for adventure. The drawing room at Onslow Place, a restful haven of quiet blues and greens, seemed an unlikely place to look for it. Yet how many afternoons must I have spent stretched out with a book on the great Donegal rug, or curled up in the embrasure of a window ? Oblivious of my mother and sisters chatting of this and that over their sewing for the needy, I sought to distance myself as far as possible from respectable society. *Treasure Island* was the magic book of my childhood. After tea on Sunday afternoons Father, seated in his big armchair, would read it aloud, doing the Squire and the Doctor and all the pirates in different voices. Though there was often a price to be paid for my excitement; dreams in which I saw the blind beggar, tap-tapping down the empty road in the moonlight, and woke up screaming. Yet all my daylight games were of fighting pirates and finding buried treasure.

Later, as a boy at school, I still wondered, with David Copperfield, if I would be the hero of my own life, or would it be some other. Then, some time during my last year, grandfather made me a present of Nansen's *Farthest North*. I turned the pages of those marvellous volumes, gazing at the wondrous colour plates, filled with a host of wild imaginings. The sheer audacity of it, with all the father-figures prophesying disaster, simply drifting toward the Pole with his ship locked in the ice, shocked and excited my timid soul. For a while I affected a 'Nansen' jacket, a distinctive garment, buttoned up to the neck. Even sported the wide, black-brimmed hat.

*

In term time I rarely travelled more than a mile or two from Cambridge. For once, however, a powerful magic had summoned me to London.

That morning I'd received a telegram from Widdop. His fondness for telegrams was notorious. It was, I fancied, an extension of the schoolmasterly habit: magisterial commands sent winging about the country, succinct, peremptory: *Tonight Stop Alpine Club Stop Recent Explorations Bolivian Andes Stop Do Come Stop*

If the character of the explorer had become for me a touchstone of romance, Conway, the lecturer that evening, looked every inch the part. A tall imposing figure with luxuriant mustachios and flowing locks, he came as close as any to the Elizabethan ideal of the 'compleat' man. Some years earlier he'd led the first ever expedition to the Himalaya. There he'd mapped the vast glaciers of the Karakoram, climbing to the greatest height then attained by man, to be knighted by the Queen on his return. Not long afterwards, he'd made the first crossing of Spitzbergen. Now he was back from South America.

What he had to say about Illimani and Aconcagua (he had climbed them both) I've long forgotten, but his concluding remarks made a deep impression on my ardent soul. Referring to some old controversy of which I was then ignorant, he remained, he said, an unrepentant 'eccentrist', not settling comfortably in some hotel, but travelling, always travelling among the mountains. He held out his dream of life as an adventure of the spirit. Each day a plunge into the unknown. He quoted Montaigne: *'What truth is it lies behind those mountain walls, that is a lie here in the world beyond?'* "Surely it is better," he concluded, "to look for what we do not know, than to slumber in the assumption that it can never be discovered, or think it not our business to pursue it?"

After the lecture we took a cab back to Chelsea. Widdop had invited me to supper. Since our climb together on Pillar I'd been rather taken up, if that is the phrase, by Widdop. I'd not long left school and was no doubt flattered by the friendship of a cultivated and amusing older man. He was an entertaining companion, with a fund of stories, not only of mountaineers, but of poets and writers and the days when, as one of the poet Henley's 'young men', he'd supped at Solferino's with Wilde and Aubrey Beardsley.

"I thought that was truly splendid," I said, filled with enthusiasm for the lecture.

"Oh, Conway is a bit of a romantic, don't you think ?" said Widdop absently.

It left me confused, uncertain what to think, for I'd expected him to endorse my admiration. As we trotted through the quiet streets I sensed my companion's mood had changed. He was civil enough, yet distant, withdrawn. It was a humour I hadn't seen in him before.

Always ill-at-ease in a protracted silence, and thinking to make conversation, I reverted to the accident on the Dent Blanche. The shock of Jones' death was still recent enough for it to have been a talking point that evening. It brought other tragedies to mind. First, Professor Hopkinson, killed with his three children on the Petite Dent de Veisivi. Now, of all people, OG himself.

"For once, Jones got it wrong," said Widdop tersely.

Startled, I remarked that as I understood it the fault, if fault there was, lay with the guide.

"That's what I mean. Guides are for tourists, not for mountaineers. The mountaineer relies upon himself."

Sunk back in the shadow of the cab Widdop said nothing more. As we drew into Tite Street I found myself wracking my brain for something, anything, that might do to lift his spirits. For I was hungry. I wanted my supper, and I didn't relish eating it with a gloomy host. Yet the mood, the atmosphere I sensed on entering the house, seemed to match that of my companion. Later, through days spent on the wards, I was to become all too familiar with that subdued, oppressive presence. It was the strain of waiting for a death. Silently we climbed the stairs, and entered a dim, high *salon*.

Designed, like the house itself, by the painter James Widdop, it bore all the hallmarks of a grandiose and eclectic style. Lamplight glinted on painted Chinese screens, bronze statuettes and lacquered cabinets. Every surface bore its accumulation of bric-a-brac: jugs, braziers, delicate porcelain tea-pots, carvings, cases of ferns, stuffed birds and animals entombed in glass. It was scarcely possible to move without dislodging some trifling knick-knack, or banging into something. I imagined the relief with which Widdop must have escaped to the rough, easy-going world of his Devon schoolboys, or his climbing friends in Wastdale. Lining the walls were prints and watercolours that grew less and less distinct as they mounted towards the ceiling. Widdop explained, in a voice barely raised above a whisper, that the room had been preserved almost exactly as when lived in by his grandfather.

At the far end was an extraordinary vaulted inglenook, with half-panelled fireplace, set in an arch crowned by an elaborate cornice. Behind the arch, at first hidden from view, sat a young woman. Pale, exhausted-looking, she rose to greet me stiffly, though with formal courtesy.

"I'm sorry my mother is not able to receive you. She is unwell."

Widdop himself passed no comment. Yet in his swift glance of enquiry, a mute communication passing from brother to sister,

I sensed their mutual distress. I knew something of the tragic family history. As a boy Widdop had seen his father struck down in a senseless street accident. Death, in the shape of cart, carriage – whatever it was – took the man and spared the child. Now it was the mother, dying by degrees.

We supped à *deux*, Widdop's sister having excused herself.

Hungry as I was, the thought of the woman dying somewhere in the house affected me. I felt I ought to have no appetite at all. Widdop, though, ate ravenously.

After supper, I learnt something of the case-history.

"It started with, of all things, a game of tennis. She loved tennis. But she was finding it difficult to serve the ball. We thought nothing of it. Even when she fell in the garden and broke her arm it didn't seem especially significant. Then she began to walk rather stiffly, cautiously. We assumed she was frightened of falling again."

Quietly he described the stages of his mother's illness: the tremors, the shuffling gait, a growing confusion. As he did so I began to recognise, with secret satisfaction at my own diagnosis, the symptoms of a progressive neurological disorder.

"Within a few months she could scarcely walk unaided. We used to put her in a chair out there in the garden."

Worst of all was the gradual estrangement; that slow, drifting away from all connection. The smile, but not *her* smile, when they approached. *Hello?* Curious, enquiring.

All this Widdop had related without a flicker of emotion. Now he picked up a photograph from a rosewood chiffonier. Wordlessly he handed it to me. Gazing out from the silver frame was a sweet-faced woman, a boy and girl at her feet.

"She has no idea who we are."

He sat, head thrown back, hands resting on the arms of his chair, staring into the fire.

I kept silent for I knew Widdop's beliefs allowed him neither explanation nor comfort. At length, rather at a loss, I remarked awkwardly that life could seem like hell.

"There's no 'seem' about it, old fellow. Look around you. It is hell. It has all the identifying characteristics. The flames are everywhere, and they are inexhaustible: the pain of loss and separation, memory of past follies, remorse – the worm that never dies, futile repentance, self-loathing."

I dare say I looked rather startled, for I remember Widdop smiled his enigmatic smile, as if he spoke of depths beyond my comprehension.

It was late when I left. I walked home slowly by the Embankment, turning the evening over and over in my mind. All the excitement, the exhilaration of Conway's lecture had evaporated. I blamed Widdop for that. To tell the truth, I hadn't much enjoyed his confiding in me as he had. There are times, in one's own youthful eagerness for life, when the intimacies of others seem an intrusion. I wasn't ready for it. I found what he'd told me oppressive in the extreme. I wondered if he'd ever spoken so to Lockhart. Or were these intimacies reserved for me alone ? It was a thought I didn't relish. As I came up to Chelsea Bridge I reflected uneasily that the last few hours seemed to have shifted our friendship on to a wholly different footing. As if Widdop had suddenly become a different person. Or else I had never really known him.

Perplexed, jolted out of my usual healthy egotism, I wondered what it was about him that made me so uneasy. Yet it seemed unjust and unmanly to hold Widdop responsible for my lack of understanding. The less I understood the more reason, I thought, to keep faith with him. There were, after all, a great many things that lay, as yet, beyond my understanding.

It was quiet by the embankment. Lamplight falling through the branches of the trees made a tracery on the flags. It was a relief to think of London spread out all around me, the vast sprawl of its streets and suburbs, its great buildings, its noble monuments. Below the parapet the river flowed, sombre, majestic. A few lights twinkled on the Surrey shore. Up ahead I caught sight of the green stern light of some barge moving silently downstream towards St Pauls. Up west, at the Cecil or the Savoy, the supper parties would still be in full swing. I fancied I could hear the faint dreamy strains of a waltz wafting over the water.

VII

Back in Cambridge after my weekend off, I got down to work again. It was turning out a frantic, disorganised muddle: Morphology three afternoons a week, two lots of Chemistry lectures, and two courses of Practical Chemistry; since one of these clashed with the Morphology lecture, I could only attend the demonstrations of Practical Chemistry before rushing off to Morphology, and returning next morning to finish off my Chemistry. Such spare time as I could find was spent in the dissecting room. We were expected to dissect every part of the body two or three times over. For all that, it was not something I shone at, for it involved the dreariest kind of grind: learning by rote.

That autumn Slater and I were sharing a neck. As usual we enlivened the tedium by discussing the progress of the war. It was going badly. No one seemed to have considered, not even as a possibility, what had soon become all too obvious: that those Dutch farmers would prove such excellent shots. Or that Mausers, fired from the cover of rocks and sangars, could cause such havoc among the ranks of crack regiments. Or that makeshift commandants, galloping their squadrons so swiftly and unpredictably over those barren African hills, should so repeatedly outwit British generals.

At the end of the first fortnight of the war the public was seriously alarmed. In the Cape Colony Lord Methuen had lost a thousand men killed or wounded. A considerable part of Natal had fallen into enemy hands. The bulk of the army was now shut up in Ladysmith, and there was nothing to bar the way to the invader.

Opinions varied as to the best way of dealing with the victorious Boers. A Corpus man slitting his way through the muscles of a leg was all for pounding away with artillery, then rolling over them with waves of infantry.

"No, no." Slater was adamant. "Outflank 'em. Edge 'em out of those damn'd trenches."

One afternoon we were at our tables when through an open upper light came the hoarse cry of a paper-boy calling out news of a terrible disaster. In Natal, at a place called Nicholson's Nek, two British regiments, together with a battery of field guns, had surrendered to the enemy.

We went to the window. A couple of hansoms had halted in the street so that the passengers might buy a paper. A knot of silent men stood in the raw, grey afternoon, reading of what – their attitude plainly betrayed it – could only be a catastrophe.

The demonstrator sent out for a paper. When it arrived he unfolded it and, after a moment's silence in which his eyes passed over the page, and with everyone grouped around him, he began to read aloud: " 'Outgunned, outnumbered, their ammunition gone, the Irish Fusiliers had fixed bayonets and were prepared to die like men – but then, no one quite knows how or where, the white flag went up. Haggard officers broke up their swords, while their men flung themselves on the ground, sobbing at the shame of it.' "

His voice petered out uncertainly. We stood in silence, the corpses on their slabs wholly forgotten.

The photographs soon flashed around the world. Columns of captured British troops marching through Pretoria. The Unthinkable. Never seen before.

*

At the end of term I returned to London. All the talk was

of the reverses in the Cape. Despite the shock men seemed determined to brace up, with that cheery resilience expected of one in the dark days of misfortune.

"We may lose the first battle," said Father stoutly, "but we invariably win the war. Wait until Buller moves!"

Buller! 'A pure flatcatcher', according to great-uncle Rufus. It was a favourite expression of his; one that did for all occasions. A horse that flattered to deceive, a bad egg in the Cabinet. *Pure flatcatchers!* Buller's features, gazing out from under a pill-box cap, appeared in all the illustrated papers. Stolid, unexcitable, they had that aura of unquestionable dependability I'd always associated with bankers and headmasters. Though any movement, to judge from the bulky figure, seemed likely to be slow.

Nevertheless, Buller was the name on every lip. A whole nation hung on that moment when the great force assembled in Natal – the greatest to take the field since the Crimean, according to Father – would roll forward to the relief of Ladysmith.

Wait until Buller moves !

The worst was yet to come. Shortly before Christmas came reports of a succession of military fiascos as ludicrous as they were inept.

'Terrible Reverse of British Troops!'

The news, borne on the shrill voices of paper-boys, echoed from street to street.

Men stood aghast as they read of famous regiments humiliated and put to flight.

Disaster piled upon disaster. At Stormberg General Gatacre, leading his column out on a night raid, and failing to locate the enemy, blundered about until first light betrayed him to the

Boers. At Magersfontein the Highland Brigade, hemmed in by earthworks and barbed-wire entanglements, were also marched out by night over ground carefully prepared by the enemy. The Black Watch lost three hundred men in a matter of minutes before bolting to the rear. At Colenso it was the poor Irish, flung willy-nilly at an unreconnoitred river-crossing, who died in droves. The blackest week, my Father called it, in the history of the British army.

That Saturday was my cousin's birthday. That evening we went out in a party to Daly's only to find the theatre closed for want of an audience. Later, at the Trocadero, the war was the sole topic of conversation. Rumours were rife that Buller had abandoned his guns in the open, and fallen back.

"It's Majuba all over again." His own supper spoilt, Father proceeded to ruin that of everyone else with direst prophecies. "All our forces checked or besieged, our garrisons in deadly danger, rebellion spreading like wildfire throughout the northern Cape. There's a real possibility the Boers will over-run all our African possessions before we can get more troops out to the Cape."

"Can the government be trusted to see it through ? That's the question," frowned my uncle Guy. He feared another craven settlement.

"Chamberlain will stick," said Father gloomily. "I shouldn't like to vouch for the rest."

Yet despite the atmosphere of crisis and disaster, I soon became aware of a strange kind of zest in the air, almost a relishing of a situation suddenly so clear-cut, so unmistakeable, as no longer to allow for any doubt or equivocation. Already Boer commandos from the Free State had taken over many districts in the northern Cape. There were stories of Dutch invaders pegging out farms for themselves in newly won Natal. The unedifying thought of British families hunted out of town after town, fleeing with their possessions piled in wagons, made blood boil. It gave point, as nothing else could, to the government's claim that it was seeking to right the wrongs committed against our own kith and kin. The universal chorus of delight from the Continent only served to stiffen resolve at home. Money flooded in for the War Fund. Hymns were published in the papers calling on God to support our cause. There was a wave of public sympathy for the common soldier. And with this sudden access of compassion came a new and sobering insight as to what was at stake in this conflict between the Boer farmer and our own rough-tongued Tommy.

As usual *The Times* echoed my Father in the matter. He read the piece out loud over the breakfast kedgeree. "Absolutely right. Haven't I said so ? Mediaevalism, that's what we're fighting. Mediaevalism, standing in the way of progress and equal rights."

My mother's glance, running defensively among her daughters, quelled instantly what might have been a mutinous retort from Agnes. They were brave souls indeed that dared express any opposition to the war.

VIII

In Wastdale, as in the country generally, most men supported the war. Though, of course, any discussion of politics was generally frowned on. Remoteness from the world of affairs was one of the things that drew us to the hills. Yet even the most homogeneous of communities will have its tensions. That Christmas those tensions came to the fore. Some, I know, were convinced Widdop had come to Wastdale with the deliberate intent of making trouble. At the same time, the situation would not have ended as it did had it not been for the presence of a group of men widely regarded as 'disloyal'.

The *Manchester Guardian*, as well as serving the business interests of a number of Wastdale regulars in those years, was also vehemently opposed to the government's war policy. It was not alone in that. But once the conflict got under way other papers had gradually fallen silent. It was the patriotic thing to do. Some had actually reversed their positions. With the about-face of the *Daily Chronicle*, C.P.Scott remained the last editor to continue opposition to the war. The 'Guardian party' (it was Widdop's term) was by no means restricted to mere readers of the paper. Scott's two boys were not infrequent visitors to the hotel. There was Spender, a journalist as radical in his politics as he was conservative in matters of mountaineering practice. Finally, and most formidably, there was Charley Montague himself. In addition to being the paper's leading writer, he acted as editor whenever Scott was attending to his duties in the House.

He was, I suppose, much the same age as Widdop. Though he looked far older. Even as a young man Montague's hair was white. Eyes deep-set in a long narrow face, a tight, rather pursy mouth, lips cramped together, gave him a severe appearance. *A radical bound in a conservative hide*, was Arnold Bennett's jibe. Mason said he looked like a chapel elder, a description which delighted Widdop.

"Absolutely ! That's what he is. The conscience-keeper of a sect."

Montague was not universally popular at Wastdale Head. There were those who'd not forgiven his fierce defence of the striking miners a few years earlier. Yet in his personal life Montague was far from combative. He was, in fact, a man of the utmost reserve. Usually, where he disagreed or was not con-vinced, he would lapse into silence. Only the slightest tremor in the muscles of his face betrayed his vigorous dissent. It was his writing, poured forth in shafts of provocative scorn, that laid bare that passionate soul.

*

I arrived in Wastdale a day or two after Christmas. Widdop had already had a full day's climbing. I'd barely settled in before he came banging on the door of my room.

"I'm getting up an impromptu concert after dinner," he remarked breezily. "A benefit for the troops. Can I put you down for a song or a recitation?"

Of course some argued later he'd no business to act in the provocative way he did. I learned subsequently that one or two of the older men tried to persuade him to forgo his plan in order not to create an 'atmosphere', though Widdop, flushed with the day's success, was less likely than ever to defer to the susceptibilities of a few pro-Boers. One's hour of triumph was not a time for compromise or retreat. Certainly, his ascent with Lockhart that afternoon of Walker's Gully had been a splendid effort. It was a year, almost to the day, since OGJ first forced the passage of those daunting walls. I'd approached it once from the top, from Jordan Gap, picking my way gingerly down loose, frightening scree, to peer into its depths. It struck me as far and away beyond my capabilities.

Evidently nothing had been revealed at breakfast that morning. As I came downstairs for dinner I heard a voice in the hall ribbing the triumphant pair that they'd kept very quiet about their plan.

"Plan ?", said Widdop. "It was scarcely a plan. The most we had in mind was a modest expedition to recover Jones' socks."

The socks in question, a spare pair, had been dislodged from the pocket of Jones' coat as it was hauled up over the final boulder, a detail seized on at the time by Widdop as if it were a shadow cast over what might otherwise have been a notable success.

"After all," he said, "what shall it profit a man if he gain the victory, yet lose his socks?"

I'd always thought of it as Lockhart's climb. He was the first to make the direct ascent of the lower section, and had gone further up the gully than any other man, only to be turned back at the final boulder. OG's triumph, I'd reflected at the time, must have come as a bitter blow.

That night, over dinner, it was a triumphant Widdop who gave a characteristic account of the day's adventure. He would, he said, a tale unfold: a tale such as to freeze up our young blood, and make our eyes start from their very sockets; a desperate tale of derring-do, with hairbreadth 'scapes in the imminent deadly breach. From the ringing tones, the flushed, animated face, it was clear that Widdop was in jubilant mood. We all prepared to enjoy another extravagant performance. And so it proved, as Widdop concocted a *tour de force* of spectacular effects: immense slabs shiny black with ice, Sisyphean boulders jammed between impending walls, a crash of falling water as the intrepid duo struggled up through freezing torrents.

At length they'd come to the crux, the pitch that had defeated them the previous year – the cave below the final boulder. Here, as everyone knew, Jones, stripping off coat and boots, had made further progress only by dint of a typically Jonesian stratagem – a rope, threaded over a chockstone jammed between the boulder and the gully wall. There was much interest in how the new ascensionists had succeeded where formerly they'd failed.

"Ah yes," said Widdop, "the crux. Lockhart, being a man of science, recognised that what the situation called for was a momentary regression in our evolutionary progress. So he contrived a simian manoeuvre. Hanging on to the edge of the boulder with his left hand, he reached back across the gully with the other, and braced himself against the opposite wall. Thus established, he simply backed up past the boulder."

He was in that state of dangerous euphoria which often follows the prolonged and uncertain ordeal of a major climb: in Widdop's case a state bordering at times on manic glee. When, after dinner, he announced that the concert would begin shortly, it was unclear whether what was about to follow represented a benefit for the troops, or a celebrating of the conquest of *Walker's Gully*. A handful of men, not much liking the look of things, drifted off to the smoke room. I went with them. It was the impulse of a moment. I couldn't have said why. But whatever it was that was about to take place in the dining room, I felt disinclined to be part of it.

In the smoke room it was a wretched evening. It was not the noise. In other years we might have sung the self-same choruses as part of a seasonal celebration. Conversation fluctuated in a desultory fashion. I fell to discussing a new pattern of nailing with Harold Spender. Lockhart chatted a while with Collie, who'd climbed with Bruce in the Alps that summer. Eventually he excused himself and went out. *To take a turn*, as he put it.

The raucous bawling from the dining room killed all conviviality. *Rule Britannia, Men of Harlech, Soldiers of the Queen*: one by one the old patriotic stand-bys made their appearance. Quieter intervals, punctuated by storms of cheering, no doubt represented solo recitations. Eventually a light, tenor voice began a rendering of *The Absent-Minded Beggar*, in which it was joined for the chorus amid much stamping of feet and banging of the table. Evidently Widdop was performing his party piece. Meanwhile Montague, in a display of icy indifference, was reading his way steadily through the Climbing Book. No doubt the patriotic bellowings from the other room evoked for him the jingoism he most dreaded and despised. Only Collie, reflecting perhaps on his forthcoming expedition up the Columbia River, sat unperturbed, puffing serenely at his pipe.

The hullabaloo mounted to a crescendo of applause and cheering. Suddenly, the door of the smoking room burst open.

There, wild-eyed, stood Widdop. In one hand he clutched a small canvas bag that jingled as he strode into the room.

"I'm not asking," he cried passionately, "for your agreement. Only for support for those not able to help themselves. We owe it to the men."

At which point, as if to emphasise that urgency of need, he shook the bag at Montague.

I've no doubt that Widdop was utterly sincere. In his own eyes, at least, he was pleading for the sinking of differences, for the cause of comradeship and brotherhood. Nor do I doubt we would all have put our hands in our pockets. But Widdop, more worked-up than I'd ever seen him, was aiming his appeal directly at Montague himself. As if to recognise an obligation. To do the decent thing. And maybe it was that, the unthinking assumption of the moral high ground on Widdop's part, that so offended. For in altered circumstances Charley Montague would surely have made his contribution. After all, he had no quarrel with the troops. For them he felt nothing but compassion. As it was, without raising his eyes from the Climbing Book, Montague remarked, in that tight, precise way he had, that such a request seemed hardly consistent with the sentiments (he would not call them principles) expressed in Widdop's recent letter to the *Guardian*.

"I must say I fail to see why, the men's lives being – as you would have it – so expendable, you should be so solicitous for the women and children."

There are some affronts to which silence is perhaps the only rejoinder. Maybe Widdop judged it so. Or else a sufficiently cutting retort failed to suggest itself. At any rate he flushed, turned on his heel and left the room.

The crash of the door behind him might have been an iron shutter slamming down across our world.

Silence returned. Glacial as ever, but for that slight working of facial muscle, Montague resumed his perusal of the Climbing Book. Only Collie seemed wholly unconcerned. Puffing at his pipe he gazed into the fire with perfect equanimity.

IX

From Wastdale I went on to the Highlands. For it was understood that, to make up for my absenting myself on Boxing Day to go off mountaineering, I should rejoin the family in the Black Mount for the New Year.

"I see no reason," said my mother firmly, "why George should be spared what the rest of us have to endure." The cold dark winter days, the barbarous plumbing, it was all too much for her.

Though in truth I found it no hardship. There was something about the house, its gloomy setting, that appealed strongly to my romantic nature. Built facing north, it rarely admitted a deal of light. From November to February the sun never appeared above the northern hills. But grandfather loved it for the view it offered of the Black Mount across the loch. Rowan, Scots pine and birch, planted as a shelter from the cold winds, now clustered thickly on three sides of the house. They were a source of great irritation to Father. Every summer there were grumbles about those trees.

"It's beyond me why you want so many. At least thin 'em out a bit. Get some air between 'em. That way there might be a few less midges."

Midges – the bane of these family visits to the Highlands.

"If it isn't rain," wailed Dolly, "it's insects."

"*Culicoides impunctatus*, to be precise," said my grandfather. "It's the female that does the biting."

My sisters, he added, should consider themselves fortunate indeed that they were spared the attentions of the warble and the nostril fly. Deer were not so lucky.

The party was fewer than usual. My Uncle Giles had fallen victim to a strain of gastro-enteritis then laying waste to SW1.

Uncle Guy had cried off too. There were, after all, no stags to be shot in January. Only a sad lack of imagination on my Father's part had seen them boarding the train at King's Cross. So my mother put it. She hated these forays north.

Given the circumstances, I found the party livelier than I'd expected. The national crisis seemed to have brought about a universal buoyancy of spirit rare at these family gatherings.

"The darkest hour comes before the dawn," said Father stoutly. "Britons are never more dangerous than when their backs are to the wall."

The foreign press had been jubilant at our discomfiture, a response which, in so far as it related to the French, he seemed to contemplate with equanimity.

"It is only to be expected of the French. Their history has been largely one of suffering defeat at our hands. As for the Russians, the most repressive of European states is inevitably opposed to the one which stands most prominently for individual liberty."

My mother was full of admiration for the tea the Queen had given for the wives and children of the soldiers at the Front.

"Princess Alexandra handed out the presents personally from an enormous tree," added Dolly.

"Her Royal Highness' sympathy for the common soldier is, of course, well known."

This struck me as rich coming from my mother. I knew she regarded common soldiers as low swaggering fellows, little better than ruffians. I remembered one of the housemaids walking out with a corporal of the Guards, a pimply Scot in tremendously long striped trousers who winked at me, and called me 'Jimmie'. He took to calling at the house in Onslow Place. Eventually my mother got to hear of his visits. She spoke to cook. He never came again.

Now, though, she was full of all the young men she knew, sons and nephews of her friends, who were joining the colours.

"Lady Ettingham did tell me that as many as three hundred members of the same London club have enlisted. They're all riding off to the war together."

Private companies of sportsmen, good riders and good shots, were springing up almost overnight.

"Many of the men are providing their own equipment," said Dora. "Some are even contributing their pay to the War Fund. I think it's wonderfully inspiring." The thought of groom and nobleman riding knee to knee in the ranks was enough to send her off into a delirium of novelettish musings. "No distinction of rank or birth," she murmured dreamily. "Kind hearts and coronets, simple faith and the bluest of blue blood."

"All that matters," said my father briskly, "is what a man has to offer."

"Giles is to join Paget's Horse," exclaimed Dolly, clasping her hands excitedly.

Agnes made a face. She had Father's wonderfully expressive look: the same clear grey eyes, lids hooded like Gothic blinds, able when words failed – or, more likely, had been ruled out of order – to convey the necessary suggestion to a jury.

I smiled as I caught her eye.

"Don't be beastly, Agnes." Dolly was rather sweet on Every. "I think Giles will look perfectly splendid in uniform."

I reflected sourly that he probably would.

All that week bad weather kept the family indoors.

I went off by myself, down the glen and up among the shrouded hills. More often than not I came back drenched, though my mood had little to do with the soaking I received.

Never before had mountaineering seemed so trivial. A useless passion.

My mother and sisters had no notion of what it might entail, except that it had to do with hills. And they hated hills. As for Father, I knew he regarded it as little more than a schoolboy recreation, an opportunity to raise a laugh at my expense with remarks about soaped poles and bear gardens, a good-natured jibe I knew not to be original.

I stayed behind when the family returned to London. Father remarking on the folly of getting wet quite so often, I needed little further encouragement to reveal, truthfully enough, that I was feeling out of sorts. My mother, fearing another manifestation of the microbes that had laid low my uncle Giles, urged me not to risk the journey. In truth, I felt no desire to return to Cambridge. At the same time, uneasiness at my own lack of enthusiasm drove me back to my books.

On the morning following their departure I settled down at the long library table with my physiology notes. I made little progress. Though the notion of Giles Every as man-of-action struck me as preposterous, the sudden transformation of my cousin had had an unsettling effect. I felt life was passing me by. The humdrum business of grinding at my books seemed wholly out of keeping with the ebullient spirit of the times. Men and women, old and young alike, the universities, even the churches had been caught up on a great wave of patriotic fervour. South Africa was the place to be. The Master, preaching in Chapel, had spoken of *that intensification of life* which was war's gift to man. Even my physiology supervisor, whose lectures on the central nervous system I was trying to get up, justified the war as a step towards the fulfilment of the Darwinian plan. Though it was Widdop who, with characteristic candour, seemed to me to have put the matter in its truest colours. *War is in the natural order of things, George. Indeed, I'll go further. All that we value most in our English way of life has, at some stage or other, been preserved on the field of battle. War has made us what we are. Some of my boys are defending those things now. I've no doubts whatsoever that the time will come for other boys to do so again.* I recalled the thrill his words had engendered. That tingling feeling on the surface of the skin. Properly speaking, I thought wearily, a superficial sensation arising from efferent impulses along the nervous system. Still, Paget's Horse had a fine dashing ring to it.

Unable to work, I got up from time to time to wander about the library, mooning among the books on the open shelves. Most of them seemed to consist of dreary anecdotes of epic stalks and legendary 'heads'. Suddenly, sensing another presence, I turned to find a silent figure regarding me from the doorway.

"I'm trying to educate myself in the ways of deer, grandfather," I said lightly, for I was embarrassed to be thus caught out.

He studied me in silence.

"Do you really want to be a doctor ?"

The question caught me off guard. What I may have said by way of reply, I don't remember. No doubt I stammered something. He nodded, turned to go.

"Those books are about men, not deer."

His voice came floating back as he retreated down the corridor.

"You'll learn nothing about deer from them."

*

During those few days, left largely to my own devices, I discovered something of what it meant to lead a solitary existence. Our only visitor was a neighbouring laird. I knew him of old. He suffered from gout. A consequence, I reflected with some satisfaction, of his own excesses, for he was a great glutton. It was his boast that only a horse of sixteen hands could carry him. All his talk was of food or drink, or of killing animals. He had an inflamed face, and a spongy swollen nose, as if engorged with all the blood he'd spilt.

Dinner was a largely depressing affair, during which I affected polite attention as two old men, indifferent to one another, addressed themselves each to his own obsession. Of the two, grandfather was marginally the more entertaining, since the withering scorn he'd always entertained towards the military had been further fuelled by the set-backs in South Africa.

"Can't shoot ... Can't ride." Paring an apple as he spoke, he punctuated each verdict with a vehement jab of his knife. Then came the story, as I knew it would, of manoeuvres witnessed in Hyde Park some thirty years before.

"In all my life I never witnessed such a damnable exhibition of incompetence. Men so ignorant of their business – scarcely able to pitch a tent. As for the Life Guards – would you believe it – put to flight by a flock of geese !"

The laird's conversation was confined largely to the merits of jugged hare. How one should hang 'em a good ten days. Above all, keep the blood: the goodness was in the blood.

Ill at ease in the great empty house, I moped about for several days.

To tell the truth, my grandfather's abrupt question, in focusing so precisely my own misgivings, had left me at a loss. Work seemed out of the question. At the same time I found inactivity unendurable. I had to get out.

The next morning I set off on a stravaig up into the Blackmount. I took the stalker's path up by the Allt Toaig. Then, from the bealach, I followed the east ridge of Stob Ghabhar, the Aonach Eagach, that runs up towards the summit. I found it icy and exciting. In places it narrowed to an arête. The snow of a few days earlier made for heavy going. A freezing wind had crusted the surface, so that I was breaking through continually. I'd hoped to descend from the neck of the ridge, where I knew of a gully just below the summit, then traverse right to reach the upper *couloir*, high and remote above the north-east corrie. Climbed a year or two earlier by Maylard and his party, it was rapidly becoming a test piece for the aspiring Scottish mountaineer. But in such conditions a solo descent of the gully was more than I cared to take on. So, from the summit I headed west, dropping to the bealach below Meall an Araich, then down again to the Allt Dochard.

To please my grandfather I'd offered to keep a lookout for deer. It was something of a seasonal anxiety, the winter roaming of his stags.

"You'll need to go high," he'd called after me. "Look for them on a windward slope."

"I know," I'd shouted back, "I know."

I was rather irritated at the instruction. I knew enough to know that. That lonely glen had seemed a likely place to find them. But there was nothing to be seen, and I turned south again, floundering through a waste of bog and tussock. I had to wade the burn to gain the track through Glen Kinglass.

Out on the loch were a pair of divers. Wet and cold as I was, I lingered to watch them, small dark figures against the dull sheen of the loch, swimming to and fro and turning in unison. Now and then one or the other would dive, lowering neck and head in a single graceful movement, and gliding out of sight. I reflected that our guest of the previous evening, inveighing against predators and vermin, would certainly have shot them.

I'd smiled, nodded, for I was ashamed, in that house with its stags' heads, its cases of wild cat and pine-marten, of my own inability to kill anything.

Out on the loch one of the divers uttered its strange cry, a thin small sound chiselled on the freezing air. Its lonely note entered my heart. Suddenly I felt a surge of longing, yet for what I could not have said. It went beyond words: baffling, larger than my grasp, a weight of yearning that seemed unendurable, inapprehensible, yet somehow bound up with the flat, steely water, the vast sweep of hill and glen. And yet a world outside, beyond the world of men.

My eyes, I remember, filled with tears.

In subdued mood I turned for home, my mind a thicket of confusion, uncertain what I was, or what I would become. Then my eye was caught by movement on the snowy slopes a long way down Glen Dochard: dozens of dark shapes picking their way slowly down to the strath.

My grandfather met me at the edge of the wood. I reported my sighting.

"Hinds," he grunted. "More snow on the way."

X

It was Father's practice to mark the start of term with lunch at his club. Begun when I first went up to Cambridge, these lunches had become something of a ritual. Though it seemed strange at first to be having the kind of *tête-à-tête* one might very well have had in the normal course of things at home, I soon realised these meals *à deux* were meant as an act of endorsement. Father thought it appropriate to set our relationship on a different footing. Extra-familial. More man-to-man. It was, too, a gesture of good will on his part. He usually lunched on sandwiches sent in from Sweetings as he laboured over a brief. Father worked hard. He was an ambitious man. I think much of his antagonistic spirit sprang from disappointed hopes. Elevation came too late to make a difference. Confined to the middle benches until the last few years of his life, he was never quite able to overcome his jealousy of the QC's who sat in the front row, the Inner Bar, as it is called. My poor Father longed to tread the red carpet of the Inner Bar and exchange witticisms with Mr Justice Darling.

Filled with misgiving, I took a bus along the Embankment. I was well aware that these lunches, however well-intentioned, constituted an informal scrutiny of my progress. It was delicately done. The subject of my studies scarcely cropped up except as the most casual of enquiries: enquiries, however, from which Mr Roderick Hazard QC was only too capable of drawing a conclusion. Lunch with father, I reflected, had never seemed less inviting.

As I crossed the Strand I looked out for the new recruiting office set up to cope with the flood of volunteers. I was astonished at the numbers lining the pavement. Curious, I glanced at them covertly as I passed. These were men about whose exploits I would be reading in the months to come. Men for whom life had now resolved itself. They would fight. They would crouch behind sangars, cursing the Boer sharp-shooters, yet keeping their heads under fire. They would ride with Paget's Horse, the red dust rising in the wake of their pursuit. Now, frock-coated, top-hatted, they stood in line. Many of them wore a slightly self-conscious look, as if embarrassed by their new identity. Ill at ease I continued on my way to Covent Garden. A stranger setting for a *viva voce* would be hard to imagine. Long known as the haunt of actors, father's club was famed for its eccentricity. I rather liked it. With its brown walls covered with pictures, the trophies in glass cases, it struck me as a kind of shabby home from home. A place where a man might unbend. In some respects it reminded me of Wastdale: the same long rectangular table, the boom of male voices, the cheery informality. Nor was the comparison with Wastdale entirely misplaced. Mason, I knew, was a member. Charley Bruce, then of Nanga Parbat fame, was rumoured to have performed a nautch dance down the long table with a peacock's feather balanced on his nose, a feat I found quite impossible to imagine taking place in Father's presence.

My sisters were deeply curious, and pressed me for information.

"I can't possibly talk about Father's club," I said, to tease them. "I'm not a member. But I'll say this much. It's not the kind of place one would expect to find a Queen's Counsel, let alone a Bencher of Lincoln's Inn."

"I dare say a great many lawyers belong to the Garrick," said Dora stiffly. Loyal to her finger-tips, she would have died for Father.

"No, Dora. A *few* lawyers, a great many actors," I said firmly.

"Perhaps there's your explanation."

Dora pressed her lips together, as she always did when Agnes was being mischievous.

"But Papa hates the theatre," protested Dolly, bewildered.

"Oh, come now," said Agnes. "Isn't this the age of the actor-advocate ? Father may have little good to say of Mr Blake Odgers or Mr Montague Lush, but we all know he secretly admires them. He'd love to tread the boards himself."

Dolly's hands flew to her mouth at the very idea.

And yet he had a presence to grace any stage. He loved to appear in King's Bench V and VI, so often the setting for cases rich in human interest, the libel actions and the suits for slander. Best of all was the Divorce Court where a man might play to a packed house of fashionable ladies. And yet his manner in court too often exhibited too much of offhanded and offensive disdain. Father had rather a taste for gratuitous confrontation. He enjoyed being rude. Agnes put it down to his being the clever second son. A common trait, she claimed, among siblings of the aristocracy.

Luncheon, no doubt, would be peppered with the usual string of irreverent remarks. Judges, QC's, even his own clients: none escaped his caustic tongue. This time, however, a single topic was to dominate the conversation. The papers were full of stories of Buller's withdrawal back across the Tugela complete with stores and equipment. Not a single man was lost. It had been, the correspondents all agreed, a masterly retreat.

It was a triumph lost on Father. "All this to-ing and fro-ing back and forth across a river," he grumbled. "He's more like a blasted ferry-man than a commander in the field. When are we going to read of a masterly advance?"

That white flag at Nicholson's Nek, the headlong flight at Magersfontein, had shaken him badly.

"It's the rifle, not the drill, that makes the soldier," he said, poking at his chop. "Do you know the annual ammunition issue for rifle practice? Three hundred cartridges a year ! And all this mechanical firing of volleys. It destroys any individual aim. It's these farmers who are teaching us the lessons, shooting accurately, taking cover, and so forth." He nodded to the waiter. "We do absolutely nothing to prepare the men for battle. And of course it's poor Tommy Atkins who pays the price. Well, thank God," he said, setting down his glass, "for these volunteers."

"Actually," I stammered, "I've rather been thinking along those lines myself. Enlisting, I mean."

Feigned astonishment was so much a part of Father's forensic armoury, I was ill prepared for the real thing.

He stared at me, fork half-way to his mouth.

"*You* ?"

For a moment he seemed genuinely lost for words.

"You can't ride. Can't shoot. What on earth use would you be ?"

My father's undisguised incredulity was, of course, entirely justified. Yet from the first exchange of shots the war had become a strange kind of mirror wherein a young man might see enacted the dream he entertained of himself. No sooner had hostilities commenced than boxed sets of stereoscopic photographs began to appear, hawked from door to door by enterprising salesmen. I had become an ardent collector of these 'battle photographs'. *The Devons charging a kopje, and facing death near Elandslaagte.* Khaki figures staggering back theatrically as if struck in the full course of their advance; the 'dead' draped tastefully with outflung arms over a convenient rock. Meanwhile, the correspondents were concocting an adventure scripted in the kind of 'death-or-glory' prose we had devoured as schoolboys, a narrative filled with the roar and crackle of Maxims and Mausers, the *gloop-gloop* of the Boer 'quick-firers'.

In the absence of victories there was an extraordinary hunger for stories of brave deeds, as if no military disaster but might find its transfiguration in some act of redemptive gallantry. One in particular fired my imagination. It told of a young officer on a hill-top, surrounded by the enemy. Disarmed, he squared up to them with his fists, had knocked down three of 'em in quick succession before a fourth called to one of his fellows taking aim, *Don't shoot that brave man !* This episode, worked out in vivid chalks, duly appeared on pavements. The young man, tall and straight, fists raised. His assailants, unkempt, hairy, with their bandoliers and Mausers. The sequel was no less dramatic. Placed under guard, the young officer subsequently snatched up a bayonet, overpowered his captor, and made his way back to the British lines.

Barely able to contain my own pride and satisfaction, I tossed some coppers into the scriver's cap. For I felt I knew him. That clean-cut Briton. If only at one remove. At the same time into my mind came a phrase, and a particular tone of voice – Widdop's voice – reserved for a very few: *The most outstanding of all my boys.*

XI

Shortly after the news of Masterman's brave deed I received an invitation to spend the weekend at his old school. It came, not via the usual telegram, but in a letter. Widdop had written at some length. Had I been less naive I might, with the circumspection that comes with greater experience, have seen an intention behind his ardent phrases. As it was, I jumped at the chance to mend matters. For I still flinched at the memory of our last encounter. I was acutely conscious of my failure to attend his concert for the troops. An impulse of the moment, by the following morning it had come to seem (in keeping with that fluctuating character which seemed to colour so many of my moods) a rather shabby betrayal.

I took the train from Paddington. As I glanced again at Widdop's letter I was struck once more by its vivid colours.

Here, in the wind and sunlight of the Bristol Channel they drink in that eager, adventurous love of country, the most precious gift we can give any of our boys.

At the same time I was put uneasily in mind of the exhortations I received when I first went away to school. *It will make a man of him,* said Father stoutly. *If he turns out a brave, honest, truth-telling Englishman,* growled great-uncle Rufus, *that's all that matters.* Though I knew very well, for all my tender years, a great deal more was expected of me than that.

Widdop's school was an unusual sort of place. That much I knew. Even so, I was unprepared for what I found. The 'Coll' did indeed stand four-square to the sea. But there was none of that veneer of venerable antiquity that even the newer schools had learnt to cultivate. No trees or courts, or creepered walls. Simply a row of what appeared to be cheap lodging houses built on a hillside battered, as I arrived, by a stiff Atlantic gale.

Widdop's 'House' took up three of the seaside villas. His quarters, like those of his colleagues, were situated among the form rooms and studies occupied by the boys. Schoolmaster's studies are, I suppose, much of a muchness: gown, mortar-board, a desk piled with Latin proses, that sort of thing. Few, though, could hope to offer a prospect such as presented itself from Widdop's windows: a tangle of bent trees above a steep-banked lane, a grey bar of pebbles, then the long line of Atlantic breakers booming in over a wide expanse of silver sand.

"They've done you proud for a view," I remarked.

"Yes," he said. "I dare say it's not much changed since Francis Drake gazed out to sea as a boy."

That the room was home to the mountaineer as well as the schoolmaster was plainly evident. Thrust among the sticks and umbrellas in the stand beside the door was a long Swiss axe. On the shelves Horace, Virgil, Livy and the rest rubbed shoulders with the classic Alpine texts, Wills, Whymper, Conway, Coolidge. On either side of the fireplace some fine studies of great snow mountains took my eye.

"Ah yes," said Widdop. "I'm indebted to Macrae for those. I expect you'll meet him later."

On one wall was a print of Nicolson's portrait of Widdop's old mentor, the poet Henley: a brigand in a black rakish hat, blue shirt and flowing tie. A large map of Natal was pinned to a side table. Little flags marked Buller's positions along the line of the Tugela. Small squares of paper in the Transvaal colours decorated the heights above the river. A lone Union Jack picked out Ladysmith in the plain beyond the range of hills.

"Two of our chaps are shut up with White in Ladysmith,"

said Widdop grimly. "They're counting on us, George. We mustn't let them down."

After a cup of tea, prepared in a little pantry, Widdop took me on a tour of inspection. We went up stairs, along corridors, through form rooms where battered desks and splashes of ink brought back a host of dreary recollections. The gale provided a mournful accompaniment to our progress, rattling windows, droning through the spaces of the walls. Then more flights of stairs. Then over the bare boards of three attic dormitories, cold, cheerless, devoid of door or curtain. The damp air held a faint, lingering odour, as of drying clothing. It reminded me of Wastdale.

"Yes," said Widdop. "We do get our fair share of rain. Generally the sort of fine sea fret we don't bother to wear a coat for."

Altogether, it struck me as a queer sort of place. For one thing, some of the boys were permitted to smoke. They carried ashplants and wore stiff, stick-up collars. Some of them even sported whiskers and moustaches, and patent leather boots.

I enquired about them, where they came from.

"They're mostly the sons of serving soldiers," Widdop told me. "Most of them are intended for the Army, or the colonial service."

After inspecting the fives court and the sea baths, built out from rocks under the cliffs, we tramped along the beach with the gale howling in our ears. I was shown the headland, now cut off by the tide, where some of the boys took their first steps on rock. Though the climbs were mostly traverses. "We might take a look at one or two tomorrow," Widdop shouted, above the gale. "Weather permitting."

He pointed to a grey blur on the horizon, barely visible through a curtain of approaching rain. "Lundy," he yelled.

"Masterman once tried to reach it in a rowing boat."

"It seems rather a long way," I shouted.

"Fifteen miles. It might have ended badly, but for a timely intervention by the coastguard cutter."

The rain arrived as we tramped back over the pebble ridge. Looming mournfully out of the hillside, the school resembled more than ever a row of out-of-season sea-side villas. A school for Spartan boys, it seemed to me.

"Yes," said Widdop, with an air of modest pride. "I suppose our appointments are a trifle primitive. I dare say the food would raise a riot in one of H.M's prisons. But boys are lazy dogs at heart, you know. They know it too. Putting up with hardship is a kind of recompense. But see for yourself. They seem hardy enough, don't you think ?"

He pointed to where half a dozen football matches were in progress: boys milling about in scrimmages, their gull-like cries piercing the raw February air. Others, returning from a paper chase, were streaming down the steep gorse-covered hill behind the House. "We keep them busy," said Widdop simply. "We send them to bed dog-tired."

After 'callover' I met a group of them for tea in Widdop's study. A 'brew', he called it: potted beef, sardines, jam and honey, scones and clotted cream. His guests, a quartet of merry fourteen year olds, faces still flushed from the football field, arrived chattering in a frank, unaffected way unthinkable in boys visiting a 'beak' at Eton.

No doubt they perished far away, and before their time. *Sed miles, sed patria*, as the saying goes. Thinking of them now, boys with whom I shared a schoolroom tea two wars ago, I'm brought face to face with the subalterns, the company commanders – ex-prefects scarcely out of the sixth form, who climbed the trench ladders and went over the top to do their duty. Boys just like those, plunged into a drama not of their own making, with the parts cast, and the lines already written.

That afternoon, though, it was the change in Widdop that struck me most. He seemed a different man. Impossible to recognize, in the genial host bustling about with cups and plates, the razor-sharp disputant of the Wastdale smoke room. Gone, the urbane man-of-the-world, the keen combative air.

"Make yourselves at home," he shouted, filling his kettle in the pantry.

'Home', I realised, with something of a start, was not Wastdale, nor yet Chelsea. Home was here. Meanwhile, as the boys grouped about the map table, it soon became clear that in Widdop's House, at least, there was a tense ferment over the fate of the men shut up in Ladysmith. All the talk about redoubts and salients, front assaults up hills, feint attacks and bayonet work among the sangars seemed on their lips no more than the colouring of a simple tale: the tangled web of war reduced to a single, desperate predicament: a pair of school chums, cut off, surrounded, hanging on through famine and bombardment. And for hero, *the most outstanding of all my boys*, fighting his way through mountain passes.

So what, I asked, over the scones and clotted cream, did they make of Buller's campaign ?

There was no immediate reply. For a moment I feared that I, an outsider, might have blundered into a matter too delicately felt to serve as the small change of casual conversation.

"Well sir," said one hesitantly, "if you ask me, the Boers don't fight fair."

In a moment the rest were chiming in with a flood of opinion, all of it scornful.

"They don't fight fair, sir."

"They slink about."

"Ask Ames, sir."

"Yes, ask Ames."

Ames, a shock-headed boy, had an uncle serving with Lyttleton's Brigade.

"It's true, sir. He says they skulk behind rocks. He says they're always running away on their little ponies. My uncle says when they capture them they make them march on foot. He says they don't like that. Ha-ha!"

Widdop, sprawled in an armchair, took little part in the discussion. Legs stretched across his hearth, a quiet smile on his face, he seemed every inch the genial host. Or, it struck me afterwards, a man at ease in the bosom of his family.

Only after the boys had left for prep did his pride and pleasure express itself in words.

"Boys just like those have gone out from here all over the Empire; Burma, the Sudan, the North-West Frontier."

"It must require a very special sort of education," I said, not without a hint of irony.

"Yes," he said, "we teach them how to live. But more than anything, they teach one another."

What 'lessons', I wondered, did they pass on to one another? What would pass for 'wisdom' in a life harsh enough by any account? Courage, self-respect, truth-telling – *that's one of our cardinal virtues*. Keeping one's mouth shut too, when necessary. Loyalty, above all.

Meanwhile the fire sank in the grate. The rain beat softly on the black uncurtained windows. "You must feel very proud of them," I managed eventually.

"Oh, more than that," said Widdop quietly. "I love them all."

I heard a lot about Masterman that weekend. No doubt imagination cast a certain glow over a history which, romantic enough by any account, seemed especially exotic on the lips of respectable schoolmasters: the rakehell father, landlord of an impoverished estate in Co.Wicklow; the wayward wife, a Dublin beauty; the wild young son who invariably turned up late via the Irish packet, a day or two after the start of term.

I saw, too, at close hand something of the *milieu* which had nurtured him – a culture of which he seemed to be generally regarded as the supreme exemplar. It was largely a bachelor establishment. Certainly none of the housemasters were married. There was a marked absence of those little touches of family life a wife can bring to her husband's House. The common room, with its tobacco fug, its sprawling figures in shabby comfortable chairs, was exclusively male. Nor did it lack for sporting prowess. The English master, still of splendid physique though turned fifty, was a rowing blue. Another had played several times for Surrey. A withered man with a limp turned out to be Macrae, the photographer. Though Widdop introduced him to me as 'a fellow Alpinist'.

"Oh, hardly that," he smiled ruefully. "I'm afraid a smashed knee put paid to all that. These days I have to make do with a Thornton-Pickard."

Widdop's colleagues were as fiercely proud of the place as he was, of its shabbiness and oddity, its difference from other schools.

"Here, a boy is what he does," the rowing blue told me earnestly. "We judge him by his actions. Every boy here knows what's expected of him. He knows what he owes to others, and what is owed to him."

Though their pride and pleasure in their ex-pupil was evident, none of them seemed in the least surprised that he should have distinguished himself.

"He was one of that rare class of boys," sighed Macrae, "who are men right from the start."

We were looking at another of his photographs, this time of a House XI. It showed a slim dark boy with turned-up collar, white scarf at his throat, a hand thrust carelessly in the pocket of his blazer, his mouth twisted in a tight half-smile. He was known as 'Hotspur' – a tribute to an explosive temper.

"Only the foolhardy," said Widdop dryly, "made jokes about his name."

'Hotspur' seemed to figure in every tale. The note of pride attending the recital of these anecdotes seemed somehow in keeping with a school which prepared boys for the army. It struck me as a place where myths accumulated. The chaplain, a cheery old fellow with several folds of chin dropping on to his clerical collar, chuckled as he recalled how Masterman had shinned up a drain-pipe and taken a tub in the Head's bathroom.

"The best of it," he spluttered gleefully, fingering the bowl of his briar, "was that the bath had just been filled for Bates."

I smiled at the tale. As I did so I couldn't help noticing that Widdop, though he smiled too, seemed to do so with a degree of irritation.

After dinner, back in his study, he handed me a letter.

"George," he said, "I want you read this."

Even after all these years I remember the first phrase that caught my eye.

'My God ! This is like Waterloo ...'

Though it was Colenso, and not Waterloo, that Masterman (for the letter was his) was striving to describe. His first battle. An adventure, by his account, as colourful as any penned by Henty or Haggard: that bizarre drill before the battle, in the half-light of an African dawn, the brigade advancing 'in fours from the right of companies', drums beating, bugles sounding, the General, sword in hand, leading the column.

'*My God! I thought. Any second now I could be killed!*'

Yet death seemed unimaginable set against the exhilaration of the moment, the swish-swish of grass, the clink of equipment, the electric air, the tensing of a thousand hearts and minds. Then the gleaming river, looped round a spit of land, men packed together, milling about like steers, a withering fire poured in from every side, that boy bugler sounding the '*Attack*', the Dublin Fusiliers fixing bayonets, charging blindly into the river.

Brave? Oh, they were brave. Sometimes a desperate kind of courage is all there is. What baffles me is that he should have written about it as he did. For it strikes me now, its vivid, dream-like quality, as the letter of a man barely in touch with his own experience. Unless, as I suspect, Masterman was unable to report it any other way. Given his education and upbringing maybe there *was* no other way to report it, except as he did.

But all that is a whole world away: Widdop's study, the patter of rain, myself at twenty, engrossed in a dream. And that letter, written in a cramped schoolboy hand:

We've taken rather a knock, it's true. And of course Hart is being blamed for the butcher's bill in certain quarters – you'll know what I mean. We've had over two hundred casualties. The Dublins, that is. More than the Seaforths at Magersfontein, if reports are to be believed. But the men! The men were magnificent. If you could have seen them, Widdop, coming off the field – bloody, covered in dust and sweat, burnt by the sun. Still under fire, yet cool as you please. No bunching. No doubling back. I could have wept with pride for them.

But would you believe it, I didn't see a single dead Boer.

Rather at a loss, I folded the letter. Handed it back.

Widdop took it from me without comment. He stuck it casually behind a rack of pipes. Perhaps his silence was intentional. The letter was, I suppose, his 'ace-in-the hole', as they say. The card to master all.

In the interval that followed, Masterman's final paragraph played over in my mind. Hart's Irish, coming off the field of battle, had acquired the image of a universal character. Men who were men as simply, as unequivocally, as a tree is a tree.

"A sudden death is as good as any," said Widdop suddenly. "Don't you think ? If I'm to die I'd sooner go as a man fully alive."

I nodded loyally. Though I registered his question, accompanied by that keen look of his, with a thrill of fear.

XII

My sister Agnes always struck me as an extraordinary young woman. We were as unlike one another, in looks and temperament, as it was possible to be. Where I'd inherited Father's dark unruly mop, Agnes was blessed with my mother's silky auburn hair with its delicate wave. The firm mouth, grey eyes clear as a mountain tarn, active elements in a face quick to register a range of emotion, betokened a character quite alien to my own cautious nature. Indeed, Agnes was wont to say that as a twin brother I was a great disappointment. Her claim of seniority by a mere ten minutes led her, even in the nursery, to assume an authority over me she never relinquished. Our journey to the park took us past a baker's shop. Even in the coldest weather there were always barefoot children hanging around outside in the hope that someone might give them something. One day, demanding the few coppers I had for pocket money, and sweeping aside the protestations of Amy, our little nursery-nurse, Agnes bought a bag of buns which she distributed among the waifs and strays.

"But they were cold and hungry," she told my mother afterwards. "They had nothing to eat."

Her turbulence marked her out early from her sisters. Obstinate when convinced of the rightness of her cause, caustic with those who disagreed with her, she dashed at all humbug with devastating frankness. *I really don't know what will become of Agnes*, my mother would sigh. Even my father found Agnes disconcerting. As an *enfant terrible* she'd been amusing. Now, however, he'd discovered that what he required in his daughters was a certain charming diffidence. Above all, he expected them to be agreeable. Agnes, though, was a born dissenter. Open, guileless, she had none of Dora's reticence. Cruelty or injustice upset her dreadfully. Then she went in for unpalatable truths.

My mother sat on several charity committees, for which my sisters undertook philanthropic work. Armed with a list of the needy and deserving, they went visiting in Battersea, calling on the women of the Shaftesbury estate. Impulsive, highly strung, Agnes' sympathies were easily aroused. She felt for others. Lame ducks, underdogs of whatever species, called for her allegiance.

It was, I suppose, only a matter of time before philanthropy strayed over into politics. One evening, the first Christmas of the war, I was hurrying down to dinner when I heard raised voices that ceased suddenly as I entered the drawing-room. Evidently Father was still dressing. Only my sisters were present: Agnes, turning away as the door opened, flushed, one hand clutching the green velvet curtain; Dora, straightbacked on the settee, her mouth tightened in a way that reminded me of Montague.

"Agnes disapproves of the war," whispered Dolly, pulling a face.

Agnes' pro-Boer sympathies were to become a closely-guarded secret at Onslow Place. A secret, that is, from Father. Though quite possibly he knew, and chose to ignore, what had so far not been aired in his presence.

*

One evening towards the end of term I travelled up to London. My last term at Cambridge was fast approaching. I was due to start my clinical studies in the autumn, and had arranged to visit the secretary of the medical school at Bart's.

Early next morning I came down to breakfast to be greeted with the news that Ladysmith had been relieved. Milly, the house-maid, was full of it. All the tradesmen had shut up shop, she said, and were marching to Chelsea barracks at that very moment.

To Father, dissecting his breakfast kipper with studied calm, the issue had never really been in doubt.

"Well," I said breezily. "Buller got there."

"Indeed. And took his time about it."

Eager to see the celebrations, I took a cab to Bart's. I was astonished at the sight that met my eyes: streets festooned with pennants, the air a sea of Jacks and Royal Standards. Every driver of any sort of vehicle had a knot of ribbon on his whip. Children walking with their nurses, even the babies in perambulators, clutched little flags.

The further east one went the denser grew the crowd. As we passed along the Strand progress grew more and more difficult. Halfway along Fleet Street I paid off the cabby, and set off the rest of the way on foot. Within moments I found myself swept up in a cheering, singing crowd flowing like a tide up Ludgate Hill. Mingled with the tumult came the piercing cries of street vendors. *Show your colours! Penny, the dear old flag.* It seemed all London was converging on the city. Everyone bore a flag or favour of some sort – medallions of Buller, Roberts, Baden-Powell and many more besides – chanting, singing, shouting, in an extraordinary ebullition of relief and joy. It was as if some long and terrible pressure on the nerve had been relieved. The unthinkable had been averted. Words of Widdop's, the nightmare they betokened of impotence and humiliation, sprang to mind. *They're counting on us, George. We mustn't let them down.*

All hopes I had of reaching Bart's had long since vanished. No private purpose could have withstood that tidal wave of feeling. Here and there men in khaki, lifted shoulder-high, bobbed above the heads of the crowd. Borne up on that same wave of pride and elation, I thought of Masterman and the chums shut up in Ladysmith falling into one another's arms. I was filled with emotion. A band of brothers. Yes, and thought myself accursed I was not there.

The crowd swept on towards the Mansion House. From somewhere close by came hoarse shouts: 'Pro-Boer, pro-Boer'. I saw a rush of bodies – a man put down – the crowd passing over him.

The sun lit up a haze of yellow dust above a sea of faces, a haze in which dark objects repeatedly rose and fell, rose and fell: hats, of all shapes and sizes, battered beyond recovery, thrown to the wind.

Over the pediment of the Mansion House flags were flying: the red cross on a white ground of the City Imperial Volunteers.

"Good old Giles," I shouted. "Hurrah for Paget's Horse."

Knocked almost off by feet in a sudden lurch of bodies outside the Bank of England, I found myself clutching at a burly smiling constable so thickly coated with the dust as to seem himself clothed in khaki. And1 all the while the great bells of Paul's pealed out in a pandemonium of joy.

The next day, having made my belated visit to Bart's, I caught a 'bus back from the city. Glancing through an early edition my eye was caught by a prominent notice set out on an inside page.

Pro-Boers in Exeter Hall tonight.
Stop the War meeting tonight.

Ought not to be allowed to meet and thus publicly condemn the war. People who rejoiced exceedingly last night can maintain their enthusiasm by going to Exeter Hall tonight and showing the pro-Boers that their sentiments are not popular.

Though it struck me as coming close to an incitement to riot, I thought no more about it, and turned the page, little thinking that the matter should so shortly be thrown back in our faces. More interesting was a paragraph describing the night's events in Cambridge. Joy had certainly been unconfined. The celebrations had continued well into the small hours. Undergraduates, flags gripped between clenched teeth, had scaled lamp-posts and church towers, torn down railings, even commandeered hawkers' barrows to feed a great bonfire in the market place.

It all seemed rather rowdy. Then I reflected that, had I been there, no doubt I would have thrown up my hat and drunk ale with the rest.

On Saturdays, as Father was usually at home, we all gathered in the drawing room. It was, of course, primarily my mother's room. As a boy at school, sick for home, it was that scene above all others I set out in my mind. It was always tea-time: the slender mahogany table set with china, Rockingham blue and gold. There would be scones and ginger cake; the dark green velvet curtains shutting off the gloomy afternoon, the great Donegal rug covering the floor, fire-light leaping on the polished fender, mother in her easy chair toasting her toes, the Sèvres lady on the mantelpiece, asleep in her armchair, one slipper dangling from a china toe.

That afternoon, apart from Agnes, who was attending an Oxford extension lecture, we were all assembled: Father, buried in The Times, my mother by the fire, her writing board in her lap. Dora presided as usual over the tea things. Dolly, bent over a sketching block, was still working her way through Ruskin's Elements of Drawing. Slowly, absorbedly, she was filling rectangles with regular lines of hatching.

Dora had just rung for a fresh pot of tea, and was replenishing our cups, when the sound of the front door bell signalled the return of Agnes. Though she seemed perfectly composed, the signs were ominous, the jaw set firm in a way that boded trouble.

She sat down, accepted a cup of tea from Dora, and plunged straight in.

"I imagine everyone has heard of the disgraceful scenes last night at Exeter Hall ?"

There was a moment of surprised silence. Dolly looked up, her tongue still caught between her teeth.

"I dare say you have, and don't care."

It was that challenging candour we all found so alarming.

"Has no one anything to say ?"

Father lowered his paper, and looked round as if to see if any one else wished to offer a rejoinder, before clearing his throat.

"Speaking for myself," he began mildly, "I strongly deprecate these demonstrations. I expect no good of them. I believe they are contrary to the best traditions of English life. However, I would venture to add that a great deal of responsibility rests with those who call such meetings. Perhaps they ask more of human nature than all history shows human nature is capable of giving."

Detached, judicious, it was a reply typical of Father's forensic habit. Though its insinuation, imputing blame to the pro-Boers, could not have been lost on Agnes.

Agnes chose to ignore it. Speaking with a kind of icy passion, she began what was evidently a prepared speech.

"This, then, is the position. The friends of peace summon a private meeting in the heart of the capital. The public is expressly not invited. Fearing there is likely to be a disturbance they ask for police protection, and offer to pay for it. The Commissioner refuses their request. The meeting is attacked by an organised mob. A free fight takes place. Blows are exchanged. There is a very serious danger to women as well as men at the meeting. All this takes place within five minutes of Bow Street police station. Yet no arrests are made, and no steps taken to bring those responsible before the magistrates."

She sipped, too deliberately, at her tea.

"And this, we are led to believe, is a free and law-abiding country."

I saw she was clutching her cup with whitened knuckles.

Father, too, invariably affected the utmost calm in the face of passion. Now, never short of a manner to fit the part, he chose the voice of shrewd experience.

"It must be remembered that public feeling is necessarily stirred at the present time. In every district there are persons who have suffered cruel losses in a war nine-tenths – indeed ninety-nine hundredths – of the country believe to be both just and necessary."

Agnes set down her cup and saucer steadily enough, though her hand shook slightly. The look on her face conveyed the futility of arguing with Father. It lamented the blindness of those who wouldn't see, deplored the brutishness of those who lacked all finer feeling. It had the effect of closing doors.

Evidently Father felt so too, for he sought to break off the engagement. Though not without a parting shot.

"You demand too much of your fellow countrymen, Agnes," he said dryly. "Naturally you resent it when they fail to live up to your expectations."

He took up his paper. Agnes flushed. Poor Dolly disappeared into her hatching. Father could be so crushing.

Dora had been coaxing the methylated burner under the silver kettle. Now she sought to mediate.

"All Father is saying, Agnes," she said evenly, "is that those who organise such meetings bear a grave responsibility for the consequences."

"And I am saying that in free England private meetings ought not to be broken up by ruffianly mobs, and that private citizens ought to be protected from being rabbled by hooligans because of the unpopularity of their political views."

Agnes rose to her feet, gathered her skirts about her, and ignoring the imploring look my mother cast in her direction, walked proudly from the room.

The door shut behind her with a soft click. Dora sipped at her tea. Father continued his perusal of the City news. Mother's pen began to scratch again at her paper.

It was as if waters had closed over a stone cast in a placid pool.

*

It was to prove a summer filled with discord. Now, in the wake of the Exeter Hall affair, came a spate of ugly incidents: windows smashed, meetings broken up, property destroyed. In some cases those regarded as pro-Boers were even physically attacked in their own homes. Charley Montague, writing his leaders for the *Manchester Guardian*, was cutting in his condemnation, not only of the incidents themselves, but of the official disregard which made them possible. In the House of Commons, Opposition speakers warned of the danger to ancient rights and freedoms. And always, in *The Times*, in Parliament, on the lips of government spokesmen, the reply was the same. The pro-Boers had only themselves to blame. For Agnes, incandescent with anger, it was almost beyond bearing. As she listened to Father laying down the law, those hooded lids conveyed an overpowering contempt.

A veritable *bellum impium*, Widdop called it. Of all calamities in the ancient world the most lamentable. The civil strife of kindred.

For us, though, the real blow had yet to fall. Poor Giles, so dashing in his uniform, found not glory, but a squalid, miserable end. And I was conscience-stricken, for I'd never liked him much.

Barely three months earlier I'd watched him going off to war. They'd marched past me, the 'good riders and good shots', club-men, sportsmen from the shires, men-about-town, on their way to the docks. Nor had I doubted for a moment that each and every one of them was a match for any number of Dutch farmers. One young volunteer had returned my salute. With his quick, eager eye, his jaunty step, he seemed the very embodiment of my own valorous dream: a life brimful of adventures, and a quick death at the end. How crass it seemed now, that ardent, foolish notion. An article in *The Times* had described the condition of the field hospitals at Bloemfontein, if 'hospitals' they could be called, for there were no nurses, and scarcely any doctors, no beds, no clean linen, not even a mattress. The fever victims lay packed together like sardines, with only a blanket and a waterproof sheet between their aching bodies and the ground.

My head was then chock-full of preparation for the Tripos. My days were spent grinding at my books. At night I lay in bed reciting, point by point, my own notes on the lymphatic drainage of the breast, the vascular anastomosis of the middle ear, the course and relations of the greater petrosal nerve. The list seemed endless.

I'd gone home for a short break, though the feeble resort of putting a few miles between myself and the examination rooms did little to halt the treadmill revolving ceaselessly in my mind, when the news arrived of Giles' death.

Poor Dolly was inconsolable.

"Mourn him, my dear," said my mother gently, "but be proud of him, too. He gave his life for his country as surely as any man killed in action."

Her eyes filled with tears. Giles was her sister's son.

Meanwhile, Father had begun his address to some celestial jury.

"To hazard one's own life for the sake of others," he boomed impressively. "Always, everywhere, it has been regarded as the pinnacle of public virtue, the *ne plus ultra*, the very latitude and longitude of our moral journey. The Supreme Sacrifice."

Sometimes a single phrase will click things into place. Or else it was so very much the kind of thing that Widdop might have said. For Widdop had sprung suddenly to mind. *A sudden death is as good as any, don't you think?* My mind went back to that evening in his study: the firelight, the soft glow of the lamp, Masterman's letter, nestling behind that rack of pipes. *Ah, the men, the men were magnificent. If you could have seen them ...*

I pictured the lolling tongues, the faces covered with black flies, the wasted limbs too weak to brush them off. The foul breath, the sickening odours, seemed to mingle with the promptings of my supervisor on the structure and digestive functions of the small intestine. *It's important to remember Peyer's patches. They're likely to become ulcerated in a case of enteric fever.* I saw the sloughs, coming away like pieces of wash-leather in the stools, tarry with digested blood. And I drew away from Widdop and my father, addicted, both of them, to a rhetoric with which it was not possible to tell the truth.

*

In June Pretoria fell to Roberts. In the euphoria that followed the capture of the Transvaal capital the war was presumed as good as won. All over England people prepared to take up peaceful pursuits again. In Cambridge the May Balls were in full swing. But out on the veldt the Boer commandos continued to fight a running war, disrupting lines of communications, capturing trains, making great hauls of prisoners and equipment.

It infuriated Father. "As usual we have pushed leniency to weakness. These guerillas are quite simply bandits, and should be treated as such." At the same time his scorn for the Opposition knew no bounds. "They cant about principle. About duty. In time of war one's duty is quite plain – to get behind the government, and behind the troops."

It must have been about that time that my mother took to coming down to breakfast. It was perhaps a measure of her anxiety, since most of these outbursts followed on Father's first reading of *The Times*. And though the rest of us might delay our appearance until Father had departed for his chambers, a repeat performance over dinner could never be ruled out.

Throughout these diatribes Agnes sat silent. Though her face spoke volumes, for our sake she held her peace.

*

That August tensions within the family were increased by a visit from my grandfather. As usual the old man stayed at Brown's Hotel. When in town he preferred to stay at Brown's, though he expected to dine now and then at Onslow Place, a prospect which filled my mother with alarm.

For weeks there had been whisperings in the press about a snap election. Now reports appeared in *The Times* that Lord

Roberts was soon to return from South Africa, a sure sign, according to Father, that an end to the fighting was in sight. Meanwhile, closer to home, hostilities were already under way. Chamberlain was barn-storming about the country, one moment down in Devon, the next popping up in Lancashire. *A vote for the Liberals*, he told his audiences, *is a vote for the Boers*. His opponents' retaliation came in kind. Whichever party in the country suffered by the war, declared Lloyd-George, one party was doing well out of it. This charge – that Chamberlain was a profiteer, exploiting the war to swell the profits of his family's armaments interests – particularly outraged my Father. A cowardly attack, he called it, th1e more so for being made under the protection of parliamentary privilege.

Grandfather could be counted on to add fuel to any flame he came across.

"It seems only fitting," he observed dryly, "that as one brother makes our wars, another should manufacture the ammunition."

He cared nothing for politics. In his book politicians were mostly rogues and liars.

"Chamberlain was contemptible as a Liberal," he went on, unperturbedly slicing a pear. "You always said so. Now he's turned Tory is that a reason to think better of him ?"

We had all been schooled to greet grandfather's provocations without comment or reaction. Not daring to look at Father I glanced instead at Agnes, sitting opposite across the table. Her face positively gleamed with satisfaction.

*

In mid-September Parliament was dissolved. The election campaign began in an atmosphere of patriotic fervour whipped up by the government. Agnes was campaigning across the river for John Burns, the sitting Member. Father knew nothing of this. Mother begged me not to let him know. Already she had extracted solemn promises from Dolly and Dora, whose loyalties must have been sorely tried. That Agnes should be out soliciting support for a Liberal was treachery enough. That it should be Burns, notorious as the man with the red flag during the dockers' strike – Burns, who had been roaring against the war from the very start. It was unthinkable.

The household went from day to day in a state of barely suppressed tension. Only a man as self-preoccupied as Father could have failed to be aware of it. Each morning Agnes set off on her bicycle for Battersea. For my mother's sake she'd agreed to make no display of her activities within the home. Though this moratorium did not apparently extend to me.

"At least escort me to the committee rooms. I promise not to inveigle you into any treasonable act."

Her face was as free from guile as mine was dubious. I had an uneasy sense I was being required to serve as proxy for this flaunting of defiance. "Do come," she pleaded. "You can borrow cook's machine."

'Cook's machine' turned out to be an ancient crock red with the rust of years, its tyres so worn as to be scarcely visible. Gingerly I hoisted it out from the area.

"I shall ride slowly," announced Agnes, pushing her bicycle on to the pavement, "out of consideration for your decrepitude."

I was rather taken aback to see her handle bars decked with bunches of blue and white ribbon. Off she went at a stately pace. I creaked along at her side. Through the park we went, then out into the Battersea Road and on past a row of neat new villa flats.

"We're going to win," she cried, her face radiant with the light of battle.

I looked doubtfully at the windows round about. Such cards as were displayed all supported the Tory.

Eventually we turned aside into an estate of small neat cottages. Here the window cards were all blue for Burns. Indeed, the place was painted blue. "This is the real Battersea," cried Agnes. "Khaki never caught on here."

The men were at work, but the women stood at the doors and greeted us with a smile. Agnes waved to them as we passed.

"The forces of progress are absolutely solid. The Social Democrats are with us. As for Rosebery and the 'jingoes', they count for nothing here."

At last we arrived at the committee rooms, located in a quiet street of modest dwelling houses. Of Burns himself there was no sign. Agnes insisted on introducing me to some of her fellow workers. She led me to a table where a group of merry girls were busy addressing envelopes.

"This is my brother George. He's rather an old Tory," she added apologetically. "But I live in hopes."

There followed a chorus of good-humoured chaffing. I felt desperately uncomfortable. Moments later a teasing, brown-eyed girl was trying to persuade me to help with the work. Greatly embarrassed, I was stammering my excuses when Agnes came to my rescue.

"One step at a time," she said firmly. "He's had shocks enough for one day."

She came to the door to see me off.

"Dear George," she said. "I'm so glad you came with me."

She bent forward, and kissed me on the cheek.

"Whatever happens, we've done our best," she cried, as I mounted the ancient crock. "We've fought the good fight."

Robust, alert, she seemed in her element. My heart warmed to see her so roused.

"If they beat us, it will be a crime," she cried, and waved. Wobbling, I waved back.

Yet in a little while, creaking back through Battersea, my affectionate regard was overshadowed by misgiving. I knew from experience that Agnes could be profoundly wrong. Sometimes the very energy of her own passionate conviction sent her careering wildly off-course. Then she would dash at nightmares of her own creation. Besides, I reflected, Agnes had the egotism of all self-righteous people. What troubled her should trouble everyone. That Exeter Hall business, when she'd set out deliberately to confront the rest of us, still grated. However much I resented Father's domineering manner I still felt that what he'd said at the time was no more than shrewd and reasonable. Suddenly I came face to face with the fact that a part of me really disapproved of Agnes. Much as I admired her forthright, independent spirit, deep down I knew I shared my father's view.

XIII

Throughout the war men continued to make the long journey north to Wastdale Head. To me that summer, its remoteness seemed more desirable than ever. Jogging those last few miles, seeing the Wastdale fells come into view, one felt restored to a different scale of things. Five farms, the deepest lake in England, a curled lip of land beyond. And behind the inn, spanning a tumultuous beck, a low arch of rough stone so primitive in its construction as to seem itself a part of Nature. In a place of such enduring forms and presences the great world, for all its sound and fury, could be known for what it was, a passing show.

One evening I came off the fells to find no more than a handful of guests sitting down to dinner. Tourists, to judge by their appearance. At least, none had the look of mountaineers. Seeing them in their cuffs and collars was a depressing reminder of the life I'd left behind in London. But no thoughts, however glum, could put me off a Wastdale dinner. I set to with a will. Then, to my surprise, who should come striding into the dining room but Lockhart. For him too it was an unplanned visit. Like me, at odds with his milieu though for different reasons, he'd felt the need to escape. "A change of scene," was how he put it.

"I was thinking I might bivouac tonight at Hollow Stones," he added casually. "If you'd care to come."

I hesitated. I'd had a long day on the hill, and to tell the truth was rather looking forward to a comfortable bed.

"You could borrow a bag from Ritson." I must have appeared hesitant, for he added diffidently, "I'd be glad of the company."

I did not know Lockhart well. I don't suppose I'd exchanged more than a dozen words with him. Widdop, gregarious by nature, loved the talk of the smoking room. Lockhart, though, seemed more inclined to silent study. Among my lasting impressions of that period of my life are days when rain fell in floods, with the wind moaning in the chimneys, and Lockhart poring over the Climbing Book: brooding on it with the absorption he might have given to a scientific paper, not so much, I fancy, for the record of discoveries made as for pointers to new lines of enquiry.

The sun was already setting when we started out. Light had dwindled in the dale. But it still lingered, green and golden, over the upland fells. Unusually for Lockhart he went slowly, I dare say out of consideration for myself. Yet, though my legs were full of miles, I felt only a little tired. I was buoyed up by the novelty of the thing. Going among the hills at night, with a bivouac thrown in, was a new experience for me. There was, too, the excitement of being in on something. Exactly what, I had yet to discover. Lockhart had given no hint of what was in his mind, though when we met in the hall before starting I noticed him stowing a rope in his rucksack.

We walked in a deepening twilight. A slight breeze kept the midges off. At first we went with the noise of the beck bustling along beside us: then, as we started up Brown Tongue, Lockhart climbing the steep cropped turf with easy stride, the fussing of water grew less and less distinct. On every side, the hollows of the hills were filling up with shadow. The visible world was slipping away. Yet what remained seemed solid and reassuring. Each soft foot-fall, the thudding of my heart, the laboured breathing of a companion, small enough matters, to be sure, yet things one could feel certain of. With every stride the feeling grew that here, in everything around me, was all that I loved best in all the world.

Gradually, as we gained height, vague buttresses reared up to our right: Black Crag, bold and dark against the sky, then, as we neared Hollow Stones, the top of the Pinnacle, caught in one last ray. We paused for a moment, our eyes fixed on High Man. The rock glowed like a furnace: first rosy red, then gold, then glowing bronze, sinking finally to ashes.

At last Lockhart halted at a large undercut boulder, and we set to work, clearing away the stones. So we settled for the night, myself stretched out in my borrowed bag, Lockhart with his back against the rock.

A great hush enfolded Hollow Stones. Due to the huge proximity of Scawfell Crag, with Pike's Crag across the way, no light penetrated the hollow where we lay, save what spilled down through the gap of Mickledore. We lay without speaking, enclosed in an inky blackness that seemed to have come welling up out of the earth, flooding the amorphous masses of the hills, the edges of which now stood out sharp and still against a luminous sky. Now and then, faint on the breeze, I caught the fleeting murmur of the beck, the bleating of a lamb. The dark bulk of the hills, the blue night filled with stars, immeasurably distant, was creating in me a feeling of strangeness. Something dream-like. Not quite real.

The day had finally caught up with me. Immensely weary, yet too tired to sleep, I lay in a kind of stupor. Still Lockhart had given no inkling of his plans. Evidently he intended to climb as soon as possible after first light. Yet his objective remained uncertain, and I wondered vaguely if he was as yet reluctant to commit himself. Certainly, I was too tired to press him.

At length my uncertainty was answered. Or else Lockhart came to a decision.

"I thought I'd take a look at *Jones' Direct* first thing tomorrow," he murmured, putting another match to his pipe. "Just a look, you know."

I fancy he may have stayed like that all night. Sitting

upright. In the intervals of waking – I slept, on and off – I had an impression of him still in that same position, pipe in mouth, gazing up at the Pinnacle Face. The great crag loomed, form without substance, a black void against the pale night sky. Lockhart seemed to be studying it intently. Moving up it in his mind.

A great crag can seem warm and friendly in the sun. Scawfell was never that. Lit by sunlight only in the early morning, or on a summer evening, it dwells very much in mist and shadow. In bad weather it could seem an awesome place. To visitors in the last century, toiling up to view the gloomy hanging crags, the dark ghylls, silent but for the *drip, drip*, of water, the shattered debris spilling everywhere, it must have seemed the realm of Chaos and old Night. In our founding fathers it awoke a turbulent pleasure, something between fright and admiration, for they were drawn like moths to a flame. Even so, they kept mostly to the ghylls, or went up obscure places well away from the fearful exposure of the face.

Then, towards the end of the 'eighties, one Hopkinson led a party from the top of the Pinnacle down to a ledge, two hundred and fifty feet above the screes. He built a cairn there on the ledge to mark the limit of his progress. A short time later, his brother, equally bold, starting from Lord's Rake, climbed some way up the left wing of the face until he too was stopped, and forced to retreat. From that time onward there had been numerous attempts to reach the cairn. Jones had come closest. Yet even Jones was forced aside by the extreme steepness and smoothness of the rock.

The customary gloom was very much in evidence that morning. A bank of cloud had built up during the night. By daybreak it hung over the Wastdale fells, veiling the highest summits, imparting everywhere a sullen grey half-light in which a crag, grim enough by any account, seemed all the more forbidding. If Lockhart had been hoping for an hour or so of sun to lift the spirits he was out of luck.

I'd done a number of climbs on the crag, including one or two of the more difficult listed in OG's gazetteer. But they mostly followed the courses set by the founding fathers. *Jones' Direct* entailed a leap into another world. Even so, I was determined not to be intimidated. It is the awestruck tourist who yields to the thrill of the wild, the savage, the savouring of which seems, at a distance, so hugely enjoyable. For the climber the opposite must be the truth. He must drive out fear by the strength of his concentration. He must maintain his integrity of purpose no matter how awesome the surroundings. Yet I knew men, stout performers on the steep rock of Pillar or Gable, who spoke of the strain here of holding on to one's effort of concentration, of the sense they had of climbing against a constant resistance, as if the crag were striving all the while to thrust them off. What struck me, as I gazed up at it, was the utter impossibility of imagining myself in such a place.

Lost in my own reflections I suddenly became aware that Lockhart had been addressing me.

"So it seems to me a climb best tackled alone," he concluded. "I hope you don't mind."

He looked at me rather anxiously. Though my relief must have been evident, Lockhart's face bore the expression of a man not wishing to disappoint a friend.

We spent some time speculating as to the line taken by Jones two years earlier. I say 'speculating', since the climb was still something of a mystery. We knew it started from Lord's Rake, and came out ultimately at the top of the Pinnacle. But no one had repeated it, and OG's account was vague as to detail.

"If you stay here you should get a view," said Lockhart lightly. "All the same, don't wander off. I'd like to feel there's someone with a rope not far away."

A slight, unconcerned figure, he went on alone towards Lords Rake.

With Lockhart now out of sight I continued to study the face. Mountain features tend to reflect whatever one is looking for. Wall, buttress, ridge or slab all too readily assume the configurations of some passage read in a book, or a description passed on by a friend. But in that flat grey light it was impossible to make out any detail. The over-riding impression was of fearful blankness. I was profoundly glad not to be going up there. At the same time, I was made vividly aware that in venturing onto the open face, Jones had entered *terra incognita*, and regretted never having seen him in action. "What was he like?" I'd once enquired of Widdop. The schoolmaster had been at his most severe. "Jones climbed like a Turkish wrestler. All grunts and grapplings." In his eyes, at least, Lockhart was incomparably the better man. But Jones had done the climbs: *'C' Gully, Walker's Gully, Kern Knotts Crack*, the fearsome *Central Chimney* of Doe Crag, not to mention the climbs here on Scawfell Pinnacle. Lockhart had comparatively little to put beside that list of victories.

Meanwhile, he had re-appeared on the terrace crossing the lower buttress that forms the massive plinth of the Pinnacle. For what seemed an interminable time he stood, poised on the very edge of Deep Ghyll, staring upward. Suddenly he began to climb.

Fluently, with an economy of effort that spoke of ease and confidence, he climbed thirty or forty feet to an overhanging lip, the crude abutment of one slab with another. Flowing movement, punctuated by periods of intense concentration – that was always Lockhart's way. Reaching into some recess he stepped up beneath the lip and, leaning backwards, his feet on the slabby wall, began edging delicately left, out beyond the barrier of overhangs: a small upright figure, hands flat on the slab, working his way across the open face in a rising line towards a grassy niche.

*

It is the man who makes the climb. In the interval between each ascent rock is simply rock. It had never seemed more so than when I stood looking up at Lockhart, himself poised, head raised, thinking maybe of Jones at the day's end, in gathering gloom, piecing a way where no one had ever been before. OGJ, on reaching these self-same slabs, had removed his boots, thrown them down to his companion, and continued in stockinged feet.

Seeing that tiny figure, alone, unroped, on the huge sweep of open slab, it was impossible not to be struck by the presumptuous enormity of the thing. Marvellous, it seemed to me. A solitary man alone on featureless rock, he seemed to me to have soared beyond the confines of my own dreary day-to-day existence. A surge of fearful joy rushed through my veins. All my heart went up to the climbing man.

From my position, so far below, it was difficult to see clearly. A thickening of the mist, grey on grey, made everything vague. Against my cheek I felt a few faint chill drops, and wondered if the mist might turn to drizzle. What stood out, unmistakable, was the tiny figure moving against the rock. Always upright, yet so sparing of effort, it progressed by slight movements of the hands and feet. Subtle pressures, delicate adjustments, were enough to win a fresh position. A slip would kill. Yet it seemed to make no difference. Always the upright posture, the upward questing look. The silent scrutiny, it seemed to me, of a man advancing on a tiger. A continual enquiry. It was almost abstract. A puzzle for the mind rather than the body. And the intentness of that mind. Poised so critically, and yet so still, absorbed, as if probing for something locked in stone. Not that the rock yielded as the man advanced: rather, he seemed to find some key, a password that made safe those few steps further.

At length he reached a second niche, thirty or forty feet above the first. Immediately above, a shadowy depression in the rock suggested a shallow corner, some seventy or eighty feet, as I guessed it, from the ledge of Hopkinson's cairn. Some distance to the left, a wide shallow groove I took to be the line of the gully climbed by the brother a dozen years earlier, and the point at which Jones had been turned aside, forced into an exposed traverse further left. But Lockhart seemed scarcely to regard the traverse. His gaze was focused upward.

*

I still recall the excitement of that moment. Suddenly I knew beyond a doubt that Lockhart's intention was to climb directly to the cairn. Not only did he dream of emulating Jones. He dreamed of climbs harder than anything Jones had ever attempted. For minutes on end I kept my gaze fixed on that tiny figure, motionless, still in its niche two hundred feet above my head. Suddenly, Lockhart began to descend.

Neat, unhurried, he came down again with the same precision and control. I put it down to the mist. Certainly, retreat seemed the prudent thing. For a lone man on sketchy rock the slightest suggestion of damp might have been lethal. I went up towards Lord's Rake to meet him, full of admiration, expressed my sympathy at his rotten luck. But for the mist he must surely have succeeded.

Lockhart shook his head at my commiserations.

"The mist," he said, "was in myself."

XIV

As the time drew near for me to start my clinical studies all my old anxieties returned. Was this what I really wanted? Each time I thought about it I was filled with panic. I'd no grounds for knowing, one way or the other. Uncertain, irresolute, it was a state of mind of which I felt thoroughly ashamed. What was my place in the world? To most of my contemporaries at Caius the thing presented no difficulty whatsoever: school, college, hospital – all, for them, was progress on the self-same path. But they had physicians for fathers. I was quite unable to say what had prompted me to pick on medicine, unless it was to thwart my own Father.

It was always assumed I would follow him into the law, a prospect that provoked much good-humoured banter from Father's brothers. Uncle Guy used to make jokes about the dinners at Lincoln's Inn. Eating one's way to a qualification, he called it. "Couldn't do better," said Uncle Giles. "Where else would a boy find a career so short in hours and long on fees." I was strongly tempted to point to his own merchant bank, but of course I held my tongue.

As my school career drew towards its close Father had attempted to initiate my legal education with extracts from the Law reports. "Now here's an interesting case," he'd begin over breakfast. I groaned inwardly. My sisters avoided one another's eye.

In due course Father showed me over Lincoln's Inn, of which he was now a Bencher. And though I did my best to appear impressed, I found this lawyers' quarter, with its ponderous wooden gates, its grimy bricks and tiny dusty windows, depressing in the extreme. It struck me as little better than the prison in which so many of its members' clients were confined.

In the end I'd won the day. It was the first major victory of my life. Though it had been a long campaign, fought out in many silent walks together along the Embankment, or over Chelsea bridge and into the park.

*

So, in late September, I left home once more. The necessity of being close to Bart's meant living in the City. For the first time I found myself tramping the streets, lodgings list in hand, searching for somewhere to live. I spent whole days looking over a succession of shabby rooms in a greasy neighbourhood, seemingly given over to butchers and slaughtermen. It was a demoralising experience. Then my luck changed. Ranging further afield – a pointer, perhaps, to some unconscious desire on my part to place myself at a distance from the scene of my daily labours – I found what I was looking for on the south side, and towards the top, of Ludgate Hill: believing, in my innocence, that the clatter of cabs and wagons, the trains rattling over the bridge spanning the hill, was a small matter to set against the view of the great west front of St Paul's. They were handsome quarters none-the-less. That I was able to afford them was due to a generous increase in my allowance, a measure of Father's satisfaction at my winning the Duckworth Prize. Perhaps he saw it as an earnest of future success. But I knew such modest achievement as it represented owed more to sheer slog, than to any flair or enthusiasm. I was already flinching at the thought of the mountain of work that lay ahead. I knew I wouldn't be able to keep up. Even so, it was a profound relief to be leaving Onslow Place.

"How lucky you are," sighed Agnes. "If I were to make myself thoroughly disagreeable, do you think father would pay for me to live somewhere else ? I shouldn't want anything very grand. A single room would do."

The results of the election had left her in dejected mood. Khaki swept the board, and she had taken it badly. All the things she cared about, the plight of the homeless, the multitudes crammed into teeming slums, had gone for nothing. In London especially, 'the forces of progress' had been ignominiously defeated: those who would have done most, rejected by those most in need.

"In the whole of England," said Agnes bitterly, "only two or three constituencies voted against the war."

"At least Battersea," I pointed out, "was one of them."

She refused to be consoled.

For Father it was nothing out of the ordinary. An overwhelming Tory victory, followed a few weeks later by the return of the City Volunteers, sealed the inevitable triumph of civilisation over brutishness and barbarism. Euphoric crowds greeted the men as they marched from Paddington to St Paul's. Father and I were in the Strand that day. We were quite unable to get through the dense throng of spectators. The crush was truly tremendous. Cheering men and women waved from the upper windows of stores and public buildings. The roof of a building opposite where we'd halted, close to St Clement Dane's, was lined with figures, leaning perilously out over the parapet in their eagerness to cheer the heroes home. Even my father, no enthusiast for popular demonstrations, was so far carried away as to add his own *hurrah* to the general jubilation. Such was the din, I wasn't able to catch his words. He had to shout them again, his face close to my ear.

"We may lose the first battle, but we win in the end," he yelled, above the ponderous thumping of the drums. "We always win in the end."

110

I smiled, nodded. Hemmed in by such fierce joy, I found I
had no strong feelings of my own, nothing except revulsion at
the memory of poor Giles, and shame at my own inadequacy.

*

Yet one man I knew seemed indifferent to the war. Indeed,
I can't remember Lockhart ever expressing an opinion. Absorbed
intellectually and emotionally in his work, he came to Wastdale
to climb.

He was often in my thoughts that autumn as the war dragged
on. It was an anxious time for me – discord at home, uncertainty
as to the direction of my own life – yet always, amidst all that
was most disagreeable and fragmenting, was the memory of
Wastdale, and of Lockhart. No atmosphere, however tense,
seemed to ruffle that air of quiet composure. Or else I pictured
him as I had seen him on Scawfell: that upright figure, alone,
unroped. And always the upward questing look. It was a thing
that spoke to me more eloquently than any words.

For weeks afterwards my mind had been engrossed by the
extraordinary composure, self-sufficiency, whatever it was that
enabled him to remain for minutes on end, poised, concentrating
on the next few moves, in a place where a mere mortal like
myself would have been straining every nerve and muscle simply
to hang on. From that day forward I'd thought of him – not as a
friend, exactly. I couldn't claim that. Yet he'd begun to figure
in that inner sanctum of the soul wherein a young man's sense
of himself is formed. Not as he is, but as he dreams of being.

A few weeks after the climb on Scawfell Pinnacle, we'd met
again. I had some business to complete in Cambridge, and

finding myself with time to spare I'd called at his rooms. I'd an idea he lived in Park Terrace. A short search along a row of pleasant villas soon tracked down a neatly printed card. *Dr.J.G.Lockhart.*

I pressed the bell. Lockhart himself answered it. He seemed somewhat taken aback to find me at his door.

"I don't get many callers," he said, as he ushered me up the stairs.

He showed me into a sunny, first-floor sitting room overlooking Parker's Piece. To say it was simply furnished is to do less than justice to the truth. Lockhart's room was the most Spartan I'd ever seen.

"I live quite simply, as you see."

Left alone while he went in search of refreshment, I took stock of the room. A worn carpet, two half-decent armchairs either side of the empty grate, another chair at a table which served as a desk, to judge by the books and writing materials set out neatly. Bare white walls. Above the mantelpiece hung a single photograph, the more notable for being the only item in a room otherwise devoid of ornament. Nothing superfluous. The *pied-à-terre*, it struck me, of a man for whom the life of the mind was all-in-all. But where, I wondered, did he keep his boots, his rope ? Shoved, presumably, in some cupboard or wardrobe. Certainly, there was nothing to suggest his life as a mountaineer.

I turned to the photograph on the mantelpiece. Standing, sitting cross-legged, or seated on chairs were a couple of dozen young men. Solemn in their waistcoats and watch-chains, as if slightly over-awed by whatever it was they'd come together to represent, they were grouped around a slight headmasterish figure with folded hands, thin-faced, studious in *pince-nez*. On either side of him sat a young woman. There was nothing to suggest who or what the photograph might signify. The setting gave nothing away – trees, the roof of a shed, a bicycle leaning against a wall. It was just possible to make out, in the foreground, the tram-lines of a tennis court. It might have been any suburban garden. I almost missed Lockhart. Frowning, seemingly ill-at-ease, he stood directly behind the central figure. His eyes were fixed resolutely on the camera. He had the air of a man determined to see it through.

"Ah, the family photograph," said Lockhart, coming in with a tray of tea. Though he spoke lightly, it sounded rather forced. "Actually," he added, setting down the tray on the hearth between the chairs, "Thomson's research group."

"That's Thomson himself," he went on, indicating the donnish figure. The note of respect was unmistakeable.

Curious, I enquired about the young women. Thomson's daughters?

Lockhart stared at me, then broke into laughter.

"No, no," he said. "*Protégées* perhaps, but not his daughters. Indeed, they may surpass us all in the end."

Listening to him that afternoon as he identified some of his colleagues, explained what they were working on, I began to see how it was no use anyone trying to understand him for whom the intellect was not in itself a thing for passionate excitement.

Lockhart had been present at Thomson's historic lecture on the electron. "Would you believe it, someone actually accused J.J. of pulling our legs."

He smiled wryly, sipping his tea. No doubt I looked rather baffled, for he began to explain, in simple terms, the current state of knowledge regarding the atom.

"They're the only material things which still remain in the precise condition in which they first began to exist. Some of us are convinced that something has to rattle inside the atom in order to explain atomic spectra."

He spoke of the speculation then exciting the Cavendish that the electron might possibly be connected with atomic spectra, that maybe Thomson had hit upon a universal atomic constituent.

"And if he has ?" I asked, trying to keep up my end.

"Oh, it changes everything."

All this was way above my head. Even so, I began to sense the proximity of a shadowy world in which momentous things were happening.

Somewhere across the town a college clock began to chime. It was time for me to leave.

We walked together over Parker's Piece. The September sun cast long shadows across the grass, where boys were playing a late game of cricket. As we went Lockhart spoke of the wider world of physics. Great things had been achieved. Greater were to follow. He mentioned names – Planck, Boltzmann – that meant nothing to me, but filled him with excitement.

At the corner of Regent Street we shook hands and went our ways, he to Free School Lane and the Cavendish, I to catch my train. I went on towards the station, my brain working with a sense of I knew not what. Yet that shadowy world was beckoning around me, mysterious and vast. On the platform, I stood as a blind man might have waited, lost in a blankness from which I was recalled by the porter's bellowing: *Liverpool Street ... Liverpool Street.*

As the train drew in I looked for an empty carriage, for I wanted nothing to break in on my reverie. Gazing from the window, with familiar fields and hedges slipping by, I dreamed of a life absorbed in some arcane pursuit: of making some discovery, obscure, known only to a handful of fellow workers, yet momentous in some fundamental way.

XV

I'd been at Bart's a month and I was all at sea. An undergraduate no longer, I was now a 'medical clerk', the lowest form, it seemed, of hospital life. The first few weeks passed in a whirl of incomprehensible activity. Every morning I reported for duty on one of the men's medical wards. Much of my new education seemed to consist in hanging about the ward picking up scraps of information, and doing such odd jobs as a clerk was thought capable of.

Two afternoons a week the physician, Dr. Squire Sprague, made his rounds accompanied by his clerks. An imposing figure, always formally dressed in morning coat, he seemed to take an instant dislike to me. On discovering where I'd begun my medical studies he advised me abruptly to put behind me all I'd learnt at Cambridge. Anatomy and physiology were not 'real medicine'.

Teaching took place at the bedside, often within such a vacuum of knowledge on my part that I could make little of what was being said. We clustered round to hear the salient features of the case discussed; its history and pathology, the train of reasoning by which Dr. Squire Sprague arrived at his diagnosis, the treatment proposed. In due course we took our first steps in clinical examination, a procedure which violated all I valued most with regard to personal privacy. Had I known what I was doing it might have seemed less indecent. But for me, struggling to transfer passages from textbooks into bodies of flesh and blood, it was a baffling business. I would stare helplessly at some expanse of torso, as empty of significance to me as any *terra incognita*, with Dr. Squire Sprague's maxim (*the first precept of the physician*) echoing in my head: *Eyes first and most, hands next and least, tongue not at all.* The eyes of the patient, sliding nervously from side to side, seemed to mirror my own bewilderment. I peered down throats. I palpated lumpy tissue. With my stethoscope I listened to confused thumps and murmurings I could make nothing of. After a ward round I would often come away despairing, convinced that my presence there was simply a hindrance to the real business of the hospital.

Overwhelmed by my new life at Bart's I saw relatively little of the family. On my first visit home I said nothing to indicate my bewilderment and confusion.

Though Father, carving the beef, had been in inviting mood.

"I dare say George finds a difference walking the wards," he remarked, to nervous flutterings from Dolly.

"Not at the table, please," said my mother firmly.

Father made a great show of clashing knife and steel, while the ghost of a smile, the merest twitch of an eyelid shared with me his bit of fun.

There was no sign of Agnes that evening, and my enquiry had been received in an awkward silence.

"Agnes has gone to Blackheath," said Dora eventually.

"Rufus is unwell again," added my mother carefully, "and poor Harriet is not getting any younger."

It was, as I thought, a tactical withdrawal. A whispered aside later revealed that Agnes had been distributing pamphlets on behalf of South African women and children.

"She gave one to cook," hissed Dolly. And pulled a face. "Father was furious."

*

After Christmas I resumed at Bart's, now as a surgical dresser. Dr. Squire Sprague had been wont to talk of the 'art' of medicine, as opposed to the 'craft' of surgery, which he seemed to regard as little more than a refined kind of carpentry. An activity for artisans. So I was curious, as well as apprehensive, to see what I would make of it. Our instruction was undertaken by a dapper, dry-skinned Scot. Spiky black mustachios, together with raven wings of hair brushed back above the ears, gave him somewhat of a diabolic appearance. He had the look of a demon king. Unsurprisingly, he was known as 'Old Nick'. His opening remarks, delivered with quiet irony as we gathered round a bed, made a deep impression.

"Our profession, gentlemen, has been described as at best a bloody and conjectural business. So let us search scrupulously, and with the closest attention, for the clinical facts."

How my heart quickened at his words. I felt for the first time I'd come face to face with the awesome nature of what I'd taken on.

MacSelf operated twice a week. In the mornings patients due to go to theatre that afternoon would serve for a theoretical demonstration of his craft. Though the surgeon's fingers, palpating an abdomen, found things that utterly escaped my touch. *No? Perhaps I was mistaken. No, it's there all right. Here. Try again.* Kindly, humorous, he let us down lightly.

Now, as I went about my business, dressing wounds, renewing bandages, I felt that at last I was doing something. As yet of small value, except perhaps to myself. Yet for me it was a new and satisfying experience. On MacSelf's 'afternoons' I took my seat on the steep tiered benches of the 'gods', hanging over the rail, a tense spectator of the drama played out below me on the table. Here was the world of intense excitement I was seeking. Often the only hope a patient had lay with the surgeons's intervention. Yet the merest slip might kill. The thought was terrifying.

Afterwards, writing up my surgical observations, I would pause, allowing my mind to dwell on those hands as, deft, precise, they went about their business. I examined my own blunt instruments. More suited to gripping rock than wielding a scalpel. Dissection was never one of my strengths.

For all that, I began to think of myself, after qualification, securing a hospital appointment, then perhaps taken on to the staff, a surgeon, with my own consulting rooms in Harley Street. After all, one should never put anything out of court. Hadn't MacSelf said as much ? "It's not so very long ago that our esteemed colleagues over at University College were telling us that the brain, the abdomen, and the thoracic cavity would be for ever closed to the intrusion of the wise and humane surgeon. Since when I have myself removed a stomach, a whole lung and large sections of the intestine."

The sly grin that accompanied his words was more than ever that of the demon king.

Rapt, excited, quite certain of my own unfittedness, amazed at my own temerity – yet for the first time in my life I really knew what I wanted to do. At home I said nothing of my new resolve. It was not for sharing. Kept to myself it would become a store of secret satisfactions, to be savoured through the months and years ahead. Thus I began to cherish day-dreams in which I saw myself, amid seething trays of instruments, intervening where the greatest in the land were powerless to act. In my consulting room I interviewed stricken politicians, grim-faced noblemen, despairing fathers, husbands, wives. All beating a path to the door, not of some suave, society surgeon, but a plain, blunt man. Yet the best in London. *What are the chances ?* A pursing of lips. *If I do it ? Perhaps fifty-fifty. If it's done by someone else …* A shrug of the shoulders.

At last it was possible to think of myself as a serious person.

All through winter the war dragged on.

As spring approached with still no let-up in the fighting it became increasingly difficult for the Government to maintain the fiction that the war was as good as over. More and more the conflict took on the character of a guerilla struggle. In parliament and at public halls throughout the country opponents of the war redoubled their opposition, often in defiance of angry crowds who came to break up their meetings. Meanwhile, I was discovering for myself how much the East End of London had contributed in blood and suffering, how many local men had fallen victim either to bullet or disease. There was much indignation at the Boers' refusal to accept that they'd been beaten 'fair and square'.

" What's the bloody point, sir – beggin' yer pardon, sir."

As the weeks passed, and it became more and more evident that the Boers weren't going to give up, the public mood grew all the more obdurate. The 'brave opponents' of Pieter's Hill and Colenso were now presented in the press as rebels and murderers. Stirring episodes, which had lent a glow to the earlier stages of the conflict, now gave place to stories of outrage and atrocity.

One day, in one of the surgical wards, I went to change the dressing of a man with an ulcerated leg. He was gazing, with bitter anger, at an illustrated weekly.

"Just look at that, sir." He pointed to pictures of soft-nosed bullets taken from a captured Boer. I flinched to think of the damage they must inflict on human tissue.

"Shoot 'em ! That's what wants doing. No prisoners. Shoot the bloody lot ! Beggin' yer pardon, sir."

*

It was my father's custom each April to mark dividend day at the Bank of England with a supper to celebrate the family fortunes. *Our harvest festival*, as he sardonically put it. Some of my aunts and cousins considered the thing in poor taste. Father was well aware of it. Indeed, their disapproval only increased the delight he took in entertaining them so lavishly. Incomparable in his disdain for fashion or opinion, he never did things by halves.

As directors, with a large holding in the firm, Father and his brothers had good reason to give thanks. They were all intensely proud of the family achievement. At the same time they viewed it with a good deal of complacency, almost as if it were the operation of a natural law. Something we Hazards were born to. Just as it was our prerogative to be victorious in all our wars, and have the moral right of it into the bargain.

For me as a boy it was always a magical night: my mother resplendent in her diamond pendant, Father in tail coat and white waistcoat. He loved to cut a dash. All the uncles and aunts and cousins would gather in the drawing room. Grandfather, though formally invited every year as guest of honour, never attended. Rufus was usually ferried over from Blackheath as a kind of proxy: a valetudinarian from the cradle, he had survived to a robust old age. Then at last the double doors would be thrown back to reveal a wondrous sight: the lofty dining room ablaze with light, the *Star of Northumbria* decked with a green garland, the long table stretched out with extra leaves, with glass and silver set out on the glowing wood, the Waterford decanters, the silver claret jug, with damask napkins and the silky gleam of laundered Irish linen against the rich warm swirl of red and brown mahogany.

Seated at the head of the table, Father was in his element. Every year his speech was much the same: secure, untroubled, its very predictability an assurance of enduring prosperity. He would begin by singing the praises of the British merchant service: *Fifty percent of the world's tonnage – a good proportion built in the Hazard yards*. Though speaking as *a refugee from marine engineering*, he reminded us that our roots lay in the thrift and toil on which the family fortunes had been founded. True, the family's control was not quite what it was. True, the private banks – here a humorous sidelong glance at Giles – had acquired a significant interest. But the name above the shipyard gates was still the same. Long might it remain so.

Then the uncles, aunts and cousins would rise to their feet, raise their glasses to the *Star of Northumbria*, and the firm of Hazard would be toasted with due solemnity.

That evening however, as we waited in the drawing room for dinner to be announced, I was feeling rather ill-at-ease. Somewhat recklessly, in emulation of Father, I'd donned a white waistcoat. It was the impulse of a moment. Now, conscious of my Uncle Giles' ironic eye, I was rather regretting it. But it was too late to take the damned thing off.

I smiled nervously at Agnes. Restored to the family fold, if not to favour, she hovered at old Rufus' side. Seated in Father's armchair the old man was still feeling the effects of his bronchitis. Sunk in gloom at the old Queen's death, we had thought him sliding into a decline from which, at his age, it seemed unlikely he would recover.

"Touch and go," he declared gravely, as we gathered round to congratulate him on his recovery. "Touch and go – until Agnes took me in hand." The old man put his arm around her in a gesture of endorsement.

Inevitably, the war crept into the conversation. Men fell into it now almost unawares, whatever the occasion.

Kitchener's offer of terms had been rejected by the Boers.

"It's great pity," Father was saying gravely, "and it will cost more lives. But the annexations are not negotiable. The Transvaal is British territory now."

The annexation of the Boer republics had brought about a problematic change in the status of the Afrikaaner population, who, if they might now be treated as rebels rather than prisoners of war, could also be thought to enjoy certain rights under the Crown.

It was a point not lost on my Uncle Giles, standing back to the fire, hands thrust under his coat tails. Evidently he was uneasy at the thought of elderly Transvaalers being forced to travel on military trains. Though he put the point with the air of a man posing a kind of forensic teaser. "You're the lawyer, Roderick. Can it really be legal, do you think, for the government to make use of British citizens as hostages? *Civis Romanus sum*, an' so forth."

Not for the first time I was struck by an erosion in that moral certitude that had so buoyed up support for the war. Only that morning further allegations had appeared in *The Times* regarding the conduct of a British general.

"To burn a town is one thing," old Rufus was saying. "To post a notice instructing women and children seeking food and shelter to apply to the guerillas does seem gratuitous, to say the least."

"The man's a brute," said Agnes fiercely. "He's a disgrace to the uniform he wears."

Had it been said lightly, with a kind of womanly disdain it might have passed muster. It was the ardour, the moral passion, that offended.

"I hope the Boers knock him off his horse," she added for good measure.

There was an embarrassed silence. A general avoiding of eyes. I looked away myself. At that moment the double doors swung open. Little Milly, bobbing prettily, called us in to dinner. The relief, as the guests paired off, was almost tangible. As the men sought their partners I caught sight of Agnes, flushed, defiant, standing in the centre of the room. I felt a rush of sympathy and was about to go forward to take her in to dinner, when I saw old Rufus gallantly proffering his arm. The procession formed up, and off we went: my mother graciously, with a swish and a shimmer of silk and satin: Father still with a face like thunder.

XVI

At last the winter session ended. After six months on the wards I was ready for a break. Ordinarily I would have been looking forward to my holiday with the keenest anticipation. Easter held a special significance for all Wastdale men. It was our great festival, the season for meetings and reunions, for savouring again the bonds of friendship and fidelity. Every Easter the great men of an earlier generation returned to their old stamping ground. And in the evenings, after the day's adventures, there would be laughter and tobacco, old victories recalled, stories of brave deeds, honourable defeats, tales apocryphal and cautionary. Yet, as I took the train from Euston, I felt only disquiet. Though several months had passed since my last visit to Wastdale, rumours had reached me of the change that had come over our community. Even Slater, not the most sensitive of men, had marked the alteration: men who'd once shared the same rope now barely speaking, the affable camaraderie of the smoke room reduced to a kind of tight-lipped politeness. Even when one allowed for the colouring Slater gave to all his tales there seemed little doubt that the open hearts of old were now a thing of the past.

It was a dismal day. The dreary skies seemed only to increase the tedium of the journey. I sat gazing out over the Cheshire plain filled with misgiving. I was in that dejected mood in which one sour reflection mounts upon another. Opposite me some Manchester merchant, with a copy of *The Times* next to a pair of yellow gloves on the seat beside him, was scanning the inner back page of the *Manchester Guardian*. The sight of the paper did nothing to lift my spirits. Scott's unpopularity was then at its height. If rumour was to be believed, every post saw his letter box stuffed full with abuse and filth. I'd heard it said that a cordon of police was posted on daily duty around the *Guardian's* offices to protect its editor from his own readers. Meanwhile, Charley Montague continued to wage his pungent and provocative onslaught on the government. He was not a man to pour oil on troubled waters.

The Manchester merchant, presumably having gleaned all he needed, suddenly crumpled the *Guardian* into a ball, and tossed it onto the floor. He left the train shortly afterwards and I was left alone in the carriage, staring out at rows of signal lights and flaring furnace flames, conscious of the crumpled sheets of newsprint, wondering what I might find at Wastdale Head. I had an additional reason for uneasiness. Widdop's mother had died a day or two after Christmas. *After a long illness patiently borne ...* I'd seen the notice in *The Times*, and had written an uneasy letter of condolence. Widdop's courteous reply reflected nothing of the gap I felt had opened between us. I was uncomfortably aware that I'd been holding him at a distance. It was as if the ugly circumstances of Giles' death had somehow rubbed off on him. Now, I was forced to admit that it seemed grossly unfair to hold Widdop responsible for that, or to feel that he was in any way implicated in its ugliness and squalor. As well as being troubled by a nagging sense of having wronged a friend, I was conscious of having fallen short of the loyalty I prized above all else. *Ideals*, I remembered Widdop telling me, *are worth as much, or as little, as the men who hold them.* In his eyes, either a man was satisfacto1ry, or he was not.

I need not have worried. Widdop's greeting was as generous as ever. Nothing could describe the rush of joy I felt on encountering that ready smile. The firm grasp of his hand.

What did it matter what a man thought or said ? What did it matter – so long as his climbing was courageous and sincere ?

That night was bitterly cold. Even in bed I felt the frost nipping my nose. Next morning the old excitement of waking to a different world was, if anything, intensified with the first shock of getting out of bed into the icy air of an unheated room.

I took a short walk before breakfast, over the bridge and into Mosedale. The cold had laid its hand on everything. Even sounds seemed somehow deadened in the freezing air. At the same time, small things took on a terrific intensity. Slender grasses the frost had thickened. Beads of water threaded on a stalk and frozen there. In a black hollow under a boulder I came across a whole fern frond encased in ice, a fresh green marvel, and I found myself wondering at my earlier gloomy imaginings. When had Nature ever betrayed me ? Stirrup Crag, sharp, distinct in a sky of icy blue, the frosted birches hanging over Mosedale Beck, the very boulders, had all the glitter of a promise kept.

Flushed, alert, I tramped back ravenously hungry to the inn.

Breakfast saw the usual excited speculation as to what the day might hold. The long cold spell had kept the gullies in condition, and there was much keen anticipation and a general sharpening of axes as parties made their preparations.

Manoeuvring me into a quiet corner, Widdop said in a low voice, "Lockhart and I are going to take a look at 'C'. Why not come along ?"

Evidently the pair were still in relentless pursuit of Jones. This time it was to be the Central Gully on the Screes. The climb had long been high on their list. Its intrinsic difficulty would have offered a sufficient challenge in itself. Though I suspected that for Widdop at least, an added attraction lay in the fact that OGJ, incautious enough to try a second attempt, had fallen from the topmost pitch. George Abraham still talked about it. In any other circumstances the very thought of entering the gully would have daunted me absolutely. Abraham's story was as vivid as it was cautionary: OGJ, bruised and bandaged, looking 'paler than the snows of Pillar'; his dire warnings: *Promise me, George, never to climb 'C' Gully. It is a deadly place.* Now, apprehension struggled with what I recognized as a rare privilege. Lockhart and Widdop generally climbed as a pair. It was unusual for a third person to be invited to join their expeditions. There was, too, a feeling of security in being included in such a partnership – one of the most powerful in the district. Besides, I reasoned, Jones climbed it when wet and rotten. We would be coming at it frozen hard.

Together we made our way along the side of the lake. It was a cold, fresh day, the light splintering off snow and water. An icy wind battered our faces. As usual Lockhart went off on his own, that slow, unceasing stride taking him further and further up the scree. Widdop was in high spirits, singing snatches from Gilbert and Sullivan, squawking back at the jackdaws wheeling out from the crags, skimming stones that bounded and rebounded over the blue-black waters of the lake. Music was one of his passions. Some weeks earlier he'd been present at a performance of the *Enigma Variations* in St.James' Hall. Now he embarked on a tale of hilarious invention, according to which the famous work had nothing at all to do with Elgar's friends and fellow musicians, but was in fact based on incidents from the life of O.G.Jones. Widdop illustrated his extravaganza with vocalised extracts from the score: Jones (*glissandi of strings*) shinning up Cleopatra's Needle; Jones (*pomposo of brass*) posing for photographers; Jones at Euston, evading the station bobby by leaping (*arpeggios of woodwind*) across the rails from platform to platform; Jones plunging frost-bitten fingers into a pot of boiling glue (*yowl of tortured cat*).

"It quite crippled them, of course. Yes, virtual claws. Though Jones always claimed they gave him a prehensile grip."

With Widdop in this mood nothing was sacred. No reputation safe. When the fit was on him he would pull down the holiest of holies. Lockhart, striding ahead as usual, seemed a dull fellow by comparison.

Laughing, singing, we had picked our way across bands of stony debris, beneath a vast vegetated cliff of crags and gullies. Our path ran out at last among huge boulders, piled chaotically above the lake. Several hundred feet still separated us from our objective. Lockhart, meanwhile, had reached the place. Dwarfed by the tremendous cliff, he was gazing up at a black cleft, narrow and fearsome. Hearts thumping, we toiled up the scree to join him. I was conscious of the wind, shrilling and booming between the crumbling towers of the crag. The change of mood was almost palpable.

"Ah, that deep ... romantic cavern," gasped my companion. "A savage place, to say the least."

Widdop was to lead the climb that day. A renowned performer on ice, he was well qualified to lead us against whatever obstacles we might encounter in the gully. I'd heard it talked of as repulsively loose, oozing moisture and choked with vegetation. This, I thought to myself as we roped up, was venturing into the labyrinth, the dragon's den. My heart was in my mouth when we came to the traverse from which Jones had fallen. Yet, secure in my companions, roped between men I most admired in all the world, it became the triumphant climax of a day to dream of: the *chip, chip* of the axe, the glitter of ice, of rock, of blue-black water a thousand feet below.

Then tramping back at dusk, cheeks tingling, flinging down ropes and axes in the hall, the eager enquiries of our friends – such, in happier times, should have crowned a memorable day.

Yet all was soured, the moment we pushed open the hall door.

We'd arrived at the tail-end of a private conversation. The discussion, literary. The voice, prim, rather tight-lipped, unmistakeably that of Montague.

He glanced round as we clattered into the hall. His face offered no greeting. There was no enquiry as to our day. Turning away, he resumed his conversation.

"Well, they beat Kipling! To be frank, they struck me as going as far in degradation as it's possible for a poet to go."

I looked at Widdop, his face still flushed from the exertion of our walk back. Flushed, too, with victory. Slamming his axe into the umbrella stand, he burst out furiously, "Henley has a perfect right to attack so-called Englishmen whose attitudes he regards as contemptible."

Montague's look of pure, proud integrity grew visibly stiffer. The mouth tightened. The muscles of the face twitched once or twice. There was a pause, an icy interval in which Widdop's outburst seemed to hang in the air.

"Nevertheless, whether you like it or not, there are Englishmen who feel that some of Henley's utterances in recent weeks have been despicable."

White with anger Widdop turned on his heel and left the inn. Shaken, I turned to see Lockhart, sitting on the bottom tread of the stair, absorbedly unlacing his boots.

A row that Easter was inevitable. Oh, men tried. They did their best. But what divided us was no mere difference of opinion. It was a clash of beliefs and values as deeply cherished as they were mutually antagonistic. And when men turn the fierce light of disdain on one another's conception of things it can only end in mutual contempt. A friend had been attacked. And since loyalty to a friend is everything, it could not go unavenged.

That night at dinner Widdop found his opportunity. Just what led up to it I cannot say. What I heard – what we all heard

– from the other end of the table, cutting across the general buzz of conversation, was a voice of passionate protest.

"For heaven's sake ! Surely even war has its laws. There are things which may fairly be done, and things which should certainly not be done."

Into the hush that followed fell a clear, bell-like voice.

"I absolutely agree."

Widdop leant forward to seek out Hastings, further down the table.

"Wouldn't you say, Hastings, from a practical business point of view, that it's quite preposterous for us to provide for the care and maintenance of enemy women and children ?"

He turned to Collie, sitting at his side.

"Did you know, Professor, that some Army and Navy Stores lists have been introduced into the camps ? I dare say your Boer *frou* will return to domestic life with a taste in corsets and silk stockings as will quite astonish her husband."

No doubt Collie was as taken aback as the rest of us. Yet even if a reply had been under consideration in that formidable mind, it was forestalled by an outraged voice – Montague, rising to his feet ... "You have no right to say such things. No one has any right to say such things. It is cheap ... contemptible ... "

Widdop sat with gleaming eye, his face flushed, triumphant.

Heavy of heart, I took my candle and went up to bed. Fresh snow had fallen. A new moon stood above Yewbarrow. It filled the little room with a pallid glimmer. Too agitated for sleep I went over to the window. Ice lay thick along the edges of the pane. There I sat, with the shock of cold air against my face, my mind in a turmoil. I thought of the portrait in Widdop's room.

Only a few months earlier I'd had Henley pointed out to me, a stout red-faced man climbing painfully out of a cab in Oxford Street. There before me in the flesh stood one of my childhood's archetypes. Yet of the piratical air and manner that led Stevenson to Long John Silver nothing survived but the crutch. That, and the imprint of pain. Was it perhaps that crippled man Widdop was protecting ? He was, after all, the loyalist of friends. It was a mitigating thought. But no, I knew it wouldn't wash, even as I considered it. Widdop was a born antagonist. Adversarial to his fingertips. *What did it matter what a man thought or said* ... How fatuous that seemed now. And what of me ? Tentative, lacking confidence in all things, I was dazed, fascinated, by the sheer fluency of his attack. That savage goading of civilized susceptibilities. To mock where it would most offend.

Ugly. Ugly. And that ugliness thrusting itself upon us in places where, in times gone by, it would have been unthinkable. Then I thought of Lockhart sitting on the stair, unlacing his boots. It was a relief to dwell on that simple, single-minded focus. I sat in a dream, my eyes fixed where the long fellside gleamed in the moonlight. There was no wind. Nothing moved. Hill and dale, empty and silent. Another world, it seemed. The glittering stars, immeasurably distant. Snow-covered hills still and silent, under a silent moon.

XVII

At the start of the summer session I resumed once more as a medical clerk, this time on the female wards. I was surprised to find that I got on much better with the male, than with the female patients. Puzzled, I put this down to the fact that, my mother and sisters apart, I'd had little experience of women. At Cambridge one saw very few. There was my bedder Mrs Stubbings, a motherly old soul in a black cloak and bonnet. Occasionally one might catch a glimpse of the Girton girls. But as they were brought to lectures in a convoy of closed four wheelers, and whisked off back to Girton afterwards, it was never more than a glimpse.

Without thinking very much about it, I'd always taken women to be creatures whose biological determination rendered them quite different from myself, being delicate and easily upset. As a boy my sisters' lives had seemed to me as dull and uneventful as those of the stuffed birds and animals under the glass domes in my great-aunt Harriet's house in Blackheath. Now, as I came to study the diseases of women, it seemed to me very likely that such differences of temperament should not be unconnected with the contents of the female pelvic cavity. This region, to the anatomy and physiology of which I'd returned with greater concentration, now came to resemble a mysterious and anarchic zone outside the masculine boundary. It was to this area that I now looked for an explanation of that *ennui* that rendered my mother, returning home from an afternoon's visiting, so debilitated that she must lie on the sofa to be read to by one or other of her daughters.

It was largely for her sake that I resolved to spend the odd weekend at home. She'd begun complaining that she

131

saw nothing of her son. My father, with a decorum wholly uncharacteristic, had muttered something about 'a difficult time of life'.

It was in the drawing room, one Sunday afternoon, that I had my first inkling of a controversy that was soon to grip the nation, with its tale of farms burned, women and children turned out of their homes, herded into *laagers*. 'Concentration camps', they came to be called. Even Father, trying to explain it to my mother, clearly had his misgivings. "It seems alien to us, I know," he said. "But what the public has to realise is that these women and children represent the eyes and ears of the enemy. Deprived of his intelligence department the Boer must capitulate before long."

For all his faults, Father was a decent man at heart. Indeed, 'decency' was part of the problem. He simply couldn't bring himself to believe that British officers and administrators could ever behave in a callous way towards the women and children of their foes. "Lord Kitchener himself has looked into the matter. The people in the laagers have sufficient for their needs. They are all quite comfortable and happy. We have Kitchener's word for that. We must rely on his assurance." As details emerged of the death rate in the camps he doggedly refused to add his voice to the growing protests. Yet he was not a callous or indifferent man. The thought of those deaths troubled him as they troubled others. But, he reasoned, the incarceration of a civilian population, carried out in wartime and in hurried conditions, must necessarily involve some loss of life. Perhaps he hoped that a month of two would see an improvement. In any case, such fatalities as had already occurred were probably due in no small measure to the insanitary habits of the Boers themselves. "They don't wash. They won't use latrines. They have a horror of fresh air. It's being said Kitchener intends to charge some of these women with manslaughter of their own children. In my view, he'd have a case in law."

The Times published details of the outlandish remedies favoured by the enemy. Father read out some of the more bizarre items from the Boer *pharmacopoeia*, presumably on the grounds that I, as a medical student, was well placed to judge of their barbarity. "Listen to this. Brick-dust and brandy, dog's blood and Reckitt's Blue, cow dung with vinegar, to heal skin sores. And how about this for measles ? A child's body daubed with green oil paint – it dies of arsenical poisoning."

His voice struggled somewhere between incredulity and satisfaction. "It almost beggars belief."

But now a figure of chaos entered his domestic world. Ironically, it was Father himself who first spoke the dreadful name within our walls.

"This Miss Hobhouse is accusing the government of the most abominable cruelty," he remarked lightly one morning over his breakfast egg. "They have deliberately left the prisoners' tents and quarters open to the north wind."

I kept my gaze fixed on my plate. Deprived of filial support my father addressed himself to my mother's loyal but puzzled smile.

"It's a point of geography, my dear. South Africa is south of the equator. The coldest winds come from the south."

Up to that second summer of the war few people had even heard the name of Emily Hobhouse. A spinster, middle-aged, the daughter of a provincial arch-deacon, she seemed a wholly unlikely focus for such notoriety. But *she* had visited South Africa. *She* had seen the camps. On her return she'd written a report describing the conditions: exhausted women and children herded into laagers, the lack of fuel, of bedding, of proper food, the multiplying sickness. This document was circulated among MPs. Agnes' radical friends had sight of it and, in due course, the gist of it was passed to her.

Indifferent to opinion, contemptuous of consequences, Agnes set out to confront the British public with the facts about the camps. She began with Milly, the house-maid. Milly, a tender-hearted soul, wept over it with Dolly. My father was outraged.

"But it's absolutely heart-rending."

It was no use. Dolly's protestations were swept aside. Miss Hobhouse was simply a 'screamer', a woman who magnified the virtues of her country's enemies and the faults of her own people.

For once my mother took a dissenting view. Just as she thought the male superior in intellect and judgement, so she believed women more sensitive in their sympathies. It was only natural for Miss Hobhouse to feel as she did. However, for a lady to engage publicly in political debate was altogether a different matter.

That she held strong views on the subject became clear later that afternoon. It was one of her sewing afternoons. Another sale of work was looming. My sisters, seated on the long low settee opposite the fireplace, were dutifully stitching away. I sat in Father's armchair, skimming through *The Times*. For no particular reason, I happened to remark on an item announcing that Miss Hobhouse was to speak that evening at the Queen's Hall.

"I must say," declared my mother firmly, "I find something quite repugnant in the idea of an Englishwoman mounting a platform to address a vulgar, gaping crowd."

"At least her eyes are open," said Agnes levelly. "She sees an atrocity for what it is."

"As to that," remarked my mother mildly, peering short-

sightedly at needle and thread, "I cannot say. All the same, it is
not becoming. It is not what one would expect of a lady."

"If it be unlady-like to tell the truth instead of seeking to
conceal it," said Agnes, laying down her work, "to bear witness
to the compunction men fear as weakness – then so be it. No
more 'ladies'. Away with them. Let us have done with 'ladies'
altogether."

Her voice ended on a note of suppressed fierceness that
seemed to threaten some defiant gesture. A smashing of
windows. At the very least, dashing the *Sèvres* figure from the
mantelpiece.

I looked up from the cricket scores. Agnes, however, merely
picked up her garment and began stitching rapidly. No one
spoke. Dolly and Dora gazed intently at their work. Mother
embarked on a lengthy rummaging through her basket. Agnes
was to be left to seethe and bubble in her own ill temper.

*

I'd had no intention, when I went up north, of getting
involved in politics. Indeed, it was with relief at the prospect of
escaping all political controversy for a while that I took the train
to Harrogate at the start of my summer holiday. I'd arranged to
stay a day or two with climbing friends, the Bartons, before
travelling on with them to Scotland. I arrived to find the whole
town buzzing with the forthcoming meeting to be addressed by
the infamous Miss Hobhouse. She'd had a busy month. Twenty-
three meetings in four weeks. *A plucky campaign*, according to
the *Daily News*. But the *News* was itself notorious as a pro-Boer
rag. The rest of the press had branded her a liar, a rebel, and a
traitor to her country.

"One can shake hands with an enemy fighting for his

people," said Father, with uncharacteristic magnanimity. "But one's own fellow country-man ... an *English*woman ... "

Father's bewilderment was understandable. The blue-print was as rigid in determining the manufacture of young men and women as it was for the building of ships. Boys were brought up to be brave and honourable. The female sex was expected to honour manly achievement. Small wonder, then, at my Father's shock at the behaviour of Miss Hobhouse, a woman who had so signally rejected her allotted role as to impugn the humanity of British officers with her allegations that they were failing to care for women and children. It was the outrage of a man, honourable enough by his own lights, confronted with the evidence of shocking facts, the result of measures undertaken in his name. His reaction was inevitable. It couldn't possibly be true. And so he turned, as did most of the country, on the accuser.

That weekend I attended my first and last political meeting. The memory remains for me a matter of shame. Well, it is enough to look back over the events of twenty years to flinch at the mistakes one made: to recognise how much better one might have acted.

Claude Barton tried to dissuade me from going.

"It'll turn ugly," he said. "You mark my words."

His warnings served only to inflame my curiosity. There were several ladies among the platform party. Yet I knew instinctively, as one always does on these occasions, the person everyone had come to see. Though there was nothing remotely exotic about her. None of the romantic mystery men used to yearn for in a woman. She was about forty, elegant, not markedly different in appearance from any of the well-dressed women whose cards appeared with such regularity on the hall table at Onslow Place. An oval face, hair the colour of ripe corn, a firm, determined mouth. She sat bent slightly forward, glancing round attentively – alert, yet in no way intimidated by the temper of an audience which, to judge from the proliferation of miniature Union Jacks, was not likely to be well disposed towards her.

I found a seat close to the front, next to an elderly white-haired man. Like many of those present he was studying a copy of a patriotic pamphlet freely distributed in the streets around the hall. I'd had one stuffed in my hand by a smartly dressed young fellow, bawling out his wares with all the gusto of a regular newsboy. 'Gross calumnies! *Shameful tissue of lies! Read the truth about the war.*' Though there were a number of ladies present, the great majority of the audience were men. Indeed, a whole cross-section of the male population of Harrogate seemed to have packed into the building. Old and young sat side by side, labourers cheek by jowl with respectable manufacturers. A large number of seats in the rear of the hall were filled with noisy parties, many of them boys scarcely out of school. Boisterous, good humoured, roaring out *hurrahs* for Chamberlain and Baden-Powell, groans for Kruger and Lloyd George, they seemed more inclined towards the raucous conviviality I associated with bump suppers than a serious public meeting.

A fair hearing for Miss Hobhouse that evening was never a possibility. All the circumstances were against it. Her chairman could scarcely have served her worse. An apprehensive figure in *pince-nez* and soft bow tie, he rose with the air of a man going to his martyrdom. A more prudent man might have contented himself with a word or two of introduction, followed by a swift resumption of his seat. This fellow, though, for all his apprehension, was determined to bear witness. *A great wave of what had been called Imperialism had swept the country. It had swept men off their feet, or off their heads, he was not sure which.* ('No, no.') *We liked to think Englishmen were always fair and just.* ('Hear! Hear!') *But a different ideal had sprung up of late, an ideal given*

*over to the worship of size and strength. During the last decade we
had added four million square miles ...*

It was offered as a reproach. It met with loud, continuous
applause. At the back of the hall someone started *Soldiers of the
Queen*. Reaching for a rolled-up banner at his feet, the old fellow
next to me mounted his chair and began waving it about in
time to the singing. On and on it went, the last triumphant
notes of the chorus culminating in deafening cheers. In the lull
the followed, the chairman attempted to resume his speech.

"Give somebody else a chance," came a voice from the hall.
(*Loud cheers.*)

Scarcely audible amid the catcalls, the whistling and
stamping feet, the wretched man struggled on with his
introduction. *The speaker who was to follow him had recently
returned from South Africa. She had witnessed dreadful things.
Disdaining popularity, she had come to speak the truth of what she
had seen. He believed he could trust our Yorkshire spirit of fair play
and open-mindedness to treat a lady with respect.*

Smiling, Miss Hobhouse rose to her feet. It was the signal
for a demonstration that lasted several minutes. Stamping feet,
the tooting of a tin trumpet, cheers for Tommy Atkins, groans
and hisses, gave place at last to another rendition of the National
Anthem.

All this while she stood, mutely regarding the scene in front
of her. Then, in the lull that followed the anthem, she got in an
impromptu observation.

"I think you will agree with me," she remarked mildly, "that
if her Gracious Majesty the Queen, to whom you have sung,
were present now she would be heartily ashamed of her Yorkshire
subjects."

It was an unfortunate beginning. Amid the uproar that
followed a deep voice somewhere in the rear of the hall struck

up with '*Wheer hast tha' bin since Ah saw thee ?*' Back came the answer, roaring to the rafters. Thud, thud, went the stamping feet. On and on went it went, the singers revelling in the well-known verses that seemed to hold a grimly jocular message for the speaker. '*Tha'll go an' catch thi death o' cold ... Then we shall 'ave to bury thee.*' Many of the audience had by this stage risen to their feet, turning their backs on the platform to witness the noisy proceedings at the rear of the hall. Miss Hobhouse remained standing, smiling, occasionally shaking her head. Two or three times she tried to speak. "I have a great deal that I am anxious to say to you." (*Groans and hisses*). "Will you sit down for a few minutes and listen to me ?" ('*No! No!*') "I had expected better of Englishmen" – a reproach which was greeted with derisive laughter. *Soldiers of the Queen* started up again. The trumpet tooted. Tramp, tramp, went the boots. The old fellow next to me again rose to his feet, and began beating time with his flag.

For the first time she seemed to lose her composure, turning first in exasperation to the chairman – *if they wanted to serve the Queen, let them behave like subjects of the Queen* – then blazing at the audience. "This kind of behaviour will do more to advance our cause than the most eloquent speeches we could deliver," she shouted, above the din. "The rest of England will read the account of what has happened here tonight with disgust. Yorkshiremen will be held up to shame."

At this, a man in front of me climbed up on his chair and begged the meeting to give Miss Hobhouse a hearing. Another fellow promptly leapt on *his* chair to shout that it was the lady herself who was responsible for the disorder. Unabashed by the cheers which greeted this sally she tried again. "I ask you to give me a quiet hearing, and then go home and think over what I have said. We have respect for the feelings and opinions of our opponents, and we ask for the same."

This was greeted with vigorous applause on the platform.
But at the back of the hall bedlam prevailed. Cheers rang out:
for the Queen, for our generals at the front.

Some wag called for three cheers for De Witt. Loud groans
were his reward. Rattled now, she hit back. She would not be
silenced. She had come to make a speech, and make a speech
she would. It was a losing battle. As the realisation grew that
she was attempting to make her speech, if only to the first few
rows, the uproar worsened.

'Rule Britannia, Britannia rule the waves,
Britons never, never, never shall - be - slaves!'

The whole audience was on its feet. Flags waved. Chairs
were knocked about. Then a khaki-clad soldier bobbed up like
a jack-in-a-box, swaying about on the shoulders of the crowd.
An outburst of hurrahs for Tommy Atkins – then a chanting
chorus of The Absent-minded Beggar; 'Pass the hat for your credit's
sake, and pay - pay - pay!'

Nothing daunted, she flashed back at them. "Yes, you gave in
your thousands then. Will you not give a few moments now ?"

She was howled down. Groans, boos, hisses, shouts of 'No,
no'. Still the high urgent voice persisted. Fragments of her
message pierced the storm. "Boer women and children ... any
less deserving ... higher considerations ... those of decency ... "

But in the hall it was all heroic story. And she was spoiling
the fun, casting a shadow over the glorious adventure, be-
smirching the self-sacrifice of countless heroes with her lies about
the camps. As the patriotic bellowings continued, several dozen
young men sporting miniature Union Jacks advanced from the
back of the hall: in their midst, the khaki-clad figure, lurching
alarmingly on the shoulders of his handlers. Alarm now showed
plainly among the official party. One or two of the ladies rose to

their feet, and were escorted rapidly from the platform.

Miss Hobhouse, however, refused to leave. For ten minutes at least she stood her ground. Head thrown back, flushed with indignation, she regarded us with anger and contempt. Though we intended her no harm. Indeed, by this stage we were oblivious of her presence. In perfect if uproarious good humour the young men continued their circuit of the hall. Round and round they went, singing and cheering, while the triumphant tin trumpet gave out *toot* after *toot*.

*

Years later, shortly before the outbreak of war, I went to call on her. Six months had elapsed since I'd returned from my third trip to the Arctic. I'd written up my notes, published a paper on Sabine's gull (*xema sabinii*) which I'd observed in its summer breeding grounds. Restless again, I set off for Italy, travelling down through Tuscany and the hill towns of Umbria, fetching up at last in Rome. There I discovered, through a casual café encounter, that *la Signora* Hobhouse was now resident in the foreign quarter. My informant didn't know where, only that she was ill, and living alone. The memories of that meeting, the unworthy motives that took me there, her scorn, the shame I felt afterwards – it all came flooding back.

I enquired at the embassy for her whereabouts. A young third secretary dealt with my request.

"She has an apartment on the Caelian Hill," he said. "That's about all I can tell you. Miss Hobhouse is not exactly *persona grata* with us, you know. Though I believe she's rather an invalid these days. Weak heart, or something. Do you know her?"

Flowers in hand, I went one evening to pay my respects. Her flat was close to the Trinità dei Monti, at the top of the

Spanish Steps. A maid showed me into a high-ceilinged room, light and airy though sparsely furnished. On a day-bed beside an open window lay a woman. She wore a long dress of some dark blue material, tinted green.

I was struck by the change in her appearance. A dozen years had taken their toll. Still the same fair oval face. But the golden hair I remembered had turned to grey. Now swept back, it seemed to confirm the jibe one still heard made about her. Indeed, I'd heard a version of it that very morning on the lips of the young third secretary. *'Certainly, she's high-principled. But they're the principles of the schoolma'am. Truth-telling, right and wrong – that sort of thing. And, like all schoolma'ams, she's always in the right.'*

She thanked me for my flowers. "If you'll forgive me," she said, "I won't get up."

I explained, somewhat shamefacedly, that years earlier I'd attended a meeting at which she'd received rather a mauling.

The grey eyes surveyed me candidly. "I hope you won't take it amiss, young man, when I say that in the main I have found your sex to be unprincipled, as well as greedy, envious, and fearful. Nevertheless, you are most welcome."

Cooped up in the heat of a Roman summer, she seemed glad of any visitor from home.

Like many invalids she was eager to discuss her condition. No longer able to climb the steps, she had to be carried up and down by men hired for the purpose. Her treatment necessitated having baths of carbonic acid, and inhaling the vapour of iodine, a nostrum which she believed gave elasticity to the arteries and helped liquify her sluggish blood. I remarked that it would have been a treatment known to ancient Rome.

"Well, as you can see, I'm almost a citizen." She gestured to the window. Spread out below were spires, domes, and red-tiled roof-tops bathed in yellow light. She pointed out ruined walls and columns: golden stone glowing between soft, sprawling shadows. "One day," she murmured, "London too will come to that."

The maid brought us *ratafia*, a plate of almond biscuits. I sat in a low chair beside her couch. The open window let in the cool air of evening. A sound of bells.

She spoke of her early life: a youth spent caring for an invalid father, the years of wandering that followed, preaching temperance to miners in the wilds of Minnesota, jilted in Mexico. No, she never considered marriage after that. "I am a cat that likes to walk alone."

She revealed these details of her life with a candour astonishing in a woman of her class and generation. My mother would have been appalled. They were, I suppose, more or less of an age. And yet her face, alert, expressive, had none of my mother's look of middle-aged complacency. High cheek bones, and a delicately pointed nose, suggested a certain tartness, traces of which occasionally flavoured her conversation.

Again and again she returned to the subject of South Africa. The champion of victims of injustice, she had become, in her own eyes at least, the victim of injustice. Her eye-lids quivered scornfully as she remembered people and events: Broderick, the Secretary for War, "Oh, yes. A slippery fellow with a fine moustache." She'd spent a long hour with him. "I told him that once the truth was known the British people would never tolerate the suffering of women and children in those camps. How wrong I was."

She spoke of war in all its cruelty and destruction: of the plight of women and children, of crass male stupidity and muddle; of authorities with no more idea how to make provision for the helpless than the man in the moon. She did not mince her words. All the while she spoke, her pale, lavender eyes were fixed on me intently. "Society will ever remain composed of two bitter enemies, Mr Hazard. And the struggle between them is very serious. There are those who wish to suppress the truth, and those who insist upon truth being made known."

By the time her tale was done shadows were lengthening in the room. A thin yellow nimbus hung over the Alban hills. The massive walls of the Colosseum, dark, ruinous, loomed against the fading light.

For her the call of conscience was paramount, and her bitterness at her treatment was undiminished.

"I had repudiated my duties as an Englishwoman. So I was ostracised by society. People turned away when my name was mentioned. Even old friends deserted me. It has been so now for years, and has done much to sour my life." Exhausted by her own vehemence she sank back on the couch.

I still cherish the hour I spent with her, though I fear my visit put a strain on her powers. I sensed a kindred spirit, no more at home in those cluttered drawing-rooms than I was myself. Years of wandering had bred in her a character wholly different from her contemporaries. She had acted freely. I admired her for that. Though there was something there I shrank from. In that bare room of encroaching shadows she had the poignancy, as well as the fearfulness, of the perpetual exile. A figure persisting on a brink. *Sans* home. *Sans* country.

"I'm so glad you came to see me," she said, as I rose to take my leave. "As for – Harrogate, was it?"

Her lip quivered slightly: a facial tremor, or the ghost of a smile.

"I absolve you." A thin hand sketched a Roman blessing. "Go in peace."

Though it was war that lay in wait. And for her a notoriety more scandalous than the last, as she campaigned to stop the fighting. She was the turning we never took: a possibility as yet unrealised throughout our long and bloody history. Though it may yet represent our only hope. That last crusade earned her the contempt of Asquith. He called it *the twittering of sparrows*.

XVIII

Among the pictures in my mother's drawing room hung a print by Millais. *Christmas Story-telling.* Unremarkable as a picture, yet for me it evokes all the atmosphere of the smoke room at Wastdale Head: the famous Papa, with his brood gathered about him, absorbed in some tale of high adventure; a handsome boy, leaning with folded arms on the back of a high chair, has a look of Masterman; another, rapt, clasping his knees as he listens, could have been Clegg. And the tale is told again: of midnight summits, and peaks ablaze with lightning, and men's bodies so charged with electricity their hair stood up like bristles on a brush, and fire mountains erupting in black inky columns that blotted out the sun. For there were men in that small room who'd journeyed to the ends of the earth. And still Clegg sits: the spellbound boy. Chimborazo, Cotopaxi, they had stolen his soul away.

*

To the Wastdale regulars he first appeared as something of a joke: the awestruck 'shepherd boy' gazing up at them on the crags. Slater had complained to me of being 'gawped at' as he was about to attempt the tricky mantelshelf on the Needle.

"It's most disconcerting, I can tell you, to be made conscious of oneself as an *entertainment.* I didn't care for it much."

Then one day, at Kern Knotts, I saw him for myself. It was the summer before the South African war. A slightly built youth in shirtsleeves and waistcoat he stood, coat slung from his shoulders, a little way below the broken boulders at the foot of the crag.

Kern Knotts was a favourite resort for parties making the best of an off day. The principal attraction was a steep open fissure, eighty feet in length, in the blank wall of the buttress. Jones, needless to say, was the first to climb it. It was another *tour de force*, a test piece for skill and muscular endurance. None but an expert would attempt it without a rope held from above. Yet, thus protected, even a rank beginner might try his luck.

I was there that morning with a party from Oxford. A few weeks earlier, one of them had climbed the famous Mummery crack on the Aiguille de Grépon. He'd heard of this Cumbrian version, and was eager to sample it for himself. Since I'd done the climb several times it was up to me to provide a demonstration. I did so, though with no great style, after which I descended the chimney at the back of the buttress to watch as, one after another, the Oxford men embarked on their trial of strength. After each attempt the rope came winging down for the next man. The rest of the party, those who'd made the ascent as well as those still to be put to the test, gathered at the foot of the climb, there to pass judgement on the efforts of their friends.

All this while I'd noticed the youth edging closer. He was perhaps sixteen or seventeen. His freckled face wore a look of wonder, as if marvelling that mere mortals should be able to do such things. At length the last man struggled out at the top. The rope came winging down again.

"That's all," I shouted.

"Can Ah have a goä ?" enquired a Cumbrian voice: a flash of white teeth in the freckled face; sandy lashes blinking.

He hadn't the faintest notion how to fasten a 'bowline'. Arms uplifted, he stood submissively as someone tied the rope around his waist. One of the Oxford men looked him up and down.

"He's rather short."

Clegg grinned back at him. "They do say good stuff laps up in laäl bundles."

He failed that day in the Crack. Long arms were needed to haul one's body out of an awkward niche a third of the way up. After a brief, clumsy struggle Clegg fell, and came on the rope. He had to be lowered off. Such a humiliation might have crushed a boy of a different class. Clegg, however, was far from discouraged. He seemed to regard his *début* that day at Kern Knotts as a tacit *entrée* to our world. He took to turning up at the inn in the hope of attaching himself to some climbing party. Some were outraged at the boy's 'brass neck'. Others were amused by his enthusiasm, the eagerness to please. There was some inextinguishable quality in Clegg. Snubbed God knows how many times, he came bouncing back, good nature undiminished.

Unsophisticated, credulous to a degree, Clegg was sometimes the butt of cruel jokes. One day, noticing a mild eruption of vesicles on his face and arms, Slater and I persuaded him to take a dip in a pool in Mosedale Beck.

The freckled face regarded us uncertainly. The water in that pool was Arctic.

"Oh absolutely," said Slater, out of the straightest of faces. "Finest thing in the world for clearing out the pores. It's a cure for every ailment. Especially if followed by a brisk trot. You'll feel thoroughly restored."

Stripping off, Clegg dipped a toe in the beck. He was in and out of the icy water in a flash, pulling his clothes on over his streaming body as instructed, then set off briskly, trotting back along the path to the inn with Slater and I, doubled up with laughter, bringing up the rear.

Though afterwards, I thought of the sunburnt arms and the

V of his chest, like a brand on the white shivering body, and felt ashamed.

Some time later I ran into him again. Finding no one to climb with at the inn I'd gone up alone to Gable. Halfway up Gavel Neese I spotted a lone figure roaming among the rocks below the Napes. Since I had a rope we joined forces. That day we climbed the Arrowhead, and then the Needle Ridge.

After that, we often climbed together. We got on famously. A sort of youthful sympathy, I suppose. To me he seemed the very image of simple happiness. Joy unperplexed. He was a great observer, relishing things I should never have looked at twice. The delight he took in the comic or the captivating often redeemed a day otherwise disfigured by failure or foul weather, making it linger in the memory, if only for a single incident or encounter.

One summer evening we came back together from Scawfell Pike along the 'Corridor' under a sky such as one never saw in London. A Stygian darkness loomed over Gable and Kirk Fell. The air bore down, thick and heavy with the storm to come. We were legging it back for all we were worth when the heavens opened. Curtains of rain came sweeping up the dale. Within minutes we were fairly soaked. Shivering, we battled down towards Wastdale with the beck, now in spate, roaring at our side. The rain fell in rods. I trudged along in that state of misery and fatigue when all awareness shrivels to the consciousness of one's sole suffering self. Suddenly, Clegg froze: nodded, wordlessly. In the lee of a boulder a mouse or vole, reared up on its hind legs, was clutching a seed-head of grass. Oblivious of our presence, it nibbled at its prize. Its equanimity, in that storm of wind and rain, was such that we both burst out laughing.

To some he was always an outsider. But in most hearts he won a place. The 'laäl bundle', Widdop called him. Cheerful, willing, he was the kind of boy certain to appeal to Widdop. Though his treatment of the lad jarred with me at times.

One evening, as we stood chatting in the yard, Widdop challenged him to run up Yewbarrow.

"There and back in under an hour would be jolly good going. Wouldn't you say so, George?"

It struck me as good going indeed for one of the steepest fells in the district. But Clegg stripped off his coat, and raced away. We watched him go, then left him to it.

Some time later I crossed the bridge behind the inn and wandered a little way along the beck to look out for the boy. Soon he came into view high on the shoulder of the fell, a tiny dot, veering from side to side with that creeping motion distant figures have on a steep hillside. Clegg was giving it all he'd got.

Widdop was one of a critical group in the inn yard watching a demonstration of the Barndoor traverse, when the boy staggered back, gasping, lathered in sweat. I was embarrassed for him, for I knew they would all think it a foolish performance. Public acclaim was the very last thing he could expect. But Widdop clapped the lad on the shoulder, at the same time despatching me to the pump for a can of water. After which they all trooped back inside the inn. The great men resumed their solemn discussions over their pipes. No one paid any further attention to Clegg.

Later that autumn there came a change in Clegg's standing among even the most stand-offish of Wastdale men, the outcome of another visit to Kern Knotts. Jones' crack had an unclimbed companion, a hairline fracture running more or less parallel to its famous neighbour. Sometime during the autumn Clegg ascended it on a rope held from above, a feat which caused a stir, to say the least. Slater, who'd tried and failed to follow him that afternoon, was deeply impressed. "It's desperately strenuous. There's only a couple of places to take a rest. You're hanging on, literally, by the finger-tips. Believe me, that boy's a good deal stronger than he looks."

Meanwhile, as the war entered its third year, I began my stint as medical clerk in the out-patients' department. If I'd not realised it before, I was now left in no doubt that I'd entered a great and ancient hospital for the sick and suffering poor. At nine o'clock every morning the doors were thrown open, and in they came: the winter coughs, the digestive disorders, under-nourished women worn down by childbirth, pale consumptives mingling with sturdy labourers swathed in bandages, old and young, the strong and the feeble, wheezing, gasping for breath, shuffling on crutches, a teeming humanity seeking help. London was full of them. Yet as fellow citizens I'd scarcely taken note of them at all. Now I had to push past them every morning in the lobby. They lined the corridors, clutching their jars and bottles, the very image of helpless indigence.

Each day I attended one or other of the consulting rooms, assisting the houseman and picking up whatever I could. Twice a week I acted as clerk to Dr. Squire Sprague. My duties included keeping his 'book': entering the patient's name, age, sex, trade or occupation, and his medical history. Usually I would be given a case or two to look at. I would make my examination in a side room: temperature, pupils, pulse, blood pressure, respiration. I looked, felt, tapped, listened. Then I would note the facts on the hospital 'slip', and form a diagnosis, which I would subsequently read out to the physician, in the presence of the other clerks. There was always something I failed to notice, some significance I overlooked. Each omission became the occasion for Dr. Sprague to dwell on the first maxim of the physician: *Eyes first and most, hands next and least, tongue not at all.*

Sometimes I reflected sourly that Dr. Sprague seemed more interested in a faultless diagnosis than in healing the sick. Even when a case was hopeless, concern for the patient seemed of less importance than that I, his clerk, should be led to recognize the clinical facts. Dr. Sprague, face expressionless, would indicate a place on a patient's back or chest. I listened to the murmur, crepitation, whatever it was, wishing myself out of the room, at the same time profoundly thankful it was the physician, and not myself, who had to break the news. He did so with the gravity of a judge pronouncing sentence, always with the same formula: *I strongly advise you to put your affairs in order.* Then he would settle himself to listen to the incredulous protestations, with every show of sympathetic attention, waiting patiently for the moment when he might usher the doomed man or woman out of the room, sometimes alone, sometimes in the company of a bewildered friend or relative – he had, after all, other patients to attend to – with a deftness as fascinating as, to me, it was repugnant.

We were learning the rudiments of general practice. The pattern of our future lives. For I knew enough by then to recognize that most of my fellow students were doomed to work as assistants in general practice until they could afford to buy into a partnership. The sheer thought of it bore me down. I felt crushed, stifled. It struck me as little better than the life of a curate.

By this stage I'd come to recognise that my dreams of a surgical career were simply that: an extravagant fancy. Unlike Slater, I hadn't the talent. Too much of my life had been wasted in pipe-dreams. Somehow I had to get free of all that. It would be a struggle. Yet I must be something that I *ought* to be, something sanctioned. At the same time I felt ashamed at my failure to respond to what was after all a worthwhile and honourable calling. Determined to acquit myself, (if only in my own eyes) I redoubled my efforts, strove in all things to be a conscientious student. I made a careful record of every case seen during the day. Each evening I wrote up my notes with elaborate thoroughness, checking my observations with the relevant passages in Osler's *Medicine*. Nothing I did could shift the conviction of my own unfittedness. This was not what I wanted for myself.

Now, in my more despairing moments, some lines we used to sing in chapel returned to mock me. The same couplet, endlessly reiterated, about *the trivial round, the common task* furnishing *all we ought to ask*. To me it seemed to announce the shutting down of life. One day, turning the pages of an old copy of *Blackwood's*, I chanced upon a passage which echoed everything I'd come to feel felt about the deadening tedium of my daily life.

Humanity is beginning to sicken at the round of ordinary humdrum existence and is eagerly seeking for new forms of excitement ...

What was a life-time of worthy drudgery beside the life of the questing spirit? Here was a voice calling me to a richer, wider world. I began to dream of a life adrift like Nansen in the ice, by distant mountains and strange seas.

*

Holidays were now hard to come by. Whenever I could I

snatched a day or two away, taking the night train from Euston, tumbling stiff and bleary-eyed out of the carriage at dawn.

Rain or shine, that walk to Wastdale in the early morning was always a joy: the sense of space and light, the sweep of fell that carried the eye upward, the companionable sound, never far away, of running water.

Sometimes Clegg was there. More often not. Yet when he was, any uneasiness I felt at my truancy was soon banished. Perhaps I saw in him a mirror image of myself, yet free of the cares that burdened me, at home in his world as I never was in mine. I felt less at war with myself when I was in his company. Even to watch him move was a restful pleasure to the mind. Clegg strode the fells with a gait that put me in mind of stalkers in the Black Mount: that same roll of the thigh, foot placed flat on the ground, easy, unhurried, the same at a day's end as at its beginning.

Several times that winter Lockhart turned up in Wastdale. Like me, arriving unannounced, he'd spend a day or two in the hills before returning to the Cavendish. "One has to clear out now and then, don't you think ? Look at things from another angle ?" The gaze quizzical as ever.

Each morning, after breakfast, he went off on his own. I made no attempt to join him. I'd formed the impression he was seeking a few day's peace and quiet to mull over his work, and had no wish to break in on his solitude. Besides, Lockhart often tackled quite hard climbs alone.

"Aren't you ever frightened ?" I asked him. "Climbing solo? I'm sure it would frighten me."

Lockhart scratched his nose with the stem of his pipe. "Oh, one learns to shut the door, you know. Besides, I fancy there's some protective mechanism in the cerebral cortex that stops a man coming too close to his actual limit. The mind wanders, the legs start to shake."

His wry smile, as he broke off, left me uncertain how to take him. "Besides," he added, "the exploration of reality must of necessity be a participatory experience, don't you think ?"

Again, he left me in the dark. Yet the whole business of climbing seemed suddenly shifted to a more profound and puzzling level.

*

After Christmas I took up my duties in the accident room. Here, in contrast to the familiar complaints routinely presented in out-patients, the variety was constant, the need immediate: hands mangled by machinery, labourers dug out from collapsing trenches, botched suicides, wives knocked about by husbands, children run down in the street. Now, three days a week, I lived in the hospital, on duty day and night, with rarely more than an hour or two of sleep. "If you're in any doubt, old chap," said the house surgeon, a gingery fellow not much older than myself, "just press the bell." He grinned amiably, and left me to it. I knew he wouldn't expect to be called to anything less than an emergency. Saturday nights were the worst. Not infrequently the police brought in a prisoner in need of medical attention. I found it difficult to tell whether a man was drunk or dying, and went in dread of discharging a patient back into police custody only to have him die in the cells.

By this stage my misgivings over my career were far advanced. Yet I was uneasy at the prospect of another showdown with Father. I'd seen little of him since Christmas. Then, I'd noticed the change in him. The war was dragging him down.

"We seem no nearer an end at the close of the year," he muttered gloomily, "than we did at its beginning."

In the Cape martial law had been declared. The newspapers told of men and women being dragged out to witness the execution of their friends, as Kitchener stepped up his campaign to crush the Boers. Father remained as staunch as ever in support of the government.

"We're fighting a guerilla war, George. One can't expect the usual observances to obtain." Since he wouldn't permit himself to call the military authorities into question, he railed against the Boers. "They must know they're done for. By all accounts they've scarcely clothes to their backs. There's nothing left for them to live off. Surely they can't go on much longer?"

There was a greyness about him I hadn't seen before, the eyes sunk more deeply in their sockets. He seemed worn. Weary. I'd always thought of him as so indefatigable. It unsettled me to see him so. But he only thrust aside my tentative enquiries.

"Had I realised," he burst out irritably, "that having a doctor in the family would mean having to submit to unsought-for medical advice ... ' He stormed off, banging the door behind him.

That Christmas too I learnt that Agnes had left home. It was Dora who broke the news to me. I arrived home on the afternoon of the first of the Christmas dinner parties to find her sitting at my mother's bureau. She was copying names from the guest list on to blank visiting cards. Menus and place cards were always Dora's task. She took great pride in her neat lettering.

"We were having tea one afternoon," she said levelly, "when Agnes announced she would be leaving home to live in Canning Town. I believe it's somewhere down among the docks."

Her pen scratched at a card. "It seems she wishes to devote her life to working among the poor." At which point she must have made some slip in her copying. Methodically she tore the card in two, selected another.

"And to think," she resumed quietly, "that Father used to find Agnes' eccentricities so amusing."

I saw that Dora's dull rectitude had kindled a small, mean flame of satisfaction.

Was I also jealous of Agnes ? Was there something in one sibling that resents another ? Would, if it could, tip it out of the nest ? Horrified at the thought of detecting in myself the ugly satisfaction I was conscious of in Dora, I was forced to recognize that Agnes's departure had fulfilled some long-cherished anticipation on my part. For I'd always half-hoped the day might come when she would declare herself, at whatever cost, and so breach the barrier that enclosed us.

No one spoke of her over Christmas. It was as if she'd ceased to exist. All I could gather, from a private questioning of my mother, was that Agnes had behaved unforgivably to Father. Bitter words had passed between them. She had packed her bags and gone.

This rooting out of my twin sister from all mention was not something I was prepared to accept.

One morning, when we were all at breakfast, I brought up her name. Father was opening his morning mail, as usual discarding what was of no interest on to the floor.

"Is there any news of Agnes ?" I enquired, as casually as I could manage. In the silence that followed, the scraping of spoons evoked a note of furtive complicity.

"She's cut off all her hair," Dolly almost blurted. She sounded quite aghast.

Father took up a knife, and began dissecting his kipper. "It would seem that Agnes aspires to look like a boy," he said, in a voice of weary patience. "I dare say, since we men can do no good, young women must become men themselves."

The irony struck me as unusually ponderous for him, though

the show of indifference was utterly predictable. It came as no less of a shock. Uneasily, I wondered how it would be when the time came for my own defection.

*

That winter, as I've said, the inn at Wastdale was usually deserted but for Lockhart and myself. One evening, there being no other residents, dinner was served to us in the smoke room. Afterwards, when the dishes were cleared away, we drew our chairs to the fire. For a while we sat in a companionable silence. I'd grown used to these silences of his. Thrown together as we were, I'd begun to understand that what I'd once thought of as intellectual aloofness was, in part at least, a painful shyness, not unlike my own. We fell to talking, mostly about mountains and mountaineering. Eventually we got on to the subject of solitary climbing. It was all part of his determination to develop in himself 'a single mind', as he put it: the capacity to concentrate without distraction, to drive out fear of what might lie ahead by focusing attention wholly on the immediate difficulties. I thought of the day on Scawfell Crag: the upright figure, and that questing gaze, a thing that spoke to me more eloquently than any words of some essential element in his nature, something remote, uncompromising.

Climbing well, he said, was like doing good science. Only with mind and body working in harmony. The comparison evidently took his fancy for, putting a match to his pipe, he began teasing out his own analogy.

"The best hypothesis excludes the most possibilities. It's the same with mountaineering. The better the climb, usually the less ways there are of doing it. With a truly great climb there will be only one way. For toes, fingers, at any given moment there will be just that point of contact, that distribution of weight. Precisely that. Then one enters one of the orders of bliss."

He fell silent. Head thrown back, puffing reflectively at his pipe, he seemed to have entered his own interior space.

My mind went back to the evening following his ascent of *Walker's Gully*: Lockhart, sitting quietly in much the self-same attitude. Now and then in the firegleam I'd caught a glimpse of his face. He was savouring those first few hours, unlike any others, when the climb is still as vivid as a dream, and to have come down successful is to be alive absolutely, to be secure in one's own life. That rapt focus evoked everything I felt lacking in myself. So far I'd spoken to no one of my own anxieties. Encouraged perhaps by the intimacy of our surroundings, the stillness of the house, the hills beyond, the dark night over all, I began to tell of the discontent that was gnawing at my life. I poured out my heart that night as I had never done before: my bewilderment as enthusiasm faded, my fear of letting down my family, the whole daunting, desperately difficult business of adult life.

Lockhart's face was hidden in shadow. I couldn't see where his gaze was fixed, yet his whole attitude signalled a profound attention to what I had to say. I had the feeling no one had ever paid me such close attention. I believed I was heard, and understood.

"Well, of course, I can't advise you," he said hesitantly, when I'd finished. He bent forward to knock out his pipe against the bars of the grate. As he did so I saw that his face, coming into the firelight, wore an expression of the utmost gravity. "But I do think one has to persevere. Fidelity to the task, you know. We all have our periods of discouragement."

From his rueful smile I gathered his own work was not going well.

XIX

In the dining-room at Wastdale Head there hangs to this day an old plate photograph of the *Eagle's Nest arête*. It shows a blade of rock outlined against the sky: superimposed upon a misty vacancy, the dark figure of a man. Poised on a spiral stair of tiny sloping holds, he clings as if to the very edge of things. Only the action of the camera shutter seems to hold him in position. A ribbon of beck gleams faintly far below. So awed was Solly, the first man to climb it, by his own temerity, he felt as if he'd committed some act of *hubris*. No inducement, he said, would tempt him to go up again without a rope. Talking it over later, Solly's party let it be known they felt unable to assume responsibility for presenting it as a route to be followed. Even Jones, who made the second ascent the year before his death, agreed that the *arête* was not to be recommended. It was one of a small number of climbs, the contemplation of which awoke in most of us a kind of holy dread. At the same time, there were a handful of men who, if only in imagination, were projecting themselves upon it. Men like Lockhart.

*

One Easter I met him in the lane. After a fine day of mountain wandering I'd come down at last to the dale. Waiting for me at the inn was a message from Clegg reminding me that I was expected for tea the following day.

"He's up at Burnthwaite," Ritson told me.

Clegg and his uncle were cutting up a tree brought down by the March gales. 'Giving a day' to one another was standard practice among the dalesmen. Though in Clegg's case I suspected it was often the pretext for surreptitious visits to the crags. I strolled up the lane to confirm the arrangements. On my way back to the inn I fell in with Lockhart. I asked what he'd been up to.

Casually, he mentioned the *arête*. "I thought I'd take a look at it," he said. He'd climbed up to the parallel cracks which gave access (via a notorious and committing swing) to the tip of the nose that formed the base of the *arête* proper. Then, soloing up the easy *West Chimney* to where it joined the top of the *arête*, he'd climbed down a few feet of the upper section.

"It's certainly very exposed," he said. "The holds slope badly. But the upper part doesn't seem so very difficult. Under ideal conditions I should love to lead it."

I'd often studied the photograph in the dining room, though I thought I'd die of fright if ever I found myself in such a place. I stammered something of the sort. Lockhart shrugged it off with a smile.

We turned into the yard to see one or two familiar figures disembarking from the hotel trap, the first of the guests expected that weekend. Others would be arriving later, walking over Sty Head.

"By the way," murmured Lockhart, as we waved a greeting, "I'd rather you didn't mention it to anyone."

He'd been spotted, none-the-less. The sighting gave rise to an animated discussion that evening in the smoke room. A growing number of the older men had begun to believe that perhaps our achievements were approaching the limits of the justifiable. Indeed, it was becoming commonplace to speak of 'the exhaustion' of the district. *Ah, Pillar, Gable*, some elder would sigh, shaking his head. *I fear the grand old crags are all played out.* There was even an agreeable kind of *Schadenfreude* in their recalling of old times. They, who had known the district in its heyday, affected a kind of sympathy for latecomers like ourselves, who could never know the joys of that early world, fresh from the Creator's hand and waiting to be explored. Among the younger men, however, a quite different attitude was springing up. Not unnaturally, they saw no reason why they should be cut off from achievement, their youthful powers and potentialities confined to what was safe and familiar. No one wanted to be told what not to climb. Besides, whatever the warnings issued by the older generation, their deeds spoke for themselves. Nevertheless, that night in the smoke room a sober voice was calling for caution.

It was a small room, able to seat no more than half a dozen. As usual the overflow sprawled on the floor, bodies propped against the wall or lying across one another's shins. I'd bagged a chair close to the fire. Clegg squatted at my feet. Lockhart sat as usual at the back of the room. Pipes were lit. The coffee went its rounds.

"I grant you difficulty and danger are not necessarily the same," said Oppenheimer. "Some exceptionally stiff passages can be protected. Others cannot. That's when difficulty turns to danger. The moment a leader, in such a situation, feels he's close to the limits of his powers, then it's time to turn back."

Several of the leading younger men were there that night: Fred Botterill, the Bartons, young Harris the Penrith schoolmaster – an ambitious fellow, he longed to be ranked with the founding fathers.

"I don't agree." Harris was vehement, but respectful. A much loved figure at Wastdale, Oppenheimer was one of the most intrepid climbers of the day.

"Mountaineering is deadly dangerous. If it weren't so we wouldn't do it. That being the case, I think one should abandon all ideas of safety first. Set up a different ideal. One may be killed. But what of it? The whole of life is a challenge. What is it the poet says? '*All may have, if they dare choose, a glorious life or grave*'."

"Harris would live gloriously, or not at all," someone murmured.

"He's been listening to Widdop," said Claude Barton dryly, to general laughter.

"No!" Oppenheimer's voice was quiet but firm. "Either one finds a safe belay, or one abandons the climb."

There was a moment's hasty scuffling among the bodies on the floor, where a cramped leg had sent a coffee cup flying.

"There is an alternative solution," put in a voice from the shadows.

A sudden silence settled on the room. Everyone was listening. Clegg, propped against my shins beside the fire, craned round to fix his eyes on the speaker. He worshipped Lockhart.

"Oppenheimer identifies risk with consequences. That's too simple. Danger is relative to skill. The more the skill, the less the danger. Therefore acquire more skill."

"And how do you do that ?" someone enquired.

"By tackling more and more difficult climbs."

"That sounds like a circular argument to me," put in another voice.

"Not circular," observed Lockhart mildly. "A methodical progression."

No one ventured a response. The fire crackled. I sipped my coffee.

"A pity, don't you think, to go out at the end without ever knowing what one's made of?"

The quizzical note in Lockhart's voice suggested he was smiling.

Early next day I called at Burnthwaite for Clegg. After a morning climbing the Napes together, we picked up my rucksack at the inn, and set off.

He'd been pressing his invitation for some time. Rather against my will, I'd agreed at last to go. I knew I'd have to eventually. I couldn't put it off indefinitely, without offending Clegg, something I'd no wish to do.

His home was in Miterdale. I'd never been there. Indeed, I don't suppose it occurred to me to wonder where he came from, or what he did. Clegg lived in another world. Whenever he came to climb he stepped across from that world into ours. At least, I thought of it as ours: the deep romantic dale, with its dark lake scooped from the rock in one tremendous lunge, the screes, the looming hills and crags. Though any stranger, coming from Sty Head or over Burnmoor, might have picked out, in the stone walls and tiny fields, in the tracks leading from one dale to another, the patterns of an already ancient community. Clegg's family had lived in the district for hundreds of years. This, and other things, he told me as we followed the bridle path through the trees and little fields above the lake, climbing towards the old corpse road crossing the moor.

"You've only to look in t' churchyards. They're full o' Cleggs and Wilsons." He stood aside for me to pass through a stile. "Ah reckon we swam ashore wi' t' sheep," he added with a laugh.

He went on to tell me some old folk-tale about the forty little sheep, wrecked with the Armada, that had come ashore at Drigg, wandered up to Wastdale, where they'd thrived and so increased that they spread throughout the neighbourhood. Though looking at Clegg's blue flinty eyes, the sandy lashes, it was Viking and not Spanish blood that came to mind.

It was a bright, gusty day. The wind bustled at our backs, driving the showers ahead of us to fall over the higher ground in a succession of glittering cascades that ceased almost as soon as they started, leaving behind a glimmering rainbow in the sky. After half an hour of uphill plodding we turned aside from the path to follow a barely discernible path, little more than a trod in the coarse wet grass. We crossed a mile of flat boggy moor before dropping suddenly into a craggy amphitheatre, where a little beck fell from the rocks, cascading down to a green glade. Beyond the glade a narrow dale opened out between bleak bare fells. "You're on our land now," Clegg announced.

We went on, level with the top of fellside, where a few polled black cattle were scattered among the Herdwicks grazing here and there on the moor.

"Are those yours ?" I asked, with a show of interest.

"Aye, though they mostly have to fend for themselves."

"They're like the Cleggs," he added, with a grin. "They do well on very little."

The path led on, winding along the top of the fellside, slanting down at last to a green strath, with a white-washed farmhouse just visible between the trees, and a few tiny stone-walled fields beside the river. We crossed a paddock, where half a dozen tups were grazing, then another, even smaller, with two ponies cropping the turf in the shadow of the house.

Dalehead was one of those long, low-roofed Lakeland farmhouses, walls a yard thick. An ash wood stood above the house. The river rippled past below. It was as remote and peaceful a spot as ever I'd dreamed of. Clegg opened a gate to a walled yard in the angle of the barn. A couple of fierce-eyed dogs who'd been kicking up a din fell silent at a word. Coming out of a dairy or outhouse was a girl of twelve or thirteen in a dirty apron. She was carrying a large jug. Her fair, rosy face darted a shy look at me before slipping away around a corner. Meanwhile, Clegg was urging me to inspect the barn wall where, in imitation of its famous counterpart over in Wastdale, he had worked out a traverse of his own. It seemed churlish to refuse to 'have a goä'. Though the tiny holds required fingers stronger than mine. Clegg was unashamedly delighted when I fell off.

Later, up in a tiny bed-room among the rafters, he showed me his few bits and pieces. In one corner lay a pair of heavy dumb-bells. He used them every day, he assured me in all seriousness. I smiled and said nothing, though it struck me as odd he should feel the need to exercise, considering the work he did. Clegg was certainly strong. At arm wrestling he beat me every time. Then I remembered something someone had told me about OGJ training for three months with heavy dumb-bells prior to his attack on *Walker's Gully*, and wondered if Clegg had picked up the same tale. Above the bed I was surprised to see a shelf of books. A small store of Alpine classics (I couldn't help wondering if he'd actually read them) given him from time to time, Clegg said, by guests at the inn: Wells, Whymper, Leslie Stephen, rubbing shoulders with, of all things, a battered copy of Mason's novel, *A Romance of Wastdale*. Had someone given him that too? Had he picked it up second-hand one market day?

We had our meal in a little whitewashed parlour. To my surprise just three of us sat down: Clegg, myself and Clegg senior, a spare wiry figure, sandy like his son. Mother, smiling, ample, and the fair-faced daughter bustled between the menfolk and a brood of younger brothers and sisters in the kitchen, whose little faces appeared from time to time, staring solemnly at me from the doorway. Tea was a truly sumptuous affair, with scones, home-made breads, some malted, some with currants, and toasted cakes served with rum butter. I reflected that the Cleggs, with their dairy and their ponies, their geese and ducks, were people of some substance.

Impassive, supping his tea, jaws munching, Clegg senior ploughed steadily through the meal. No stranger to paternal atmospheres, I sensed the silent disapproval, stifled by my presence. Clegg meanwhile was prattling on about the Alps, which of course he'd never visited. The King of the Belgiums, he let fall, was a famous Alpinist. Dr. Hazard (he insisted on calling me 'Doctor') also climbed in the Alps.

"Not at the moment," I said ruefully. "I wish I did. I don't have the time." I was embarrassed by this turn in the conversation which I'd soon seen for what it was. Indeed, it annoyed me rather. I felt I was being used.

Above the mantelpiece hung a sepia photograph. The grandfather. Wiry in shirt-sleeves and waistcoat, with long side-whiskers, he stood clutching a climbing pole six or seven feet long. Clegg had explained that in years gone by he'd taken tourists to the top of Scawfell Pike.

"Did he ever climb the crags ?" I asked the father, thinking to draw him out a little.

Clegg senior shook his head. "He'd mair to think on," he said scornfully.

Thoughtfully, I sipped my tea. It had never occurred to me that Clegg might have been as much at odds with his own father as I was with mine.

XX

Twice a week I attended the celebrated Bartlett's lectures on forensic medicine. Familiar to us as the author of Bartlett's *Medical Jurisprudence*, his name was well-known to readers of the sensational papers. He figured in many grisly tales of midnight exhumations, of organs removed by lantern-light in mortuary chapels, and of subsequent appearances at the Old Bailey, upon which he would descend like some *deus ex machina*.

He was a big man with great bushy eyebrows, thick wrists that cut through bone in a trice, and an arrogant manner born of supreme confidence in his own abilities. If, for my old tutor at Caius, everything came down to atoms and molecules, then for Bartlett life and death were mysteries which, at the last, resolved themselves into pathological anatomy.

"This is the only time, gentlemen" – gesturing for the corpse to be uncovered – "when you see the entire medical or clinical condition of the patient laid before you. Not in the ward. Not in the theatre. Here, on the slab."

As if only the dead were to be trusted. Unlike the living, whose prognoses were never certain, they did what was expected.

Bartlett shared the scorn for general practice which was common in the hospital, and his poor opinion did nothing to revive my flagging spirits. He was withering about the vast numbers of deaths, the true causes of which, he claimed, utterly escaped the family doctor.

"In the GP's book there are only two causes of death among the old. If they fade away over several days, it's bronchopneumonia. If they go out like the electric light then it's myocardial infarction." The shrubby eyebrows bristled at us scornfully. "Believe me, gentlemen, a myocardial infarction covers a multitude of sins."

It was a claim given some weight by the daily visitations of surgeons and physicians descending the stone steps to the post mortem room to discover just what it was that had killed their patient.

I hated post mortems. I hated the cheerful brutality with which the demonstrators went about their business. There was about their acts of casual butchery a reductive quality that revolted me. Their very jauntiness somehow conveyed a horrible knowingness. They carried out their duties, these rag and bone men of the human body, like fellows who were not deceived. They peeled away a man like an onion. And the conclusive manner in which they chalked up their findings on a slate conveyed an air of indubitable finality. A kind of Q.E.D. As if the whole human enterprise had been exposed for what it was. A sham. A swindle.

Sometimes the body might be that of a patient I'd attended. There was one in particular, a famous street 'character' from whom I used to buy the *Evening Standard* on the corner of Ludgate Hill. Admitted, treated and discharged, he'd collapsed in the street the following day. They brought him in on a handcart. He'd died within the hour. As we went to work I found the man still obstinately alive in my imagination: his chirpy banter, mocking the headlines of the day; his hoarse news-vendor's cry rising above the clatter of carts coming down Ludgate Hill, even as we were taking him to bits, searching for signs of the haemorrhage, the ruptured aneurism or perforated ulcer: a thing infinitely more significant than the human being. More potent too, since it had killed him.

One day the clatter of boots descending the stone steps was unusually heavy. MacSelf had brought his 'firm' with him. He nodded to me in his friendly way. They had come to inspect a coarctate aorta. In life they'd noted the hypertension in the upper body, the absence of pulsation in the legs. Now, *post mortem*, they would see for themselves the actual lesion. Holding the dead man's heart in his hands, a finger under the aortic arch deftly demonstrating the obstruction, MacSelf fell to musing on the surgical procedure whereby, given the possibility of establishing some collateral circulation, the stenosed portion might be re-sectioned, followed by anastomosis of the two ends of the vessel. Then he shrugged. "Purely conjectural, of course." And smiled, as a man might, admitting something quite beyond his skill.

Yet I knew he dreamt of expanding the surgical conquest to hitherto unexplored parts of the body. Meanwhile, he had his task and he kept faith with it, probing the lumps and lesions presented on his rounds, the causes of which were usually to be found in some localised dysfunction; some obscure con-striction, the failure of a valve, a concretion here, a perforation there. Things which to me had come to seem banal. Mere mechanics.

Even if I'd been good enough, I knew now that surgery could never satisfy me. I hadn't that kind of mind. I wanted passion, reverence before the mystery of life. Not this curious, patient toil. No doubt I took a hopelessly romantic view of myself. Yet I longed for some single self-proclaiming act – to climb a great mountain; to cross a desert – through which I might confront my destiny. Meanwhile, Father's enthusiasm for my career seemed to be growing. After all, medicine could be a lucrative business. Honours, too, lay in store for the successful. He had, I knew, begun to cherish dreams of consulting rooms in Brook

Street, a glittering practice.

The greater his enthusiasm the more irked I became. If I'd chosen a character for myself, my father had simply circumvented it. Had wrapped it in a frock coat, strung a gold watch across its chest, and set it up in Mayfair.

"Barrister or surgeon," he said to my mother, "what does it matter, so long as he's the best."

Success in life was very much his notion of a man's chief aim and duty. And, by most people's standards, my father enjoyed a successful life. Yet I knew his was a disappointed career. I've no doubt I contributed in large measure to his disappointment. For I had no particular desire to succeed at anything. But for life itself, all its magical enticements, its wonders and sensations, my appetite was unbounded.

*

My daily journey took me by Paul's Churchyard. A familiar sight, often encountered in the close, and for me increasingly an object of peculiar horror and fascination, was a giant beggar. A strange figure in black topcoat and hat, massive head and shoulders forlornly elevated above the hundreds hurrying hither and thither, he spent his days trudging back and forth between Piccadilly and Cheapside, stopping every now and then to utter his suppliant's cry for alms. Unmistakeable, amid the hubbub, the tramp of feet, the rattle of cabs and carts, that shrill monotonous sing-song: *Poor blin. Pit' the poor blin'*.

Now, as my anxieties about my future grew, he seemed an admonishment sent by Providence. Here, in all its horror, was life as a fixed fact: the *tap, tap,* of an iron-tipped stick, the placard strung round the neck, hand outstretched for the coin pressed in the palm: *Poor blin', pit' the poor blin'*.

Lockhart had talked of fidelity to the task. My heart told me he was right. But what if the task proved to be one for which I was utterly unsuited ? Besides, I saw all too plainly what lay in wait – a lifetime of drudgery in a two-dimensional world, where men dragged out the length and breadth of their days, but never looked up. Never raised their heads to the heights. The more I contemplated the crabbed ugly world of work, the keener my hunger grew for something more. There had to be a different life from that. There must be something more.

I knew I had to speak to Father. And yet disclosure seemed unthinkable. In my frustration I veered between guilt, at the thought of his reproaches, and resentment at his failure – refusal I called it – to perceive my own misgivings and anxieties. And yet I found it difficult to think ill of him for long. The uneasiness of our relations had less to do with him (he was constant enough in all things) than with my own fluctuating emotions. In many ways he'd been a good and generous father. He made me a very decent allowance, in return for which he expected me to work hard and to meet my expenses. Even my mountaineering, I reminded myself, could not have been possible without his generosity. Agnes had achieved her liberation after a long subjection, culminating in more or less open civil war.

"If it comes to it," she told me fiercely, "I shall break with him."

She'd done exactly that. She had leapt into the flood, and let it carry her away. I shrank from that. Too frightened to let go, I was hanging on to what, I knew, would drag me under.

Christmas without her had been miserable. On Christmas morning Father, registering one of his bi-annual visits to St Stephen's, led the family to Divine service. The streets were filled with people: whether whole families on the move, or young men and women hastening by themselves, all carrying brown paper parcels. There were olive branches in profusion. But no visitor came to our door. The firelight flickered and danced on the walls as of old, catching the evergreens twined in the gasaliers and the bunches of holly over the mantelpiece, where Millais' *Christmas Story-telling* – the rapt boys, the decorous, attentive daughters, Papa caught in that dramatic gesture – seemed to mock our celebration. It had, in any case, long been a masquerade: one in which all the players had donned the obligatory disguise. Agnes had thrown off hers, and the consequence had been devastating: my mother and Dolly almost in tears, Dora a study in malignant rectitude, Father, grey and worn, carving the goose.

*

Not long after Christmas I'd written to Agnes suggesting we meet for tea. I had in mind Slater's in Piccadilly, or perhaps one of the cosy tea-rooms around Bond Street. Her reply came by return of post. It was brief, and to the point. A Lyons' tea-house would be quite grand enough. The one in Cheapside would do very well. She would meet me there at four o'clock.

The tea-house was busy. I went upstairs into a spacious gallery with a lofty ceiling and rather fussy flowered wall-paper. I chose a table facing the stairs. As yet I had no clear idea what had actually precipitated Agnes' break with Father. Though the root cause was clear enough. For men and women of our class there was never any doubt with regard to what to do, or how to judge. Honesty, courage, tenacity – qualities admirable in a son – were, in a daughter, wholly unbecoming. In women the key virtue was fidelity.

In Father's eyes Agnes had violated that fidelity. I still hoped, somehow or other, to bring about a reconciliation. But then, as I saw her coming up the stairs, I felt suddenly at a loss. As if it wasn't Agnes but a stranger coming down the gallery towards me, an unknown woman in a soft-brimmed velvet hat trimmed with blue ribbon, and a long brown coat.

"Dolly tells me you've become a missionary," I said as I rose to greet her. Instantly, I regretted it. For I suddenly saw with a shock that Agnes was as unsure as I was; that she didn't know where she stood with me.

There was little to be seen, under the low brim of her hat, of the shorn head which had sent such shock waves through the family. Agnes, my mother always said, was the only one of her girls who had 'come true' to the Parrinder colouring. That auburn hair was her pride and joy. As if to satisfy my curiosity, or else in defiance of the conventionally coiffeured woman taking tea all around us, Agnes took off her hat, stretching her neck and tossing her head in an odd little motion, not unlike a pony. Her hair settled round her head like a russet helmet, level with the lobes of her ears. The effect was startling, to say the least. Stripped of the soft full mass of wavy hair that gave women of our class their female grace and dignity, her face seemed unusually exposed and vulnerable. Yet, for all that, Agnes looked nothing like a boy.

Abashed at my clumsy greeting, I tried to make amends by complimenting her on her appearance, a pleasantry Agnes flipped aside with a dismissive shrug. "I wear my hair like other women at the Settlement. They haven't time to bother with such things, and neither have I."

We sat in an awkward silence as a neat young waitress arrived to take our order. At length I asked about Canning Town, and the Social Settlement.

"We're the coming thing, George,' she said briskly. "We're

springing up all over London. Bethnal Green, Toynbee Hall in Whitechapel, Bermondsey, Walworth, Camberwell – wherever we're most needed."

She paused, as the waitress set down the tray with our tea things. "And we're not missionaries," she added reprovingly, "or 'superior persons'. Simply neighbours, fellow citizens, trying to live simple, helpful lives."

However coolly she'd set out to conduct herself during our meeting, there was no restraining her enthusiasm for this new life of hers. "There's so much to be done, George. So many things that need improving – street lighting, the water supply ... And what about poor people having access to a lawyer ?"

Over tea she gave an account of her activities. They struck me as ideally suited to Agnes' sympathies and disposition as they were alien to mine: lodging complaints, organising public meetings, giving lectures on the French Revolution. "Oh, and we run a club for factory girls."

She fished out some Brownie snaps for me to see. Young women, clad in belts and sombre uniform, drilling with clubs.

"We had a Christmas party, with toys for the children. That was very jolly. We even have a regular hospital and dispensary. When you're qualified, you must come and work with us."

I smiled uneasily.

Meanwhile, she had embarked on a spirited account of her battle, on behalf of an old woman, with a slum landlord who wanted to evict her.

"E's tyken all me doors orf o' their 'inges," she wailed in a passable East End whine. "I gave him a piece of my mind. I told him my Father was a QC and a Bencher of Lincoln's Inn, and that I should go to the High Court directly unless the doors were restored."

Our eyes met as we laughed together, and I knew we were

brother and sister still. Then, as our laughter faded, she glanced
down at her cup. "How is he ?"

"Much as you'd expect."

She toyed with her spoon. "It isn't true that I assisted the
enemies of my country. I waged war against them. Against
those who have brought us to the pass we find ourselves in today."

Her voice, low and earnest, was as passionate as ever.
Silently I reflected that if she'd said as much to Father I wasn't
surprised he took it badly.

"He feels you brought the war within your own home."

"And what of the homes of South African women and
children ?"

I gazed at my cup.

"Oh, he was extremely civil," she went on bitterly. "Since
he was providing me with food and shelter, he'd be obliged if I'd
be so good as to refrain from expressing my political opinions
while under his roof."

She put down her cup. "Well, I thought, to hell with all
that." Agnes tilted her head defiantly, at the same time drawing
down those Gothic lids in the familiar way. "I shall make a life
for myself."

The bleak finality in her voice shook me rather. Her face
looked pinched, lips pressed together as if screwed down tight
against some pain. I saw that her eyes were filled with tears.

I began casting about for something to say. Meanwhile,
Agnes was putting on her hat. She had, she said, to attend a
lecture at the Birkbeck College. She took my arm as we went
down the stairs. In the street I summoned a cab. Agnes protested.
"The 'bus will do just as well." But I insisted.

"Don't cut yourself off completely," I said, as I helped her
into the hansom. The thought that any of us should write one
another off was more than I could bear.

With sudden warmth she hugged me to her. "Dear George," she said.

*

Meanwhile I still had my post mortems to perform. I slit, sawed, trepanned, eviscerated, weighed liver and lights – by now as serviceable a butcher as any – and always hankering after mountains – to be breathing mountain air, and not the odour of cadavers. Visits home turned into an ordeal, as I became convinced that it lingered, faint, sweetish, on my hands and clothing wherever I went. Even into my mother's drawing room.

I longed to open my heart to her, to enlist her support. She'd never approved of my studying medicine. But it seemed dishonourable to go to her, and not to Father. Besides, my mother had worries enough, without my adding to them. For all that, she was quite firm in her judgement. Agnes had brought matters on herself. "She was always such a difficult child," she sighed.

I saw that we were facing different ways: that the child my mother anguished over, and the young woman with whom I was slowly coming to terms, were separate people.

Agnes and I met from time to time Either in my rooms, or over tea at a Lyons' or an ABC. Somewhat shamefacedly she confessed that she hadn't seen mother for six months. It was a delicate situation. I could quite see that. For my mother to leave the house for a clandestine meeting with her daughter might seem too much like a disloyal act. On the other hand I saw no reason why Agnes shouldn't visit Onslow Place while Father was in court or at his chambers. But Agnes didn't think it fair to do so. It would place my mother in an impossible position.

"Besides," she went on hotly, "why should I be forced to feel furtive and surreptitious ?"

She failed to add what passed though my own mind: that Dora would almost certainly have felt it her duty to tell Father.

I'd tried, without success, to bring about a reconciliation. One evening, as we sat together after dinner, I revealed that I'd seen Agnes, that we met from time to time, and that while she was happy in her new life it was still a matter of great pain for her – indeed, for me as well – to be separated from her family. Surely the ties of kinship, bonds that joined us together, were stronger, more deserving of sympathy and acknowledgement, than whatever it was that divided us ? (That she was so very much her father's daughter was a blunt truth I felt it best to keep to myself.) Father, sipping gravely at his port, heard me out in silence. When the time came for him to dismiss my appeal he chose his words with judicial deliberation.

"Agnes has consistently placed herself among those who have sided with the Boers, who have found no fault with any of their actions, who have never once protested against any of their atrocities, whilst taking every opportunity to bring charges against their own country men. That being the case I feel I cannot welcome her under my roof."

Calmly he refilled his glass, pushed the decanter in my direction. That done, he settled back in his chair, puffing out a cloud of smoke from his Havana. The sunken eyes, set at a distance, seemed to proclaim the operation of disinterested justice. Only the current of anger – deep, cold, something I'd never seen in him before – betrayed his pain.

XXI

On the last day of May the Boers finally surrendered. It was Sunday morning when the news began to spread. One by one the church bells began to ring. It soon became clear this was no call to worship. Before long, all the bells of the City, St Paul's, St Clement's, St Mary le Bow, St Martin's, just across the way from my rooms on Ludgate Hill, were ringing out the news. On and on they went, a wild cacophony of jubilation.

My mother and sisters had already left for church when I arrived at Onslow Place. I found Father looking over a brief.

"Well, thank God it's over," I said, as I listened to the bells.

"I fear it may drag on for years," he replied gloomily. "Indeed, except in a formal sense, it may never be over. If Roberts is to be believed it will need a garrison of at least thirty thousand men to hold down South Africa."

That evening I had supper with Widdop. We met in Soho, at Solferino's. From the bunting, hastily erected in the streets, to the waiters sporting patriotic red, white and blue ribbons, it was clear that victory was in the air that night. At last it was over. It had been the longest, bloodiest, costliest war in a hundred years.

Throughout the final stages, with rumours of peace conflicting with reports of the latest ambush, Widdop had been implacably opposed to any negotiation with the Boers. *There is only one satisfactory way to end the war. By winning it. After all, we have no need to end it.* Now, with the fighting over at last, he was already contemplating the next phase.

"Yes, we must hold on to the new Crown colonies. That is as it should be."

"But surely," I protested, "the Boers will want a restoration of self-government ?"

"Out of the question. We must re-structure Africa as Bismark re-structured Germany."

Evidently Widdop found my grasp of affairs jejune, for he set out over supper to give me a brief lesson in *realpolitik*, which he seemed to regard as part of an inexorable and bloody struggle for existence. "Throughout the history of the world great nations have always behaved in accordance with this law of life. Remember your Virgil: '*Tu regere imperio populos, Romane …*' "

But why? I asked. To what end ?

"What need of an end ? Power is its own end. Strength consists in the exercise of strength. Muscles that aren't used grow flabby. They waste away. Empires are like businesses. They can't stand still. They must expand or they will dwindle. To relax, or even slacken one's efforts for an instant would be to fall behind. And we would cease to be top turkey, as our American cousins put it."

"By that law," I said half-humorously, "our climbs must get harder and harder."

"Of course. And our achievement is thereby the greater. Only by surpassing himself can Man hope to have a future. Otherwise he's at a dead end. Strength and virility must be constantly renewed. That's why each generation must strive to surpass, in daring and courage, the one before. Otherwise, the species will sicken and die."

"Believe me, old fellow, mountaineering is a rite of life."

I was stirred by his words. Widdop still had that power to excite. There was something intensely thrilling in his evocation of exalted destinies, of lofty forces at work in human affairs. For a moment I sensed the enormous satisfaction, the relief even, at the thought of submitting to his 'laws of life'. At the same time

I wondered what it was about him that disturbed me so.

Meanwhile, London was filling up for the Coronation.
Edward VII was to be crowned that summer, and we were to
have seats overlooking the route of the procession. At Onslow
Place life was a ferment of excitement. There were trips to Bond
Street for tours of the bonnet shops. All the talk was of hats and
dresses, punctuated by my father's groans (*I shall be ruined*) at
the expense. My heart sank at the thought of the outcry likely
to greet the revelation of my wasted years at Bart's. For my
determination to abandon medicine was now fully formed. Yet
in my apprehensive state of mind an abrupt disclosure still seemed
unthinkable. What I imagined, what I was reaching out for, was
a quiet, sympathetic meeting of minds, as we sat together over
lunch. I'd gone through the scene a dozen times: Father, kindly,
receptive, smoking his cigar; me, opening my heart, making clear
what was no more than the plain truth – I was just not cut out
for a life in medicine. Again and again I went over my lines. At
the same time I was all too conscious of certain gaps in the script
– gaps which Father, no stranger to the rhetoric of denunciation,
was more than capable of filling.

Then, when I'd finally screwed my courage to the sticking
point, I hit on the very day, as ill luck would have it, *The Times*
carried details of the Coronation Honours. I don't know if Father
felt he had reason to expect anything for himself. He usually
affected a kind of non-conformist scorn for what he referred to
as 'petty trumperies'. For all that, he seemed to have spent the
morning combing through the List. Scattered among the CBs
and the KCMGs were the names of several contemporaries from
Lincoln's Inn, and his irritation allowed no room that day for
airing anything else.

A few days later I set out determined, come what may, to get it over with.

"Watch out," hissed Dolly as I arrived. "We've got the mulligrubs again."

Politics apart, nothing in our household gave rise to such heat and passion as the theatre. For my mother, in all things else a model of wifely compliance, the theatre of Irving and Beerbohm Tree shone, a beacon of colour and romance, in what must otherwise have been a life of stultifying monotony. Ellen Terry's Lady Macbeth was one of her most cherished memories. It had the status of a family heirloom. I had myself seen the announcement that Sarah Bernhardt was to perform a number of roles at the Garrick theatre. The prospect of an appearance by the great French *tragedienne*, as well as arousing widespread interest and excitement, had stimulated my mother's recollections of Madame Bernhardt in her prime. Not unnaturally my sisters were agitating to be taken to see her. None of this was of the slightest interest to my Father. He was generally bored at the theatre. While he might enjoy an occasional evening at the Gaiety or the Lyric – entrancing girls, a catchy tune – anything other than light entertainment was more than he could endure. His audible groans so embarrassed my mother she'd virtually given up theatre-going altogether.

The discontent flared up again over the soup.

"I'd dearly love to see her as Francesca da Rimini," said Dolly dreamily.

"I'm shocked, to say the least," remarked Father mischievously, "that any daughter of mine should express an interest in such a subject."

The rebuke drew my mother into the fray. "The theatre is in their blood," she asserted firmly.

Her grandfather had run away from home to become an

actor. Failing at that, he'd turned his hand to theatre man-
agement, a profession in which he showed himself possessed of
a shrewd business brain. Mother's rents included over a thousand
a year from the Duke of York's in St Martin's Lane.

Meanwhile, Ellen Terry stalked the boards once more.
Father groaned, Dolly and I avoided one another's eye, as my
mother embarked once more on that never-to-be-forgotten
performance, no detail of which ever escaped her telling: the
great Byzantine robe covered in beetles' wings, the rich chestnut
braids reaching almost to the ground, the sleepwalking scene,
played without the assistance of a candle, a prop considered
indispensable by every other actress.

The performance over, Dora began the delicate business of
recovering lost ground. Calmly, rationally, while expressing no
opinion critical of Father, she set out the grounds requiring their
attendance at the Garrick. Everyone would be going. The King
himself was almost certain to attend. Not to go would be quite
eccentric. It was fast becoming the chief topic of discussion in
every drawing room. One was sure to be asked about it – who
wanted to be thought an ignoramus or, what was worse, a
Philistine ?

"Besides," she concluded, "cultivated people really do have
a duty towards Art."

To all of this my father listened gravely, albeit with a gleam
of amusement.

"Art," declared my mother loftily, "knows no frontiers. I
have no patience with the 'little England' insularity that chooses
to sneer at foreigners. Sarah Bernhardt belongs not simply to
France but to the whole world."

"Do you suppose she really sleeps in her coffin ?" enquired Dolly.

"With or without a candle ?" Father was often at his most
insufferable when flippant.

Silent, uncomfortable, I sat through these exchanges knowing my sisters were wasting their time. Whatever they said he
would not engage with them. He would not take them seriously.
It succeeded, more than any display of anger, in rendering him
utterly inaccessible.

"It's really too bad," stormed Dolly. "I don't suppose we shall
ever get the chance to see her again." Flushing, biting her lip in
frustration, she sat for a while. But it was all too much. Her
eyes began to fill with tears. Suddenly, flinging aside her napkin,
she rose and scurried from the room.

Dinner dragged on, a frosty agony in which every scrape of
a knife or fork jangled the nerves.

Only Father appeared unconcerned. Though his affectation
of indifference couldn't quite conceal a glint of triumph. Ill at
ease though I was, I felt the relief of a burden lifted from my
shoulders. Any confession that evening was now quite out of
the question.

Though later that night, undressing for bed, I was overcome
by the sheer futility of any appeal to Father, the impossibility of
turning aside his scorn and anger. After all, I had nothing to
offer, no other suggestion as to what I might do with my life.
And what then ? I would have no career, no means, no live-
lihood. I flinched at the thought of his reproaches, seeing myself
branded as of all characters the most contemptible in his eyes –
an idler and a wastrel.

The next morning I came to a decision. I sent a telegram to
the Black Mount, and set off north.

*

At Bridge of Orchy a trap was waiting. Jogging the miles
with a silent ghillie for companion, it struck me that echoes,

even of the most stirring events, must penetrate grandfather's Highland fastness as the noise of something infinitely distant. I thought of the times when we'd come north, bringing our wars right into his house. How he must have longed for us to go – longed to be left alone again to resume the passion of his life. Swaying with the motion of the cart, I sat, my eyes fixed on the hills of the Black Mount, constant, unchanging. There was something infinitely restful in that quiet contemplation. I felt profoundly grateful to be there. The ghillie hunched on his seat, the rattle of wheels, the pony's hooves on the mountain road – suddenly I was a child again, seeing the winter hills coming into view across the loch, eager for my first glimpse of romantic spires and turrets rising among the pines.

For Agnes, it is still a sight to shudder at. A dark wood about a house, brooding, self-enclosed. And so it seemed. Yet in winter hinds would come right down to the edge of the trees. Sometimes we made stealthy patrols to watch for them. I was a small boy then, and as much in awe of the wild wood as I was of grandfather. He seemed to me very old and powerful: an old wizard, lord and creator of everything around us. A magic place it seemed to me: rank upon rank of dark trunks receding into the gloom, the pallor of snow, small gem-like birds flitting from branch to branch. I dare say there were many occasions when we saw nothing: grandfather, a finger raised to his lips, myself scarcely daring to breathe as we waited, motionless. If I looked at him he shook his head, raised that finger to his lips. *Be still. Be silent.* And he was right. Be as one with all that lies around you, and it will happen. The mysterious thing.

It was grandfather's habit most evenings to walk the boundary of his wood, where a clearing offered a vista of glen and lonely hills to the north and west. Here, on a flat rock, the old man sat to make a last inspection of his property before retiring for the night. So Agnes used to put it. Now we sat together, while the last of the sun dropped below the Black Mount. I was content to listen to the burn, flowing strongly after a night's rain. A slight breeze held off the midges, which had been troublesome in the still air under the trees. Meanwhile, grandfather carried out a lengthy scrutiny of the glen. He made no attempt at conversation.

He had greeted my arrival without comment. His silences, so unnerving in a family party, now seemed a relief. How much he knew of family affairs is difficult to say. He rarely made direct enquiries. We put it down to his indifference.

All my life he had lived among these hills. He left them only when he had to, and then for a few days at the most. *No forest thrives without the forester,* he told me once. *That's where he must keep his heart. Among the hills and the deer.* I tried to think of him as he must have been in the years before he came to the Black Mount – ship-builder, man of business – but I couldn't. None of that made sense. I'd only ever known him as grandfather: a solitary, strange old man who'd somehow got free of the rest of us.

As I looked at the face, intent, broken-veined from years of wind and rain, I saw how deep the roots of his life went down. Suddenly I knew grandfather was a happy man – a man absorbed in the task life had given him – that his was the perfect life – a life above all others.

Silently he handed me the glass, and pointed down the glen. "East of the burn," he said.

Following the direction of his arm I spotted a bounding motion among the stones that stopped just as I caught it with the glass. For a moment it seemed to gaze at me, stock-still, as I held it in the glass. A young stag. Perhaps three years old. Antlers poised above the light golden head. For one astonishing moment we were face to face in the 'O' of the glass, eyeing one another with a directness which, had it been face to face, would have discomfited us both, and yet was a plain, simple kind of seeing of what was there. Then it was off again, effortlessly bounding down between the stones.

"Every time I go to the hill," grandfather murmured, "they teach me something."

He talked about the life of a stag. Some big old fellow. August was the best month for him. "He's in condition. Free at last of the velvet. He feels cool and comfortable. No itch of sex yet to trouble the blood and make him restive. He goes up the hill alone with a younger protégé. Up where the grass is sweetest. Where the breeze keeps away the flies. Just the two of them. There he'll spend the days eating and sleeping. His young friend will see he's not disturbed. He may be shot, of course. But he'll know nothing about it. He dies in a moment."

He spoke as if it were the best Fate had to offer: the gift coming without warning. Out of the blue summer hills.

He began to fumble for his briar. "Tell me something. Is your heart in this sawbones business?"

I took a deep breath. "No. Not really." I didn't dare look at him.

"Then don't do it, boy. Give it up."

I heard the scrape of a match, then the acrid scent of the strong shag he favoured flooded the air.

"What sort of life ... " he grunted, between puffs, "do you really want ?"

The answer came to me in a flash. With total conviction. Never, it seemed, had I been more certain of anything.

"*I want to live like this.*"

*

188

I travelled south again, steeled for the confrontation. Yet somehow I knew the consent I needed had been given. Within the week I received a summons to my father's chambers. I was kept waiting. To this day the smell of a waxed floor brings with it the dismal hour I spent in that waiting room, turning the pages of old copies of *Punch*. Eventually Greatbatch, my father's clerk, came to fetch me. I followed him up the steep narrow stair, acutely conscious of my boots clattering on the bare boards.

Greatbatch knocked, ushered me in. What followed was curt and painful. My father scarcely looked up from his papers.

"I understand that you no longer wish to pursue a career in medicine. A sum of money is to be made available for whatever it is you wish to do with your life. That is all I have to say. Good afternoon."

*

A month later he was dead.

He'd set off on a sudden visit to the Black Mount. I can only guess at his reasons. He'd taken the night train from King's Cross. At Edinburgh the next morning the sleeping car attendant found him dead in his bed. A constable came round from Walton Street to break the news. God knows I have travelled in some remote places. Yet never before or since have I experienced so profound a sense of being alone in the world. It was a bleak and lonely moment.

Mother's fortitude astonished us all. As to her innermost feelings, I cannot say. She'd chosen the face that suited a widow best. She put it on with her widow's weeds, and wore it for the rest of her days. Agnes was devastated. Composed, dry-eyed, she stuck out the funeral. Afterwards she collapsed in my arms.

If I'd taken little thought for the pain and loneliness she

must have felt, it was because I'd envied her. She had the heat of her convictions. Besides, in time he would, I knew, receive her back.

Now, as we clung to one another, shaken with her sobs, a spasm of rage swept over me at his abrupt withdrawal. *That is all I have to say. Good afternoon.*

Yet anger did nothing to lessen the guilt I felt – the entirely irrational conviction that my own defection had somehow precipitated Father's death.

XXII

In due course I went back to Bart's.

"At least qualify," my Uncle Guy had urged. "It's no bad thing having a profession to fall back on. Besides, you'll feel the better for having seen it through to the end."

Old Rufus was equally emphatic. "Take your degree, my boy. Take your degree. There's many a rum corner of the world where a stranger would not be welcome, but a doctor is received with open arms."

There were times when, chastened by Father's death, I wondered if this resumption of my studies represented an attempt to appease his angry spirit. For I still suffered that bitter anger, severing, estranging. He'd seemed a man so in control of his life that even the taking leave of it could not have been anything other than purposeful and deliberate. For all that, I went about the wards with a quiet mind. I knew now that my life was destined for something other than medicine. Sometimes though, as I sat bent over Osler or Walsher's *Surgery*, the impulse to get out – anywhere – was overpowering. I would set off east of Ludgate Hill, wandering below London Bridge into Wapping and Shadwell, past narrow streets closed in by cranes and the tall masts of ships. I stood on Tower Hill, watching the ponderous bascules of the bridge lifting on the open river, thinking that I might get a ship myself when I was qualified. Sometimes, if it was wet I called in at the Missionary Museum in Blomfield Street, lingering among the cases filled with strange artefacts and outlandish gods, or Stevens' Auction Rooms in Covent Garden, where I mingled with prospective bidders examining bronzes from Benin, silken coats from Bhokhara or Samarkand, mum-mified cats from ancient Egypt, a stuffed crocodile, a canoe from the South Sea islands, a captured Mauser or a flag from the Transvaal.

Such things were like siren voices, singing me to a richer, wider, world.

I can't recall how it came about that I found my way to the reading room of the Royal Geographical Society. Perhaps some good angel steered me to Saville Row. Unaided, I should never have guessed at the existence of the wondrous world concealed behind that elegant facade.

The library was on the first floor. Apart from the librarian seated at his corner table, it was often deserted. Here, under a rich frieze of painted jungles, forests, burning deserts, I browsed among the shelves and cross-cases. I fingered globes, examined maps, eyed all manner of strange objects and artefacts. I stared and stared at everything. The walls were hung with portraits and photographs of the great explorers, exemplars all of that daring and resourcefulness the age demanded. Freed from the boredom, the daily silliness of social relations, they'd explored their deepest desires. Leaving behind them all that was comfortable and domestic, they'd climbed mountains, crossed jungles, ventured their lives in search of the Pole or the North West Passage. Silent, enigmatic, the bearded faces looked beyond me, their gaze fixed on the far distance – the focus of all I burned to experience for myself.

Here, one afternoon, I came upon a man standing at the table on which were displayed the latest books of travel and exploration. Though his back was turned towards me I knew instantly that tall figure, those flowing locks. It was Conway. He looked up with a friendly smile at my approach.

We got into conversation. Shyly, I confessed to having been at his lecture at the Alpine Club three years before. He enquired, courteously, if my own 'field of activity' lay in South America.

Flattered by such an attribution from one so eminent, I opened my heart to him that afternoon as, a few months earlier, I had opened it to Lockhart: my uncertainty as to the direction of my life, my desire to travel and so forth – though I dare say Conway had no difficulty in diagnosing for himself my irresolute state of longing and confusion.

"Well, there's real work to be done," he said, "in the Arctic. For a young man like yourself."

Meanwhile the librarian had begun to cast meaningful looks in our direction. With an apologetic smile, Conway took my arm and steered me towards the gallery of the map room. How long we spent together, an hour, a few minutes, I cannot say. It was one of those epiphanies of which a man may expect to have, at best, perhaps two or three in a whole lifetime, yet without which a life never gets going. There, in that light airy space under the glass roof, we stood together, while down below us in the map room, a row of rare globes attended like worlds in waiting.

I spoke of my admiration for Nansen, at which Conway pointed out something which, in my romantic hero-worship, had escaped me completely: that in both his Greenland crossing and in the voyage of the *Fram*, Nansen had been addressing particular scientific problems. Dark eyes alight with enthusiasm, Conway went on to describe the strange phenomena of that northern world as a man might speak of the unfathomable and the infinite. He was like Lockhart in another region of arduous endeavour. The same urge to puzzle out the hardest questions. To follow where the footprints stopped, and go beyond them. And yet I saw it was his child's sense of wonder, rendering him indifferent to hardship and discomfort, drawing him ever onward, that was the source of all his boldness. Conway was a man entranced by all he saw.

I walked home in a dream of crimson rivers flowing over veins of jasper, of seas with the consistency of porridge, of ice volcanoes and pink snow, and skies not blue but a thin, radiant primrose: *the true light*, Conway called it, *of the far North*.

Though later that evening, as I sat over Osler, my heart sank into my boots. For I knew that I was utterly unqualified for the life of an explorer. Tentative, chronically uncertain, curious about everything, sure of nothing, I had no idea what was needful to live such a life: what things were true and important, and what were not.

*

I had been dreading Christmas at home – the first without father. So I was mightily relieved to discover that my three-week stint as Obstetric clerk was scheduled for the Christmas period.

Mother had taken the blow of Father's death better than any of us expected. It was as if Fate had at last cast her for the role which she was born to play. For weeks afterwards the house echoed to the weeping and wailing of a ghastly chorus of aunts and cousins. They maintained an almost constant attendance upon her. Patient, stoical, she endured having her hand held, and sat dry-eyed through all their lamentations.

Now that Father was dead she had expected Agnes to come home again. *To lead a normal life* was how she put it ... I thought it unlikely. Nevertheless I carried out what I took to be a commission and raised the subject with Agnes.

"No," she told me firmly. "I love mother dearly, but I could never again live at Onslow Place."

For mother this double defection was another cross to bear. Though I suspect Dora was secretly relieved. Faithful beyond the grave, she could not easily forgive.

In the weeks after the funeral I saw a lot of Agnes. It was I suppose a kind of mutual grieving, albeit the grieving of conspirators. We had not wanted him to die like that. Yet both of us knew, given the fore-knowledge, it could have made no difference.

Our meetings were filled with memories of Father. Obscure moments. Little acts of tenderness. How hard he worked – how, over dinner, the head with its silky curls would droop lower and lower – his laughter when, as a child, she had amused him so.

"I dream he is alive again," she whispered. "We go out walking. Silly, really. What would we say to one another ?"

Her voice trembled forlornly. We had come face to face with the chastening truth that childhood and youth, so singular to oneself, are spent in the midst of other lives, to whom they may have been a bitter disappointment.

A week before Christmas I took up my duties as Obstetric clerk. To this day I have the impression that all babies are born at the very dead of night. A porter would come to wake me. Half asleep, I tumbled out into the street. If I was lucky there might be a neighbour or a relative to act as guide. Black bag in hand, I passed uneasily through dark courts and alleys, wondering if old Rufus's 'rum corners of the world' where a doctor was received with open arms extended to Skinner Street or Lockup Lane. The work was never-ending. I would come back from one delivery, only to find an anxious porter waiting to dispatch me to another. Countless times I went astray; was re-directed; got lost again; groped my way up black stairwells, flinching at the smell. I'd heard old physicians speak of childbirth as a perpetual wonder. Even Clegg, who must have birthed hundreds

195

of Herdwicks, talked of lambing as of some transcendent mystery. Perhaps I was too anxious, or too tired, to see it. Or else there was something missing in myself. Try as I might, I could never separate the event from its surroundings – sordid rooms, the sweetish stench of bed-bugs – and the joy of new life as like as not eclipsed by despair at another mouth to feed, and no money coming in. Sometimes, coming back to my room dog-tired, shaking the bugs from my clothes, I wondered how Agnes was faring, and whether Canning Town could be any grimmer than parts of Clerkenwell or Spitalfields.

Then, in the New Year, I had a letter. It was alive with savage indignation. Agnes had resumed her political activities, this time on behalf of the hat-box workers.

Half-a-crown a gross. That's all they're paid. And out of that they must provide their own paste, their own needles and thread. And these women make up just one small section of a vast army of sweated labour slaving away, too frightened to ask for better pay and conditions. There are thousands of them, George. Shirt-makers stitching away hour after hour for a miserable pittance – lace-workers sitting up all night ruining their eyes – little seamstresses in West End establishments working behind drawn blinds long after the hours allowed by the Factory Acts. Persuasion fails. All appeals to decency – to better nature – fail. Something must be done. I have started up a Union. At present we are small, disorganised. But I intend to make it into something. One day I shall march them to Trafalgar Square.

Her letter concluded with a derisive postscript:

PS: I was introduced to the heroic Masterman. Six feet in height, lean and handsome, with health and strength written in every line of his manly face. Is it true he is to leave the army ? Surely such a figure should be for ever slaying dragons and rescuing fair maidens. Ha-ha!

XXIII

Meanwhile my own encounter was not long delayed. It came about as a result of one of Widdop's telegrams: *Masterman At Wastdale This Weekend Stop Do Come Stop.*

Widdop's old pupil was now a celebrated figure. Who had not heard of Masterman's Scouts ? *There really ought to be a picture of them,* Widdop had joked, as we stood in the queue at Madame Tussaud's, *in their slouch hats and bandoliers among the footer teams on the refec wall.* I saw how it appealed to him. That cat-and-mouse game with the Boer commandos. Hunting, and being hunted. Though it struck me, as we shuffled along with the fathers, the grandfathers and their excited charges, that some scenes of childhood excitements are best left un-revisited. The Boer War notables were grouped together in a single *tableau.* They sat, or stood, each the waxy embodiment of some daring episode. They might have been gathered together for some historic photograph, except for a curious lack of connection, each figure stiff, motionless, eyes unfocused, as if lost in some private reverie.

The object of our visit turned out to be a slim, elegant figure sitting with a casual grace as if at some *soirée,* legs crossed, one arm thrown carelessly over the back of a sofa. He was smoking a cigarette. He wore the full dress uniform of a captain in the Dublin Fusiliers. On the wall behind his head, a map of South Africa: on a table, his sword and shako. Head thrown back, he gazed as if at some unknown questioner. The glassy face wore a tight half smile.

We stood with two small boys and an elderly clergyman in an old-fashioned chimney-pot hat. From a small boy's point of view, I thought, there wasn't much to see.

Widdop, though, was gazing with something akin to reverence. "It's him to the life."

Bored with sedentary heroes, the boys tugged their guardian off to the Chamber of Horrors.

"You can see in a moment what he is," Widdop added softly. "A man without a mask."

At a loss for something to say, I remarked that I thought it a pity not to see represented the daring rescue that had won the DSO.

"It should have been a VC," murmured Widdop.

Years later, in the Northern Cape, I was to receive a first-hand account from a man who'd ridden with Masterman's Scouts: one Potts, a lean leathery little man with bleached hair and vague blue eyes, who'd married a Boer wife, and settled out there among his former enemies. Mere matter of fact he made it sound. A plain tale, plainly told. "We were chasing Smuts. We'd ridden into this *donga*. Well, the b—— was waiting for us, and we were dashing away when Paddy Boyle's horse got shot from under him. The Captain wheels round, rides straight back through a hail of bullets, grabs hold o' Paddy, pulls him up on his own horse and brings him safe back out."

"A brave act indeed," I murmured.

"A man like that. Well, you'd follow him anywhere. Luck o' the Irish. That's what we used to say. He'd a charmed life, you see."

Not long afterwards I was to discover for myself how men cherished their ikons of protection. Which officer would get you killed. Which seemed fated to survive.

"Aye," said Potts reflectively. "The Captain knew no fear."

*

Easter was still several weeks away. But with the shadow of Finals creeping ever nearer, a break now seemed more than welcome. At the time I was acting as dresser to MacSelf. As I was only required in the theatre on Tuesdays and Thursdays, I arranged for a colleague to cover my cases for a day or two, and took the train from Euston early on the Friday morning.

Tea, set out in the drawing room, was an unusually sumptuous affair. I wondered if Widdop had arranged for Ritson to lay on a special 'brew', as he called it. He'd certainly been keeping the telegraph busy down at Westward Ho, to judge by the numbers wolfing it down. The Barton brothers, Harris, Oppenheimer. Slater, too, was there. There was also a small separate party of undergraduates, the *protégés* of Professor Armthwaite. The 'Guardian party', I noticed, were conspicuous by their absence.

Tea was generally an occasion for light-hearted conversation. That afternoon an unaccustomed quiet prevailed in the drawing room, an attentive hush in which the clatter of tea things was more than usually noticeable. Though men got up from time to time to replenish cups and plates, all attention focused on a casual, confident voice.

"Certainly this new smokeless powder confers a cloak of invisibility on the rifle-man. He's just not there." The accent, more English than Irish, held only a faint suggestion of a brogue. "You stroll about in the sunshine, enjoying the air, the view, the song of the larks – then a bullet whines past your ear. And then you realise, with a start, that someone is actually taking a pot-shot at you."

It was my first sight of the living Masterman. The real thing. It gave me quite a start. A different setting, the principal character in *mufti* rather than 'best blues', the moustache a trifle thicker, coarser – yet it was as if the effigy at Madame Tussaud's had sprung suddenly to life: as if some essential element present here, lacking there, was animating the slim elegant figure, now gesturing with that arm thrown over the back of the sofa, picking off questions with casual ease.

"That's right. You can't see him. You don't know where he is. Most likely he's a good half mile away. Perhaps more. But he's got you in his sights. It's a bit of a stunner, I can tell you."

The face, tanned, leathery, was the face of Africa. A network of fine lines told of eyes constantly screwed up in a fierce light. His chief impression ? Oh, fatigue. Soldiering had something in common with mountaineering – long marches, climbing hills, carrying heavy loads. What did he remember ? Smells, mostly. The Boers ? An odd-looking bunch in those hats and black frock coats. Like a lot of seedy undertakers.

"Though to do them justice," he added, as the laughter died away, "unlike our own senior officers, they improve with age. The more elderly the rifleman, the deadlier the aim. They rarely missed their mark."

Death and destruction had been his constant companions. For months at a time he had survived from one day to the next. Yet it scarcely seemed possible that the humorous fellow in our midst could be one and the same with the man who had endured such dangers and privations. Only when pressed about the guerilla war did the airy insouciance of the performance give place to a more serious note. The sunburnt face looked thoughtful. The lines about the eyes creased into a frown.

"I'll tell you what," he said eventually. "The most unsettling thing was the sheer unpredictability of the whole business. You try to look as far ahead as you can, work out consequences, think through possibilities, and so forth. Usually, though, you have to make a decision very quickly, with insufficient information and no sure sense of the likely outcome." He sipped at his tea, before replacing the cup carefully in its saucer. "It's like trying to see into the mind of a largely invisible adversary," he went on. "You learn to be watchful, without knowing what it is you're watching for. The upshot is that you tend to distrust appearances. You look, instead, for what's hidden. The result is you become mistrustful of yourself."

He looked round, as if to be sure he was understood. "It's almost as if there's another person to take into account, another set of intentions to be on one's guard against."

At that moment there came a fumbling at the door. Since I was nearest, I got up to open it. It was the maid with a fresh urn of tea. Some men got up to move towards the table. Others were still engrossed in the questioning of their guest. I was pouring myself another cup of tea when I heard a curious voice raising the subject of the farm burnings. I glanced round. For a moment Masterman seemed to hesitate. Then the leathery features twisted into that tight half-smile. Perhaps revelation had gone far enough.

"Well now," he said briskly, stubbing out his cigarette. "What about this famous Barndoor Traverse ? Will someone show me how it's done?"

That Widdop had plans to enliven the weekend I was in no doubt. He buttonholed me the moment tea was over. He was wearing a new suit of curious orange tweed. "I want you to be one of the scouts," he said. "Masterman, of course, will be the other."

A few moments later I was formally presented. Widdop introduced me as 'your fellow fugitive'.

"Hazard's a good go-er", he added benevolently.

I remarked, as we shook hands, that I believed he'd met my

sister. Frankly, I'd been stunned by Agnes' postscript. It seemed an encounter as unlikely as it was incongruous.

"Ah yes, of course. Miss Hazard," said Masterman politely.

Since he said nothing more, and I was still ignorant of the circumstances of their meeting, we were left smiling at one another, rather at a loss.

Widdop, meanwhile, was already moving among the other guests, recruiting as many as he could cajole or bully into taking part. In those days man-hunting was still popular at Wastdale, at least, among the young. It appealed to one's pride of speed and stamina – moving unseen over rough country, taking others by surprise. By the next morning Widdop had enlisted eighteen 'sentries' to hold the line against the two of us. Before he led them off, immediately after breakfast, he went over the rules once more for Masterman's benefit.

"They're much the same as at the Coll. My chaps will keep at least half a mile from the objective until two o'clock, unless they're actually chasing you. If two of them, within a hundred yards of you, call on you to surrender, you're caught. To put one of them out of the game you have to collar him." He handed us our red armbands, wished us 'Good luck', and went out to muster his men.

It was a bright sunny morning, with excellent visibility. I reflected that it would favour them more than us.

"A pity, really," murmured Masterman, as we watched Widdop leading his troops out of the yard, "not to climb on a day like this."

With the Cambridge party still clattering about the hall, preparing to depart, we sat down to a pot of coffee in the morning room. Since we were not to start until ten o'clock, we had ample time to lay our plans. Masterman had spent some time the previous evening poring over the map. As a guest of honour, he had the choice of objective. He'd picked a summit almost as unfamiliar to Widdop as to himself: Steeple, an airy adjunct of Scoat Fell. Our task was to reach the summit of Steeple without being intercepted. Now we turned to our map again, and fell to studying the ground. It resembled a letter E (its spine the long ridge running from Haycock, in the west, via Scoat Fell to Pillar) tilted forward to rest on rather curved, and broken arms. It offered advantages to both sides. From Widdop's point of view, its very remoteness virtually ruled out an attempt from the north. On the other hand, it offered us a variety of approaches. The two main valleys each side of the central arm – Mosedale, to the east, and Netherbeck – afforded a choice of climbs to the ridge. However, anyone taking these valley approaches would be highly visible, at least in the early stages.

Masterman immediately set me to working out the likely disposition of Widdop's 'vedettes', as he called them. Some 'captains' favoured placing their men in a defensive ring around the half-mile perimeter, then waiting for the scouts to attempt to break through. However I felt pretty certain this would not be Widdop's tactic. He would position his men so as to command the approaches, try to make visual contact, then fall back in a tightening ring, until we were close enough to be taken. Privately, I favoured a flanking manoeuvre: creeping round under the cover of the eastern arm, via Beck Head, round the back of Kirk Fell, and thence along the High Level Traverse to Pillar. However, this plan had one glaring weakness. Black Sail Pass, a crucial point on the approach, was sure to be guarded.

I was pondering this difficulty, when Masterman traced a line on the map. "How about this ?" His finger followed the central arm, formed by the two high ridges of Yewbarrow and Red Pike. It was certainly direct. Moreover, it had the advantage of concealment. Even crossing the summit plateau of Yewbarrow

we would be hidden by the rocky rampart of Stirrup Crag at its
northern end, while the steep descent followed a line so devious,
among cracks and chimneys, I felt sure we wouldn't been seen.
However, that would bring us to Dore Head – a full furlong of
open ground without a shred of cover.

"Well," I said doubtfully, "I think we can get down Stirrup
Crag without being spotted. Crossing Dore Head is another
matter."

I suggested the Beck Head flanking manoeuvre.

Masterman shook his head.

"It's the obvious thing to do," he said. "Widdop will expect
us to go that way."

I said I thought it more likely he would expect us to split
up.

"Then we stick together – at least, until we get within
striking distance. Two heads are better than one."

At ten o'clock we set off for Yewbarrow. Despite the warm
day, Masterman had donned a well-worn Norfolk jacket, with a
bulky game pocket running right round the back of the coat.
"Right," he said. "Lead on."

We crossed the bridge over the beck and went straight up
the fell. I made the pace, though any local knowledge I might
have had went for nothing amid that terrain of stony bracken,
bilberry and sliding scree. Sweat was soon stinging my eyes. I
wondered how Masterman was faring. He must be fairly stewing,
I thought, in that Norfolk jacket. We reached the summit in
just over an hour. Feeling quite pleased with myself, I glanced
back to see how Masterman had found the pace. "By Jove, that
was quite stiff," he said obligingly. Though he looked not in the
least put out.

Glad of a cooling breeze, we set off across the summit plateau. Here, in a wide depression, we were safe from spying eyes. All around were bare sunlit heights. Every detail stood out sharp and clear: Gable and the Napes ridges, the Scawfells speckled with snow, even the pools and gravel beds of Mosedale Beck meandering far below. Masterman pointed out Armthwaite's party, mere dots climbing the fellside on their way to Black Sail Pass.

The descent from Stirrup Crag was over rock, via a line of steep cracks and chimneys. We were about half-way down when, mysteriously, Masterman called a halt. "Can we just hang on a minute ?"

Settling himself in a convenient nook, to my surprise he produced a small pair of field glasses, and began scanning the fellside across the head of Mosedale. "No sign of the enemy."

For several minutes Masterman continued his silent scrutiny of the fellside opposite.

"All this must seem rather small beer to you," I said eventually. Though as a rule I enjoyed man-hunting immensely, I was conscious it must seem rather a schoolboy game to him.

"On the contrary," he murmured absently. "I intend to take it very seriously."

Armthwaite's party were by now strung out on Gatherstone Head, toiling up towards the pass. Masterman was watching them intently. Then, quite suddenly, came a shrill double blast of a whistle, echoing among the hills. Masterman handed me the glasses. To my astonishment I saw that one of the tiny figures plodding upwards seemed to be wearing a red armband.

"I thought Widdop would look for us among the civilians," murmured Masterman. He seemed gratified.

"But surely ... " I stammered. "How on earth ... "

I didn't quite know what to say.

"Oh, the young men were only too willing. You know – entering into the spirit of things, and so forth."

Masterman smiled at me disarmingly. There was a fresh outbreak of whistling across the head of Mosedale. Widdop's men were massing for a capture at Black Sail.

"As soon as they realise they've been had," I said, "they'll come racing over here."

"Ah, but they can't. Not until two o'clock."

Masterman handed me the map. I looked at the half-mile perimeter pencilled round Steeple. It effectively isolated each arm of the E. Widdop's men would have to descend into Mosedale, then climb two thousand feet of rough fell to get to us. Suddenly I saw the cunning in Masterman's choice of our objective. I wondered if Widdop had tumbled to it. If not, he would be rueing it now. Whatever men he'd deployed to cover the western approaches by way of Netherbeck were similarly cut off. That left the Dore Head sentries. Whichever way one looked at it Dore Head was the key to any approach over Red Pike. We studied the map again.

"You know the ground," said Masterman. "Where would you put them ?"

"Two at Gosforth Crag, to cover Overbeck," I said. "They're too far off to trouble us. Two for sure at The Chair." This was a rocky vantage point on the edge of the stony plateau of Red Pike, three or four hundred yards from where we lay concealed. I gazed across at The Chair. Any sentries posted there would have us in full view as we toiled up towards them. Down below us at Dore Head a few sheep were cropping the short turf of the col. Sure we were being watched, I felt a tingle of suspense. I wondered what I might have felt had the sentries been armed with Mausers.

Meanwhile, Masterman was spying the ridge. "No sign of life."

"They're bound to be there."

"That's something we shall have to risk," murmured Masterman. "I'll go first. If I'm taken it'll give you a chance to get through. Don't forget, they think one of us is already in the bag. Good luck."

Stowing his field glasses, he eased himself down the last few feet of crack and was off, bent double, scudding away over the turf. In less than a minute he had disappeared among the rocks of Bull Crags opposite. I followed – sprinting for all I was worth – expecting at any moment the blast of whistles – flinging myself down at last, gasping, heart pounding, behind a boulder. Moments later I heard a rustle of vegetation. It was Masterman. "Well done," he hissed. We took stock of our position. We were now once again well concealed on the eastern flank of Red Pike, about a hundred feet or so below the ridge, and surrounded on every side by wild cataracts of crags spilling down into Mosedale. What Masterman now proposed was an adventurous traverse crossing the precipitous fellside until, at a point level with the summit, we could scramble up to the ridge safely within the half-mile circle, and so head for home.

I thought it a dubious tactic. And so it proved. Faced finally with a barrier of crags there seemed nothing for it but to scramble up to the ridge.

Moments later we heard the sound of voices immediately above us. Our position seemed hopeless. "If we can scrag just one of 'em," whispered Masterman, "that'll do. What we need is a diversion."

He looked round, pointed to a run of small scree, twenty or thirty yards away from where we were crouching, under the rim of the escarpment. "Go down there, and make some noise. Bob up and down a bit. Leave the rest to me."

Descending as instructed, I gave the scree a good clattering.

There came a shout from above. I bobbed down behind a rock. Then came two excited voices, one of them Slater's, followed shortly afterwards by a startled exclamation, a flurry of boots scattering stones, the sound of a scuffle.

"O.K." sang out Masterman. "It's all over."

I stood up, to see a somewhat dishevelled Slater rising to his feet. Seeing his comrade had been 'captured', the other sentry surrendered without further ado. Together we walked the few hundred yards down the ridge of Red Pike. Masterman chatted amiably, casual observations about this and that, to which Slater responded rather stiffly. He was plainly unhappy with his treatment. At the wall passing over the summit of Scoat Fell we parted company. Our 'prisoners' went off to report to Widdop, while Masterman and I descended the gentle slope to the col. A few yards more, up the final *arête* of Steeple, and we were standing on the tiny top, with only the summit cairn barring the drop to Ennerdale and the silver Liza, winding far below.

"We may as well have lunch while we wait," said Masterman. Dropping down on to the turf beside the cairn, he proceeded to unship a number of packages from the pocket of his jacket: bread and butter, potted beef, chocolate, chicken legs. "I'm afraid some of it's rather soggy," he said apologetically.

Luncheon over, we shifted round to follow the sun. Masterman had discarded his jacket. Looking at him sprawled on the turf, eyes closed, his back propped against the stones of the cairn, Widdop's words came to mind: *You can see in a moment what he is. A man without a mask.*

I wondered what he was doing here. His tall slim figure put me in mind, like no one I'd ever met, of Kipling's lines about Kamal's son: *'He trod the ling like a buck in Spring, and looked like a lance at rest'*.

Lying there, arms resting at his sides, he seemed to lack all guile. And yet an evening of talk and laughter in the smoke room had done little to make things any less perplexing. Honour, my Father liked to say, was conferred by one's peers. But here, Masterman had no peers, only admirers. There were men present who'd been in one or two tight corners. But none of them had fought a war. At the same time, good form frowned on personal disclosure. So had ensued a conversation which bobbed brightly back and forth over the surfaces of things. Questions were asked, to which manliness could return at best a casual, self-deprecating answer. And war remained as much a mystery as ever.

"My cousin Giles went out," I said. "He died of enteric. I wanted to go myself. I suppose I was wondering how I would shape up."

"The universal question," murmured Masterman. "On the boat going over all the talk among the men was of how they were going to go down there and hammer those farmers good and proper. As we got closer to the Cape there was a good deal less of that. Conversations started up, then petered out. You saw men staring into space. Like me, I suppose, they were wondering how they were going to stick it out."

Masterman lit a cigarette. "It started out quite a decent war," he mused. "Bloody, but decent. Then those Dutch farmers changed the rules. In the end we had to do away with rules altogether."

I don't know to this day why Masterman told me the things he did that afternoon. I don't know whether it was a sudden warming to me, his 'fellow fugitive' as Widdop put it, or to revenge himself upon an innocent, or whether, on impulse, he decided I should be told. Perhaps I brought it on myself.

Remembering the question he'd avoided the previous afternoon, I plucked up the courage to put it to him again. This time he never turned a hair. The farm burnings ? Rather like, he imagined, the Border raids of old.

"I dare say remote farmsteads up in the Cheviots felt much the same as those Boer women when they first caught sight of our dust. Always women, by the way. The men and all but the youngest boys were off on *commando*. They looked on as we burnt their homes. Sitting on their sticks of furniture, with their arms round one another. Mostly silent, amid all the squealing and squawking. But they watched us, those women. They watched what we did as we wet the grain, fired the ricks and wagons, cut the throats of the pigs."

Casually, Masterman lit another cigarette. He blew out a stream of smoke which hung in the air over his head. Eyes closed, face lifted to the sun, he might have been soaking up the peace around us. Somewhere a lark was trilling.

"I sometimes think of those tales from history one read as a child. You know the sort of thing: Bruce and the spider, Drake playing his game of bowls, Alfred burning the cakes. What, I wonder, will the British schoolboy read in years to come ? Will there be any mention, do you think, of Masterman laying waste the crops – slaughtering the cattle – digging up the dead."

For an awful moment I thought I was being asked something which required an answer. I was still scratching around for something to say, when he resumed.

"You stop at a farm. You discover a plot of freshly turned earth. The woman declares it to be the grave of her young child. She buried him herself two days earlier. Suspecting a cache of arms you order your men to dig. Mother wailing, thrashing about. Has to be restrained. Men uncover something wrapped in a blanket ... "

The reality he described consisted mainly of things, often quite insignificant, randomly disposed, recorded without emotion or judgement: dust, the scent of eucalyptus, the stillness of hot afternoons, the African rain.

"It falls in floods. Even mules and horses can scarcely hold up their heads. The noise of it drowns all conversation. Vision too. All you see is a yard or two of earth disintegrating in front of you. Washing away before your eyes. I dare say you've seen nothing like it."

It was less a narrative than a chronology, a recollection of things happening – sporadic, fragmentary, since war moves in no direction, reaches no objective.

"We were crossing the wild Woodbush country north-east of Pietersberg. The sort of land left blank on your maps at home. Arid, empty, littered with dead mules and horses. A dead land through which we chased the Boer.

"I was feeling particularly wretched. A day or two before I'd lost my Basuto pony. My poor Blanco. He blundered into a dried-up pool. The men did everything they could to haul him out – heaving, cursing. Useless. He'd sunk to his haunches. Ears laid back. Eyes rolling. A nightmare. In the end I shot him."

Masterman broke off. His eyes opened a moment, then closed again. I noticed that the lark had ceased its trilling.

"We must have ridden forty or fifty miles without making contact. Towards nightfall we crossed an interminable plateau in driving rain. On and on through a tangle of stones and heather. We came down at last to a valley bottom, where we tumbled from the saddle. That night I slept like the dead. Next morning I woke to the most extraordinary thing. *Déjà vu*, I think it's called. A murmur of running water – the ponies stirring as they cropped the turf – a sward, pricked out with tiny yellow stars, smooth as any bowling green. It was like a dream. All around me things I *knew* would be there – the brook I might have bathed in – a hanging combe – the granite tor. It was pure

North Devon. We could have been camped in some grassy hollow up in the hills of the Torridge. Melbury, or Buckland Brewer way.

"We broke camp, and followed a track climbing the combe on the far side of the valley. I came up behind our pickets, jogging along in a kind of dream, half-expecting, as we topped the rise, to see the Coll down below, with the Burrows and the Pebble Ridge, and Lundy a blue smear on the horizon. Instead, I found myself on the brink of a tremendous fault. Grey crags marching away on either side as far as the eye could see. Bays, headlands, dark woods hanging above interminable slopes of rubble. Far below it was Africa again. The same dreary dun-coloured expanse stretching away into the blue distance, and the inevitable mountain wall one never reaches, which I used to think must mark the edge of the world.

"The track fell away below us, zig-zagging down between trees and boulders. I looked for smoke, without expecting to see it. The air's so clear a camp-fire's instantly detectable. I pushed out the pickets, left and right. Then I set off down, leading the men in single file.

"It's the silence you notice. Beyond the clink of harness, the clatter of hooves and stones – silence. No one speaks. It's as if each man has left a space around him for the ambush that could come at any moment. But nothing happened. We'd reached the plain, and were deploying when a single shot rang out. Somewhere a horse and trooper went down together. There was the usual confusion. Men cursing – horses rearing, plunging. But the fusillade never came. Nor even another shot.

"Only afterwards did it occur to me to wonder what he was doing there. Alone, on foot, in all that wilderness. Nothing we found on the body afterwards gave any clue as to who he was, or where he came from. What did become clear was that he'd fired his last round at us. His bandolier, the magazine of the Mauser we picked up afterwards – empty.

"It's a mystery to me why men do the things they do. He could have surrendered. Or stayed doggo in the bush. But no. He'd one round left, and he had to fire it at a *rooinek*. That was what did for him, of course. Even in that thick scrub he must have known we would flush him out in the end.

"So he broke cover and set off, running for his life. A tow-headed farm boy. Perhaps sixteen. At the Coll I suppose he might just have started in the Fifth. He ran, stumbling now and then, his mop of hair bobbing this way and that above the bush for almost a mile. We trotted after him. For there has to be a chase. Without a chase, Hazard, the game would be up."

Suddenly I knew that I was listening to a tale without a meaning, unless the point was that there was no point.

"In the end I shot him. A good shot too, from stirrups. I checked it afterwards. Not more than a point or so off centre, in the back of the skull. I think I shot him because of my poor Blanco.

"That was the end of it, more or less. At least, as far as my part in it's concerned. The end of The Great Boer War."

Masterman's voice, neutral, matter-of-fact, ended as it began.

I had been looking out over Ennerdale while he was speaking. Now I glanced down and saw that his head was turned towards Scoat Fell. I followed the direction of his gaze. A hundred yards away a little group of figures had appeared on the ridge. They started down the slope towards us, Widdop unmistakeable in his orange tweed. "That was a smart piece of work," he called out cheerfully. "Getting Armthwaite's man to act as decoy."

I rose to my feet. Masterman, making no effort to get up, squinted at his old master from among our debris of wrappers.

"I've never forgotten a piece of advice the Head was fond of giving us," he drawled lazily. "When you come across a variation from the normal, always meet him in an abnormal way. The corollary is equally true. When you know your opponent is expecting something, make sure he's not disappointed."

XXIV

Feelings were mixed about Masterman that weekend. Some men, following Widdop ('*Stalkiness*', *we call it at the Coll*), agreed that the recruiting of Armthwaite's man had been a smart piece of work. Others thought it smacked of sharp practice: that it offended against the true spirit of the contest. Deeper than that, though, lurked a sense of unease. It was as if an actor, playing a famous part, had made an inappropriate gesture. Struck a false note. Slater, in particular, was upset about the manner of his scragging. He objected to the unnecessary force with which it was carried out. He was particularly aggrieved about being dropped on from behind.

Behind, I suggested playfully, seemed the best place from which to drop on someone.

But Slater was not to be jollied out of it. It was not, he repeated stiffly, what one would have expected. I was reminded, furtively it seemed, of the disclosures Masterman had made to me. Why had he chosen me, I wondered uneasily, for his revelations. I wished he hadn't told me those things. I didn't know what to make of them, and not knowing made me uncomfortable and resentful. Masterman had shown me the private face of war. All I knew was that it had no meaning for me. Nor could it have had any meaning, since war is unlike anything except itself.

Only now, in the aftermath of another and more terrible war, is it possible to see how all our mysticisms of heroism end in self-estrangement. And that Masterman was no different from those other boys at the Coll – plunged into a drama not of his own making, with the parts cast and the lines already written. He was a man locked in a single dimension. To have acted differently he would have needed somehow to have stepped outside it. But in his world there was no 'outside', except that of the renegade, the deserter.

At the time, though, I had other things to think about. Finals were drawing near. I'd already approached MacSelf, and asked for a few days' leave to make up for the holiday I hadn't had at Christmas. I thought it prudent not to reveal my true reasons. He'd made no objection, and in due course I travelled up to Cambridge. After the clinical, the last of my examinations, I decided on the spur of the moment to call round at Lockhart's rooms. I'd seen nothing of him for months. He'd not been at Wastdale for the Masterman weekend. "He's burying himself in his work," said Widdop. "I gather it's coming to some sort of head."

I pressed the bell, though with little expectation of finding Lockhart at home. So I was pleasantly surprised to recognise, through the stained glass panel, an unmistakeable figure.

"I'm surprised to find you in," I said. "I rather expected you'd be at the Cavendish."

"I was working rather late last night," he said, forcing a smile.

I was quite shocked by his appearance. The austere face, that had seemed to me to reflect a mind so completely focused, stripped of all superfluities, wore a stretched, exhausted look. I thought Lockhart looked ill.

"I must go in later though," he said, as he went off to make some tea.

The Spartan room was as bleak as before, the bare walls eschewing all decoration. It offered little comfort for an ailing man. Then I noticed an addition. Propped on the mantelpiece, mounted on stiff card, was Abraham's photograph of Scawfell Pinnacle. A line of white dots traced Lockhart's ascent three years before, the traverse of the gangway under the overhangs, the climb up to the first and second niches. There the dots stopped. Thinking back to that display of solitary skill and courage, I began to see a tenuous affinity with the room. It spoke of some essential element in Lockhart's nature, something austere, uncompromising, that seemed to repudiate the whole character of the age we lived in with its deep *horror vacui*: the houses you couldn't move in without banging into something, dislodging some trifling knick-knack. Again I thought of that upright figure, alone, unroped, that questing gaze, and felt confirmed in my own – what shall I call it – faith more than belief, less a faith than a barely perceptible intimation, of how infinitely beyond what we ordinarily thought ourselves to be, our real being really was.

Then Lockhart returned with a tray of tea things, as before. This time the tray held, in addition, a plate on which lay a few anaemic-looking biscuits.

Naturally, I asked about the photograph. I'd not been deceived in my guess at his intentions. Lockhart dreamed of a climb so straight a man might drop a stone from Hopkinson's cairn that would land at the very spot from which he'd started. Talking of it seemed to restore some of his old nervy urgency.

"Someone will do it," he said gravely. "It's the natural line." It would have all the elegance of the very best hypotheses, the sort one knew in one's bones were right. "The best solutions," he added, "are always simple."

Shyly I confessed my conviction that any climb on that dreadful face was quite beyond my powers. I dare say I'd expected him to shrug it off with a smile. Lockhart, though, frowned un-expectedly. The pale face assumed a thoughtful, serious ex-pression.

"Every man has his own limit, George," he said earnestly. "Maybe in searching for it he extends it."

I bit into a biscuit. It crumbled into dusty, oaty fragments.

When, I asked, would he be going to the Alps ?

"Not this year, I'm afraid," he sighed.

From what I gathered his work was pressing him hard. Lockhart was setting up experiments to determine the density of electrons in a metal. *The field effect,* he called it. Thomson himself had proposed it. He tried to explain what was involved.

"First one prepares a thin film of metal. Then an electric field is applied perpendicularly to the film. The idea is to disperse the electrons in the surface area. In theory, anyway."

I regret to say I found it rather dull and disappointing. Refusing a second biscuit, I asked about Widdop.

"He's going to Zermatt," said Lockhart mildly. "I believe he's taking his friend Masterman with him." As to their plans, he had no idea. "I dare say they'll go for the Zinal Rothorn," he said indifferently. "The Dent Blanche, perhaps."

Preoccupied with his research, Lockhart had little interest in the affairs of others. His own work was what mattered most.

"I'm trying a new tack," he said. "I must stick at it."

He could not have known then what was only to become apparent years later; that Thomson's project, though theoretically sound, was altogether beyond the capacities of the equipment then available. He had set his *protégé* an impossible task. Despite persistent attempts, the expected effect failed to materialise. Poor Lockhart got no result.

On the train back to Liverpool Street I took stock of his news. So Widdop was taking Masterman to the Alps. I can't say I was greatly surprised. Then, for no particular reason, I remembered Agnes' ironic postscript: *Is it true he is to leave the army ?* Certainly I'd heard nothing to that effect. The cool confident figure holding court in the drawing room at Wastdale scarcely suggested a man on the point of abandoning his career. If it were true, surely Widdop would have known ? Gazing idly from the carriage window, I wondered if he'd been told what Masterman had disclosed to me.

I still wonder sometimes how much Widdop understood. Of war, modern war, he had no conception. All over England schoolmasters were winding up boys like Masterman, setting them down in India or Africa, never dreaming they'd come whirring home.

Even so, he must have known something was wrong, and did what he could – what he thought best. For life itself there could be no remedy. Yet a friend might offer support. And maybe the bitter ways of fortune are sometimes best forgotten in the well-judged blow of an axe, the absorbing business of placing a nail just so. I do not seek to belittle Widdop. If this late war has taught us anything it is that there are traumas for which only the most extravagant of illusions will suffice.

One thing, though, is clear. When his old *protégé* came home from South Africa, Widdop – sensing something was gone wrong in him – sought to lead him back to that state of grace in which men start and from which they fall away. He took him off to the Alps.

*

That summer I was too engrossed in my own affairs to trouble overmuch about the lives of others. Mentally I had already cast off the shackles, marvelling at the irony by which qualification should be the instrument that released me from a career in medicine. I returned to finish my stint as MacSelf's dresser, not expecting to be called upon to perform anything more demanding than sponging away blood, and handing up the surgical instruments. A brutal shock lay in store.

It was my first day back in the theatre. MacSelf was

preparing to remove a fatty tumour from the neck of the patient. I had taken up my usual position slightly behind his elbow, and had handed him the scalpel, when his registrar asked if he was aware we had a qualified dresser on the firm.

MacSelf looked sideways at me. "Is this true ?"

I nodded.

Macself handed back the scalpel.

I stared at him. At first I thought he was joking. Then, with horror, it dawned on me that he was perfectly serious.

He gestured invitingly. "Now's as good a time as any."

No doubt it was kindly meant. As operations go, it couldn't have been simpler. I had to start sometime. How better, than under his eye ?

That was not how I saw it at the time. Such a brutal introduction – without warning, with no chance to prepare myself. It was wholly out of character with the kindly consideration with which he'd always treated me. In a daze, I took up the knife. Inwardly I was shaking so much I wondered if I would be able to hold it. Up to that point I'd scarcely taken note of the patient. Now I saw it was a young woman. Blissfully anaesthetised, she seemed utterly remote from the drama about to enfold her. She might have had no connection with the anterior triangle of the neck, on which I was now desperately trying to focus my attention. I could scarcely see for the sweat stinging my eyes. I was acutely conscious that a slip on my part might carry the blade through the carotid sheath, and thus make a clean sweep of artery, vein and vagus nerve. It was the most frightening moment of my life. I still have the impression that I carried out the operation without drawing breath – perhaps because only when I'd got her safely sewn up was I able to breathe freely.

That summer the world lay at my feet. I was in the grip of a feverish anticipation – that wholly consuming excitement at the prospect of adventure, which only those who have known the condition are likely to understand. I was going to Spitzbergen: a region of extraordinary interest, according to Conway, only indifferently explored, and rich in every form of life. There would be peaks to climb, maps and surveys to be made, animals and plants to be observed and studied. There was probably no district in the whole archipelago which would so well reward the season's work. All this was to take place in the next university long vacation, which coincided, more or less, with the short Arctic summer. I had a bare twelve months to prepare for the task ahead. My head was filled with a mass of details all clamouring for attention. I studied maps. I drew up lists of stores (Conway laid great emphasis upon a liberal supply of tinned brown sugar). I drafted letters to agents in Tromso enquiring after the commissioning of a suitable boat. At Edgingtons I discussed the design of tents. I placed notices in the personal columns of The Times inviting enquiries from interested men. Endless agonizing over the composition of the party had finally resolved itself in favour of a botanist, an ecologist, some strong sledgers, a surveyor and geologist, and an experienced Alpine mountaineer. I myself would serve for doctor and ornithologist. In all this, Conway was my enthusiastic tutor. His sessions of practical advice were punctuated with memories of the far north: of sea fogs and Brocken spectres, of toppling bergs thrashing about like dying whales, and pack ice growling along the side of the boat as one lay in one's bunk. *There were times, I can tell you, when I was jolly glad to find myself still in the land of the living.*

It was my first experience of 'expedition fever', that sustained anticipatory excitement that grips the mind to the exclusion of all else. It had nothing to do with the thought of fame or fortune. Had Conway assured me, then and there, that no one would give two hoots for our explorations it would have made no difference. It was the glamour, the romance of the thing that bore me up. Agnes used to twit me about what she called my 'mania for adventure': *Every day a plunge into something new.*

Her teasing was affectionate, for she loved me dearly, yet I knew she thought it irresponsible. Well, we were different, she and I. Different, yet yolks of the same egg: she, swayed by youth's generous impulse to identify with all the world; I, bound by a kinship with all wild and lonely places.

*

On Monday afternoons I usually went to tea at Onslow Place. I knew, the moment I arrived, that something had happened. A subdued Millie showed me into the morning room. Mother was sitting at her writing table.

She rose, her face grave, to greet me. Instinctively I thought of Rufus.

"George," she said gently, "I've afraid we've received some rather sad news." She'd had a telephone call from my Uncle Giles. "Your grandfather died early this morning."

I was too stunned to take it in, my mind still insisting mechanically, *No, it's Rufus.*

Tea took its course, a subdued, melancholy ritual: Dora, impassive as ever; Dolly, weepy-eyed, her head bent over her stitching. She wept for any death, irrespective of the corpse.

"You must go, of course," my mother sighed.

That night I took the sleeper north. Though sleep was a long time coming. I lay in my berth hearing the drumbeat of the wheels, my mind drifting back to the expeditions of my childhood, and the romance of that journey: drifting off to sleep among the huddled roofs and chimneys of outer London, waking, as the train hauled itself towards Rannoch Moor in the dawn light, past wastes of peat and heather, silent lochs like vast sheets of pewter stretching into the distance, the wild-looking men waiting for us in the hills, the short, stocky figure who might have been a robber chief, except that he was my grandfather. And, in my awe-struck eyes, unlike anyone else in all the world.

My Uncle Guy greeted me in the library.

"He was fishing," he said, as we went upstairs. "It seems he stumbled, fell into the burn, and took a chill. Then pneumonia set in."

We halted beside a door. As my uncle's hand closed on the handle I felt a tremor of alarm. Never before had I set foot in grandfather's bedroom. We went forward into a velvety darkness. I sensed, rather than saw, a lofty ceiling, curtains drawn against the light. My eye was drawn to the figure, motionless in the great bed. I gazed down at an eroded face: eyes sunk deep in the skull: hooked, beaky nose. No hint, there, of serene old age. It was as if death had stripped away the last of life's concealments. Shrunken, withered, he had the look of some mountain raptor, denizen of stony heights, of mummifying winds and blinding light.

Just five of us gathered in the library. As well as my uncles and myself, there was the young doctor from Glenorchy, and the gouty laird, more apoplectic than ever.

"Awfu' shame," he kept saying. "Awfu' shame."

None of my aunts was present. None of my cousins. Giles had arrived the previous day.

"Rufus wanted to come with me," he said. " 'It'll be the death of you,' I told him."

From outside the windows came a crunching of gravel as the ghillies gathered, caps in hand, to pay their last respects. It was a brilliant morning, sunlight dancing on the water, greenshank piping, as we carried him to the old burial ground on a tongue of land above the loch. Below us, where the wind was whipping up white horses, the light was dazzling. Never could death have seemed so peripheral, so out of place. The glen seemed to vibrate with vast currents of energy flowing and driving everywhere, bundling up the clouds on the hill, setting the gulls screaming out on the loch. We were putting the turfs on him, yet the rocks, the sand on the shore, even the air, seemed charged with his presence.

I thought of him casting a fly where the current swirled into the burn, eyes narrowed against the glare off the stream, that deft down-turn of the wrist ... Up on the hill he was lying flat in the heather, watching a hind washing its calf ... He preferred animals to human beings.

I stayed on after the funeral. My uncles seemed anxious to get away. There were still matters to be attended to, and I was glad to volunteer. I saw them off, then walked in the woods about the house. I sat for a while in the clearing, on the flat stone where we'd sat together the year before.

My mother loathed him. My sister Dolly thought him *a perfectly horrible old man*. It made no difference. He had been the corner-stone of my life. I couldn't believe he was gone. It didn't seem possible. He was so vividly present to my mind: that way he had of screwing up his eyes, brows bristling, as he stared out at the hills; the rough, still-Northumbrian voice: *In the wild nothing dies of old age. When an animal is too old or weak to fend for itself something else will kill it.*

Final infirmity – for him the worst that could befall a man. I was glad he'd been spared that.

That evening the dour Glaswegian housekeeper served my solitary meal. "The maister always sat to his supper in the library. Nae doot ye'll be wantin the same."

Through the windows fell thick slabs of yellow light: the long, lingering light of a northern summer. The wind had dropped. The house was wrapped in a great stillness. No sound of a world outside. Only the furtive scraping of my knife and fork. The soft slow ticking of the library clock. As I ate my supper I tasted something of the silence and solitude of grandfather's life. Only a great intensity of purpose, I reflected, could have withstood that solitude. Slowly, surely, it stripped away his other selves, and left him with his task.

Towering shelves held the great collection of books and periodicals, most of them bound in volumes: *Nature, Land and Water, The Field*, to which he had contributed countless articles, the basis of his definitive work, *The Red Deer of the Scottish Highlands*. Box-files contained the papers and cuttings, a vast assemblage of extracts and clippings relating to the natural history of the region. In front of the table where I sat stood the tall glass-fronted bookcase devoted to his game books and field notebooks: pages filled with meticulous drawings and observations; sketches of curiosities made to illustrate some condition or effect in Nature – bones, tiny skulls, a comb from a wasp's nest, ancient tree roots washed out of the peat, antler forms. All minutely observed. Every day he spent on the hill was logged in painstaking detail. The work of half a life-time. Yet all this was merely the husk, the outer semblance, of the mystery that was his life. Suddenly I was overwhelmed by the slightness of my own knowledge, and the vastness of what there was to be known. All I found in my own life was illusion. I yearned for some contact with a reality other than my own, some dimension of existence in which it was possible to imagine that stifling ignorance at last dropping away. Or was that too only an illusion?

Above the fireplace hung his portrait, painted relatively late in life. I'd never liked it. I thought it a travesty of the romantic figure I'd treasured from childhood. Now I saw it presented him as he must have seen himself – something of a contradiction. He sat in a wooden armchair, an urbane figure in country tweeds painted against the loom of the Black Mount. His face was raised to far horizons, or else in contemplation of the mountain wilderness that moved him so. The setting sun cast a yellowish light on lean, leathery features: an English gentleman, confronting his own imminent extinction with unwavering eye.

How much of a man's life, one hears it said, is a journey round one's father. Yet my own father, so formidable when I was twenty, seems to me now a figure from another age. Strange, abrupt old man. All my life I have been answering to you.

A few days later I left the Black Mount, for ever as I thought. Years were to pass before I saw those hills again. Next morning, on the platform at King's Cross, I was hailed by a familiar voice. It was Slater, his carroty hair aflame. Now married, and soon to take up the post of assistant surgeon at St Thomas's, he seemed more than usually full of himself. He insisted on taking me to breakfast.

"But I've had breakfast," I protested. "I haven't," said Slater. "Come on."

Some minutes later I found myself sitting irritably over a pot of tea while Slater wolfed down ham and eggs. He was full of news, and eager to acquaint me with the new sensation. It concerned a new climb up the long steep slab projecting to one side of the Central Buttress of Scawfell. It was not a feature I'd ever heard remarked on as worthy of attention. That Botterill strayed on to it, as I learned later, was something of an accident. Failing to get started in a corner crack, where the slab lay up against the buttress, he was driven to try its outside edge.

Slater and his new wife (at which point I gathered he'd actually taken her on honeymoon to Wastdale) had been among a small group gazing up in wonderment. Now he gave a rousing account of what followed: Botterill advancing up the slab via fingery lesions, mere slits in the rock, ice axe clenched cutlass fashion between his teeth. At length, reaching a small niche, Botterill had cleared it of vegetation and swung up to sit in triumph, squatting like a monkey on a perch.

"All of a sudden he must have noticed us. At least, he noticed Muriel, for he raised his hat to her. Can you imagine it ? In such a situation ? It struck her as so comical a thing she burst out laughing."

Yet had Botterill fallen, I reflected, he must surely have been killed. Eighty feet above his second, belayed at the base of the slab, he was far beyond the point at which the rope could be considered a safeguard.

"I dare say it'll put Lockhart out no end," Slater added mischievously. "He's dying to do a new route on Scawfell."

He looked at me slyly from under his pale lashes.

As I sipped my tea I reflected I'd never cared that much for Slater.

It was mid-morning by the time I got back to Ludgate Hill. On the hall table, delivered that very morning, lay a telegram from Widdop: *Come for lunch tomorrow stop Garrick stop something big.*

I'd no idea Widdop was a member of the Garrick. Though it came as no surprise. I was uneasy at the thought of lunching there again. I hadn't been there since Father's death, and hadn't thought to go again. All the same I was curious to know what Widdop wanted. *Something big* had exactly that note of drama I'd come to associate with him.

I'd no idea when he expected us to lunch. He hadn't suggested a time. One o'clock seemed civilised to me. Nevertheless I turned up good and early. As a consequence, I had almost hour in which to kick my heels.

I sat in a curtained recess set apart from the members on the other side of the partition, turning the pages of *Punch*, waiting for Widdop as, in the past, I'd waited uncomfortably for Father. Widdop knew nothing about my proposed expedition to Spitzbergen, and I was wondering uncertainly whether or not to volunteer the news. He was bound to ask what I'd been up to. I decided, rather than risk exposing my plans to Widdop's unpredictable response, to keep it to myself, at least for the time being. Suddenly the curtain swished aside and a spare figure strode to greet me, hand out-stretched.

"George, I'm so sorry ... "

Widdop had a lean hard look about him. It was the look, unmistakeable, of a man recently returned from a season in the Alps. Still uttering apologies, he ushered me up the stairs to the dining room. Luncheon got under way amid a casual exchange of news. I mentioned my grandfather's death.

"It was rather a shock," I said. "He'd had a fall."

"It comes to us all, George." Widdop, though, spoke with

the carelessness of a man in proven condition, a man possessed of a mind and body he knew he could count on.

It had been, by any standard, an outstanding season – the Täschhorn by the Teufelsgrat, the Zinal Rothorn, the traverse of the Ober Gabelhorn, the Dent Blanche. Of his own part in these triumphs Widdop said little. Though he was full of praise for Masterman, whose first season had been 'absolutely outstanding'. I was reminded of the loyalties which lent such fierceness to Widdop's friendship, reflecting that he'd never ceased to speak of his old protégé in terms unchanged from schooldays. *The most outstanding of my boys.*

So far Widdop had made no reference to the purpose of our meeting. The revelation, when it came, was so casual as to seem almost studied.

"The thing is, George," said Widdop, leaning back to signal to a waiter, "Lockhart intends having another shot at reaching Hopkinson's Cairn."

He scribbled his signature on the bill, then clasped his hands and eyed me across the table.

"I want you to come with us."

I was dumbfounded.

"It's never been done," I faltered, too staggered to know what else to say.

"Ah, but it will be," he said firmly. "We shall do it."

Widdop's voice, the emphasis he placed on that inclusive 'we', his gaze – frank, challenging – admitted no possibility of failure.

Suddenly I was seized with an enormous excitement. At the same time I remembered my last sight of Lockhart. That strained, exhausted look. How was he, I enquired, as casually as I could.

"Lockhart ? Oh, he's fine. He's in tip-top form."

XXV

In Wastdale I heard more about Lockhart's summer.

"He's been up here a lot these last few weeks," Ritson told me. "He's here now. Camping in our field."

The reports of his climbs, all of them hard, are still to be seen in the Climbing Book, entered in a small neat hand. One in particular, a lone ascent of Savage Gully, strikes me now as reflecting his state of mind: a mixture of finely calculated transfers and fierce committing moves. Thwarted, disappointed in one direction, Lockhart had begun to push himself unsparingly in another.

Not long afterwards Lockhart himself arrived back at the inn. He'd been for a walk. He didn't say where. Flushed from his exertions, he looked a different man from the pale ghost I'd visited in Cambridge a few months earlier. He greeted me warmly, but made no mention of the attempt on Hopkinson's cairn. Though I was itching to talk about it, I had to look for another topic of conversation.

Casually, over tea, I brought up the subject of Rutherford's election to the Royal Society.

"I imagine you must have known him," I ventured.

I'd read in *The Times* that before his move to Montreal, Rutherford had also worked at the Cavendish under Thomson. Anxious to air my few, newly-acquired scraps of knowledge (the article having included a paragraph on radioactive emissions), I ventured some remark on the subject of the strange phenomena which, as I understood it, had been puzzling physicists since they were first observed some years earlier. Hadn't Rutherford propounded an explanation wholly at odds with the accepted view ? (It was, of course, a radical advance of the kind poor

Lockhart would so dearly have loved to achieve.)

He seemed to take my enquiry at face value.

"I've always thought it had to be explained in terms of a divisible atom," he said. "Though that's quite contrary to the principles of chemistry. Now we have a solution. And it's beautiful. Quite beautiful."

No words of mine could convey the way he said it. His face was full of wonder and admiration.

The inn was half-empty that weekend. Though the autumn term had not yet begun, a week of wind and rain had brought summer to an end. Signs of the storm were still evident in the dale – the lake a dull, soupy brown, fragments of green ash twigs strewn about the lane. Scarcely a dozen of us sat down to dinner on the Saturday evening. Widdop, Lockhart, of course. An unexpected visitor was Slater, snatching a last break before taking up his duties at St.Thomas's. Masterman, looking fit after his season in the Alps, greeted me amiably. If he recalled his disclosures with any embarrassment, he gave no hint of it. Again I wondered if he had spoken as revealingly to Widdop.

A propitious omen, as it seemed, was the unexpected presence in our midst of a figure from the Golden Age. Years had passed since the day when, spread-eagled upside down on the Y boulder, I first set eyes on Prebendary Iremonger. Then old beyond years, he seemed no older now.

Among a handful of others, mostly known to me, was a large man with a penetrating voice. I asked Widdop who he was.

"Oh, Professor Somebody-or-other. Lockhart knows him."

He was a newcomer to the district, a fact for which he seemed to feel some sort of apology was required.

"The Pen-y-pass is more my stamping ground," I heard him explaining yet again to Masterman.

Earlier that day, as a preparation, we'd repeated Abraham's climb on the West wall of Pillar Rock. Clear skies had promised well. We'd set off in flinty sunlight, between fells heaving up rust-red, silver-birches a bright gold above the beck. But the foul weather earlier in the week had left its mark. The crag was in poor condition, the rock coated an evil green. I, for one, found it an unnerving sight, though Lockhart appeared quite unaffected. If it troubled him, he gave no sign. He banished it, just as he banished those nagging anxieties that offered so much distraction to my own mental life. *One has to*, he once told me, *if one is to go on climbing.*

We came back with an hour or so of light remaining. The deep trench of Wastdale, as well as the shoulder of Lingmell beyond, was already sinking towards night. Clearly visible above the gloom of Hollow Stones, picked out by the westering sun, was Scawfell Crag: the Pinnacle thrusting forward from the black shadow of Deep Ghyll, grey rock faintly tinged with gold. I felt a frisson of excitement. A thrill of fear and eagerness. I turned to glance back at the party, and saw Lockhart, deft, sure-footed, picking his way among the stones. There was something inexpressibly comforting in the sight. Hands in pockets, coil of rope about the shoulders, he seemed to have touched some deep core in himself: a man assured of his life. I found it heartening beyond words.

Dinner that evening was a light-hearted affair. Though we were few in number, the atmosphere was jolly. Widdop, as usual, was in high spirits. Though neither he nor Lockhart made any mention of the purpose which had brought the four of us together, there was nothing unusual in that. Most men were fairly cagey when it came to a new climb. After an estimation of the merits of Abraham's climb, conversation turned to some droll event that had taken place that summer on the Wetterhorn. The long table rang with high good-humour: the laughter of men at home in their world, and at ease with one another. There was much ribbing of Slater, not three months married. "We see before us," declared Widdop, "a man so bored by the comforts of connubial bliss as to prefer the prospect of sodden breeches and a slicing wind."

Seated at the end of the table, I was to some extent cut off from the merriment. My efforts to share in it were frustrated by the professor, lecturing Masterman and myself on some aspect of classical philology. Since we were indebted to him for the claret we were drinking we felt obliged to listen. He was an academic of a sort I never much cared for: one of those dons whose interventions steer any conversation in the direction of their own specialism. On and on he droned, while further down the table the laughter, fuelled by Widdop's quips and sallies, flourished infuriatingly just out of earshot. Meanwhile the professor was warming to his theme.

"When you come to think of it, in the Greek word *aretê*, which we translate as 'virtue', one can hear the clanging tone of Ares, god of battle. So it seems an odd joke indeed that the word 'virtue', which originally meant virility in a man, has come in our times to mean chastity in a woman."

He paused to refill his glass.

"The Romans knew better. Thus, on the first page of Caesar's *Gallic Wars*, the word '*virtus*' means courage and martial valour. Just the kind of thing a military man would fear in his enemy and desire in his own men."

He turned towards his neighbour, evidently confident of agreement. Masterman, toying with the stem of his glass, looked thoughtful. "Believe me," he said quietly, "a battlefield is a place of terror. Every man, without exception, is afraid."

He lit a cigarette. "It seems to me," he went on, "that bravery has very little to do with indifference to danger, which is a negative thing anyway. More than anything it's a matter of disposition. Of moral force. Poor Hensley taught us that. The best of men. We lost him at Taba Nyama. He'd been in it from the start – Dundee, Farquhar's Farm, Colenso, and the Sudan before that. To say that he was much loved is to do less than justice to what we felt for him. He was our rock. To the men in his company he was a father-figure. There were no lengths he wouldn't go to, no trouble he wouldn't take where it concerned the welfare of his men."

Masterman took a sip of wine. "Hensley saw to everything – right down to the condition of their feet," he said, with a grimace which set us laughing. "I expect every regiment has its little core of officers like Hensley. There will be more dashing fellows. But they never last – the philanderers, the hard drinkers. They flash into view, dazzle us all for a year or two, and go their way. Usually they get into some scrape or other, and that's that. The rocks remain rocks."

After dinner the older men gathered as usual in the smoke room. Others headed for the billiard room. Fully expecting Slater to come looking for me, I slipped out into the hall. I was in no mood for his antics. A few moments later I found myself beside the beck at the back of the inn. Everything was gloomed over. Already the first stars had begun to glitter above the dark rim of the hills.

I walked without any thought of direction, wandering on past Row Head, and part way up the lower slopes of the fell. My mind was full of Masterman's eulogy for his dead officer friend. It was, I reflected, Widdop's own ideal. To be a man as simply, as dependably, as rock is rock. Widdop thought Masterman was a rock. How I envied it. That constancy. I wondered if they had any objective existence. These 'rocks'. Or were they simply necessary fictions ? Not the thing itself. Only an image of the thing. The lodestar of my childhood had been the Henty hero. Newbolt wrote poems about him. Haggard and Stevenson found in him the image of a universal character – that figure on the fringe of vision, crossing the jungle clearing, at the edge of the glacier. He haunted all our boyhood dreams. But Masterman, it struck me, had been paying tribute not primarily to a brave man, but to a good man. What was it about the good that moved us so ? That drew us towards them ? I thought of Hensley, and suddenly I remembered something Lockhart had said about *fidelity to the task*.

And what if the task was an illusion ...

Far off, across the lake, the lights of a farm stood out, a lonely glimmer against the black fellside. Below, away to my right, I heard the murmur of Mosedale Beck. There was something reassuring in the sound – some sense, I suppose, of the known, familiar. I caught sight of the inn, a pale blur below. Laughter round the fire, the company of friends – suddenly they seemed the dearest things on earth.

Some memories never fade. The scene that greeted me as I opened the smoke room door is still vivid after twenty years: the Professor, all smiling enquiry; Masterman, long legs stretched out across the hearth; Lockhart, a little apart as usual, turning the pages of the Climbing Book, and Widdop's voice, neutral, non-committal:

"It's simply a cairn on a ledge. We hope to climb up to it. That's all."

Then, unexpectedly, a dry ancient voice broke the silence.

"I was there," it said. "Though not ... er ... one of the party."

Turning, I caught a glimpse of snow-white whiskers, a purplish face half-smiling from the wing-chair.

The old clergyman embarked on a meandering account of the building of the cairn, and the many attempts to reach it from below. We listened in respectful silence – the Professor, with every show of wishing to contribute.

"In the eleventh century,' he began, as soon as the old man had finished, 'men embarking on your sort of enterprise would quite likely have had recourse to the *Sortes Virgilianae*."

He gazed around expectantly. In the fire a log collapsed in a small shower of sparks. No one offered a response.

"What might that be ?" enquired Masterman eventually.

"In the middle ages," began the Professor, "Virgil was thought to have foretold the coming of Christianity. It won him the reputation of seer *non pareil*. Accordingly, on the eve of some great or perilous venture, the men of old would summon Virgil to discover the fate of their expedition."

"I shouldn't think Ritson's library runs to a Virgil," remarked Widdop ironically. "How about *Barrack Room Ballads* ?"

"It should be a lofty poet," said the Professor reprovingly. "Or at least a poet of lofty aspiration. Someone remote from the mundane world."

"Milton, perhaps?" suggested Iremonger. "I think I might know where to put my hand on Milton."

Widdop groaned.

"Right, Milton it is !" said the Professor briskly. "Now. We shall need a key, and the book, of course."

"And a table," added Iremonger. "The book should be placed on a table. Though if, ah ... I remember aright, the key has to be inserted by a child or virgin."

"Or a clergyman," concluded the Professor. "Clearly Dr.

Iremonger is our man."

As there was no suitable table present in the room Masterman offered to fetch one. He returned carrying a small folding card table, and the key to the front door.

Meanwhile, the Professor was explaining the procedure. "We must have a direct question. And it must be something on which we're all in agreement."

After some discussion a form of words was settled. The Professor wrote them down.

What fortune awaits Lockhart's party ?

"It's, er ... my understanding," said Dr. Iremonger softly, "that those putting the question should, er ... sign their names. Isn't that so ?"

"In blood, no doubt," murmured Widdop.

"Ink will be quite satisfactory." Clearly, the old man was enjoying himself.

Masterman, sitting in Collie's chair smoking a cigarette, looked on in mystified amusement.

One by one, somewhat self-consciously, we added our signatures to the paper.

Solemnly Iremonger held up the key for our inspection, rather like a conjurer exhibiting an object with which he intended to perform some sleight of hand. He then placed it, not, as one might have expected, more or less in the middle of the volume, but right at the front. Holding the key carefully in position, he conveyed the book to the Professor, offering it with a slight, sacerdotal inclination of the head.

The old man was bent upon making mischief. Of that I had no doubt.

The Professor opened the book. I watched his eyes scanning the lines. The silence seemed to go on for ever. Face expressionless, he scanned them again.

Then, in a flat, matter-of-fact voice, he began to read aloud:

"Him the Almighty Power
Hurled headlong flaming from the ethereal sky,
With hideous ruin and combustion, down
To bottomless perdition, there to dwell
In adamantine chains and penal fire,
Who durst defy the Omnipotent to arms."

For long seconds no one spoke.

At length Widdop, whose expression throughout the Professor's reading, bore a gleam of fixed amusement, roused himself to mutter something about 'the unfailing thud' of Milton's metre. Other than that, no one had anything to say. The firelight flickered shadows to and fro across the walls. Slater and his friends, banging about in the billiard room, seemed a whole world away.

"Well," said Masterman eventually, uncrossing his long legs, "if it's to be adamantine chains and so forth on the morrow, I think I'd better get some sleep."

Flinging his cigarette into the fire he bade us all a genial 'Good night'.

That weekend I slept in an unfamiliar room right at the top of the inn, isolated at the end of a corridor. I lay for a long time without undressing, staring at the ceiling. From time to time I felt a dull anger directed towards the Professor. I'd been irritated, earlier that evening, by the presumption with which he, a civilian, had offered to instruct Masterman in the manly virtues. There must be, I thought, some self assurance peculiar to academics that rendered them immune to the ordinary sorts of circumspection. I'd even felt nervous on his account, fearing an outburst from Widdop. Now I cursed the entirely uncharacteristic forbearance that had spared the man to entangle us in his wretched girls' parlour game. In the train, the day before, watching the Wastdale hills gradually coming into view with that familiar mixture of apprehension and excitement, it had dawned on me that I was travelling towards the most serious undertaking of my life. Now Scawfell Crag loomed, an enormous shadow, between me and the future. Indeed, there *was* no future until the next day's business was concluded.

Why on earth had I agreed to do it ...

I stared at the wall, where the candle flame threw a soaring shadow up the plaster and across the ceiling. Now and then, as the flame juddered, the shadow of the ewer lurched grotesquely. I was struck by the sparseness of the room, a thing I'd never been conscious of before at Wastdale. Chair, washstand, basin and ewer: it brought to mind the bare room in Park Terrace. Where, I wondered, did he keep his rope, his boots ? Shoved out of sight. Out of mind, perhaps. Then I remembered the photograph propped on the mantelpiece – the line of white dots that went so far, then stopped.

The sleeping house was wrapped in a deep stillness. Only now and then some soft sound broke silence. The creak of a door. A stealthy tread on a loose board. Sounds which, in my wakeful state, I found vaguely reassuring. My mind returned to the foolish act of sortilege we had engaged in earlier. Strangely, I could remember nothing of the Milton. Not a line. Only an unmistakeable impression of menace that even the Professor's monotone mutter failed to neutralise. Well, a big climb always entailed fear, always uncertainty as to what lay ahead. But usually there was courage too, and fear was made supportable by the comradeship of friends. I was determined not to let them down. I made up my mind not to be intimidated. Not to be cowed into seeing the crag as an awestruck tourist sees it. Look at it like

Lockhart, I urged myself. Look for the line. Forget the rest, and concentrate on the line.

But Lockhart had retreated.

Alone, unroped, he'd come within seventy feet of the cairn. Success had seemed within his grasp. And he retreated. At the time I'd put it down to the conditions. Yet, as we went down together to the inn, he responded to my attempts at conversation in mono-syllables, or not at all. Silent, dispirited, he was totally cast down. *The mist, he said, was in myself.*

At the time I'd made nothing of it. I'd put it down to that self-deprecating habit. Even so, I couldn't believe it was fear. No frightened man could have climbed down over a hundred feet of steep slabs in safety. Besides, climbing for Lockhart was too much a matter of calculation for fear to enter into it. A difficulty offered itself, one worked out a solution, tested it, and so on, step by step, until one reached the top. It was his 'methodical progression'.

Yet what if some sudden uneasiness that painstaking mind could neither shake off nor ignore ...

No one had climbed there since OGJ. And what if, looking up at dozens of feet of rock, he was struck by the uncertainty of what lay ahead, the fact that only one man had passed that way before – and that man notorious for his recklessness, who might have avoided disaster on some desperate passage through good fortune. And even his luck had run out in the end.

Speculations a climber's mind should have shoved aside ? Yet suppose Lockhart's sceptical intelligence had asserted itself. Somewhere that questing gaze had encountered a gap, a discontinuity. *It wouldn't 'go'.*

Stiff with cold, I lay in a kind of stupor. Thoughts came and went seemingly of their own accord. He said it was a climb to do alone. Now he wanted a rope of four. A *strong team*, as

Widdop put it.

Again the crag loomed in my mind, grim, forbidding, skeins of wet mist drifting between its tilted buttresses. I studied the huge upheavings and collapses, the rubble spilling down below. Extraordinary, to think that anyone could ever conceive of it except as a scene of chaos and confusion. Suddenly I saw that rock was simply rock. All dreams, all aspirations, fell short of the reality. One encountered that on the face. Just as one made the crucial discoveries only on the face.

Somewhere a clock struck remotely. I lay staring into a void in which nothing took shape. There was nothing there. Simply rock. Blank rock, on which the mind could make no impression. And maybe sometimes it came down in the end to that: to the recognition that one could make no sense of things. And what took over then ? I thought of Widdop. Provocative in all things, he commended *reck-lessness*. Literally, not reckoning the loss. Jones and Botterill pushed on regardless. That kind of careless daring was not in Lockhart's nature. Then I understood something I hadn't grasped before; saw it quite clearly; saw it, not as a limitation in the man, but as profoundest truth. At some deep level, Lockhart did not trust himself. And he was right. Something in men was not to be trusted.

The guttering candle eventually caught my attention. It had burnt down to its socket. Shivering, I undressed and slipped into the welcome warmth my body had impressed between the sheets. For a while I hovered on the borders of sleep. From time to time thoughts of my companions drifted sluggishly through my mind ... Masterman, his long legs stetched out before the control, so reassuring in a second man ... Hitherto I'd seen in in them an integrity I could never hope to emulate. Now it seemed I scarcely knew them at all.

XXVI

I have tried, times without number, going over the events of that night, to assure myself that my misgivings were well founded. Yet to this day I have never been able to think of what followed, except as an act of sheer funk.

Had it been one of those mellow autumn mornings – soft shadows, that low, slanting sunlight delighting the senses with anticipation – things might have turned out very different. My night thoughts might have dissipated with the vapour rising off the fells. But the day dawned overcast. An edgy wind rattled the leaves outside my window. Instead, as darkness faded and grey light spread slowly through the room, my fears took on a hard-edged presence.

I knew I couldn't climb that day. At the same time I was filled with panic at the thought of facing Widdop. For I knew it had to be Widdop and no other to whom I broke the news. Miserably I ran through lines that never seemed to serve, however I phrased them. *If it's all the same to you, Widdop, I'd rather not climb today ... Actually, I think I'll give it a miss ...*

I strove for a casual, airy delivery. For I knew there could be no question of concocting a bogus excuse – feeling out of sorts, that sort of thing. In the end it came out as a shame-faced mumble.

We'd come face to face on the landing as I was returning from the bathroom. Widdop, of course, was perfectly decent about it. At first he said nothing. He looked at me intently – a long steady gaze. I felt like one of his boys.

"I do hope you're not allowing last night's nonsense to affect you, George ?"

"No, no." I was well aware my hasty disclaimer carried no conviction.

241

"No, not at all."

Another silence. The same long level look.

"Well, naturally, no one would wish you to climb if you don't want to."

There was only kindness in his voice. He even broke the news to Lockhart, collecting his shirt and breeches from the banisters.

"I'm afraid we shall have to manage without Hazard," I heard him saying, loudly enough for me to overhear. "He's feeling rather off colour this morning. Naturally, he wouldn't want to hold us up."

Quietly I closed my door. I sat awhile on the edge of my bed. Profoundly ashamed, and yet profoundly grateful, I could have cried for very relief. It left me with a sense of indebtedness to Widdop that nothing could obliterate. I feel it to this day.

I went down to breakfast. To do so was a matter of such pride as I had left. I had let myself down in front of my friends, and the thought of skulking in my room only seemed to compound the offence. No, I couldn't do that.

Kindness completed my humiliation.

"Last night's tapioca pudding?" enquired Slater with a grin, as I picked at a piece of toast.

"Oh, what bad luck," said Masterman.

His lean face reflected only concern at my disappointment.

Clegg showed up after breakfast. He was carrying a brand new Alpine rope.

"I hope it's the real thing," Widdop called to him as he stood at the hall door.

"Beale's," Clegg shouted back. "It came up on the train from London."

Proudly he displayed the blood-red thread of worsted twisted with the strands.

There was a quite a crowd in the hall: Iremonger, stovepipe hat in hand, the Professor, fussing over the bags. They were leaving together that morning. The trap was waiting in the yard to take them to Seascale. Lockhart was hunting through a pile of ropes when Masterman came bounding down the staircase, almost cannoning into him. Widdop had gone over to inspect Clegg's new rope. Now he came back with the youth in tow.

"I've asked Clegg to come with us," he announced to Lockhart.

"It's your rope he really wants," sang out Slater from the landing.

As I looked at the boyish figure, blinking sandy lashes, grinning his delight, I felt ashamed of my fears, which had already begun to seem as foolish as they were cowardly. For I knew I had deprived myself of more than an adventure. Clegg, though, could hardly believe his luck.

I went out into the yard to see them off.

"Don't let Slater scoff all the cake," was Widdop's parting shot. "We shall expect a decent brew when we get back."

I watched as they set off down the lane. "Good luck," I shouted again.

Only Clegg turned to wave. For a while I lost them as they crossed the fields. Then they re-appeared, climbing through the bracken, Lockhart drawing ahead as usual, the other three bunched together as they rounded the shoulder of Lingmell. Last to disappear was the tall figure of Masterman. I hung about the inn for a while – I felt I had to keep up Widdop's pretence that I was feeling 'out of sorts' – until Slater offered to take me for a walk.

We set off towards Sty Head, turning aside to take the Corridor route to Scawfell Pike. It was a cold grey day, with a blustery wind gusting in our faces as we toiled over the stony summit of the Pike. I wondered how they were faring in that wind. On our way down to Mickledore we cut across to the Pulpit Rock for a view of Scawfell Crag. But though the Pinnacle was plainly visible we saw no sign of Lockhart's party. It was not until we came down into the green hollow below Mickledore that I spotted them.

There's no mistaking a dead man at any distance. There's a candour, a nakedness of attitude that fixes the attention. Mostly the fallen look what they are. Stricken. Shocked at their fate. It was, then, a mark still of innocence, or else of *naïveté*, that my first thought, on seeing my friends stretched out among the stones, should have been that they were sleeping.

Masterman, in particular, seemed almost alive. Flung down like that, he could have been in the throes of violent struggle: his stare lit with the rictus of intense effort, or else the urgency of some desperate communication. He might have been on the point of gasping something out.

Clegg was still breathing. All entangled in his new rope, I saw at once that he was terribly smashed-up. He grinned up at me.

I took his hand in mine. He whispered something. I bent low, put my ear to his mouth.

"I need ... a piss."

I sat with him while Slater went for help. Though the poor fellow was altogether beyond any aid that men could render. He was in such dreadful pain I was reluctant to question him. Yet something was troubling him. The head, shifting restlessly, seemed somehow separate from the shattered body. I mistook this restlessness for pain, not recognizing what later was to become all too familiar in dying men – that summoning of strength to launch fragments of words, squeezed out on the shallow, sighing breath.

"Dr. Lockhart ... tired ... changed places ... with the Captain ... "

How long he'd lain on the scree before we found him, I cannot say. It was almost midnight when we finally got him on to the hurdle. He was conscious all those hours. He spoke very little. Mere mutterings. Nothing that I could make sense of. Most of the time his eyes were closed. If they opened they fixed themselves on mine.

The slow hours passed. Now and then came the cry of a bird or animal. I sat clutching Clegg's hand, my mind drawn fearfully again and again, then sheering away from imaginings I desperately wanted not to contemplate: Masterman dropping like a stone – the rope snatched from Lockhart's hands – then Widdop, plucked from the rock – poor Clegg's sheer disbelief, his sense of utter abandonment, knowing his turn had come ...

It grew dark: that close, dense darkness of the hills at night. Gradually Clegg's face faded with the light. I kept hold of his hand.

The rescuers arrived at intervals. First up was a boy from one of the farms. A lantern, bobbing over the brow of Brown Tongue – then a youthful voice hailing through the darkness. *You don't want to see this*, was my first thought. I believe I half rose, thinking to cut him off.

Impossible, in that darkness, to bring away all four. Yet some instinct demanded we do everything in our power to rescue the living, hopeless though we knew it to be. For Clegg, incredibly, was still alive. He moaned as we put him on the hurdle. He was so entangled in his rope we had to cut it from him to get him free.

It was a nightmare journey: lanterns flashing on the scree, on the white, drained face, boots stumbling against stones, the night so black and ground so steep and rough that with every step one felt on the point of plunging into some pit of darkness.

It took four hours to get back to Wastdale. Clegg died on the way down.

Women from the five farms were waiting in the yard as we carried him to the barn. Twenty years and a multitude of corpses have failed to dim the memory of that scene: the pony stirring in its stall, a startled bird flapping up in the shadows of the rafters, a rustle of straw as we laid the body on the ground. There, with the lantern light flaring on a ring of faces, amid scents of hay and dung, Slater and I pronounced him dead. It was my first certification as a qualified physician.

I sat for what must have been a good while by his body. Though I was aware of Slater waiting in the shadows, the flare of a match as he lit his pipe, I couldn't summon up the strength to go. Exhausted, drained of all emotion, I sat on, my mind a jumble of impressions ... the shepherd boy, coat slung from a shoulder, gazing up in wonderment ... that battered copy of Mason's novel – what was it called ? *A Romance of Wastdale* ... the spellbound youth, sitting at my feet.

I knew he had died the death that was meant for me.

As to what happened, who can say ? It is the man who makes the climb. In the interval of time between each ascent, rock is simply rock. It will become whatever he makes of it: conceder of grudging, minimal concessions, or pitiless inquisitor. *The mist was in myself.* Faced with that sudden, terrible draining of conviction – realising he couldn't continue, recognizing the appalling position they were in, Lockhart might very well have turned to Masterman. The war hero. A tall man with a long reach. He might see them through. After all, they weren't so far from the cairn. Only that final slab. Somehow or other the exchange was made. Somehow, Masterman climbed up into that fearfully exposed position. Stretching, shaking, grabbing for the good incut. He had no technique, according to Slater. Ten years later, when Herford finally climbed up to the cairn, the scratches on the rock were still visible. The ugly marks of sliding nails.

In the inn afterwards we waited for first light to return for the dead. A frightened girl, roused from her bed, lit candles, and set fresh logs among the embers of the kitchen fire. A handful of silent men, we clustered round the hearth.

"Eh, dear o' me." Ritson shook his head over and over again. "It were all he thowt about. I couldn't say how many times Dr. Lockhart borrowed my glasses and went up Hollow Stones. He thowt o' nothin' else."

In his eyes it was beyond all understanding. "He were so set on climbing it, d'you see ? And he thowt he were the man to do it."

They must have *known* it would happen sooner or later-those dalesmen struggling up Brown Tongue with lanterns and hurdles: men profoundly conscious of irascible gods that buried ewes alive, and sent the killing frosts at lambing time. For them it was a thing too obvious for words.

For us it was something never reckoned with until it happened. And our clinging, all through the years that followed, to our valorous reveries – our denial of darkness , our insistence, as the storm-clouds gathered, that there was no darkness. Yet all our adventures were with death. We laughed at it over dinner. We tiptoed round it, we teased it with our ropes. We were David against Goliath, Peter against Hook. We were all manner of things. But we had no knowledge of ourselves: of what we were, of what we were not. We were like characters in a work of fiction. We could not know what would happen next. Even our climbs were a kind of fiction: part of a continuous tale we told about ourselves – not as we were, but as we dreamed of being. Though we were curving, even then, towards our dreadful future.

And what if some high excitement, a thing so exhilarating, so beyond everything ordinarily to be accomplished ...

But we never talked about that. We couldn't talk about that.

Geoffrey Young, so often asked to speak these days at dinners, continues to represent the old Wastdale spirit. For him it remains a timeless place, eternally present: a place free from envy or malice, where mutual sympathy, springing from adventures shared, seals a bond between loyal and generous hearts.

For my part, I cannot see that life can ever again be as it was: or that the old, gentlemanly decencies – the Loyal Toast, passing the port after dinner – will somehow muddle through.

No, I do not seek to jeer. If, after all that has happened – four years of war, a million dead – such things seem obsolete, it may be because we have entered a different world, one that can never again be trusted. Of one thing I feel certain. No one watching us, as we carried down the bodies of our friends that day, could ever have imagined what confidence we once placed in our institution of manly courage; or what sweetness and nobility there used to be in our intercourse with the mountains and with one another.

In that morning when the world was young.